Why am I looking at him again?

Kate tried to will away the hot blush rising up her neck, but its heat continued to climb until she knew her cheeks were bright with it. She tried to look away but couldn't. And she had the awful feeling that if she didn't listen to what he had to say now, he would haunt her, his constant presence weighing on her like a ball and chain, until she did. If she remembered anything about him, it was his persistence. Much as she hated to give in to him, even for a few moments, she did.

"All right, you win. It's nice to see you again, Lucas. What have you been doing for the past *fifteen* years? And what, pray tell, brings you to Houston?" She rattled off the questions in a low, cold voice that made them more insult than interest.

"You've changed a lot, Kate. Or should I say Ms. Evans? You used to be so soft, so sweet."

"What did you expect?" she demanded, her cold tone ignited by a sudden surge of anger. "I used to be a naive eighteen-year-old girl. But even naive eighteen-year-old girls grow up. Eventually."

Her flare of temper caught him off guard. What *had* he expected? Years ago he'd been drawn to her inner strength and determination as well as to her clear sense of right and wrong, her honesty, her integrity. And although he'd walked away from her for what he believed were all the right reasons, she had every excuse to be angry. But he had to get her past it. He had to convince her to give him another chance. Too much was at stake. Her life was at stake.

Dear Reader,

The weather's getting colder, and the holidays are approaching. Why not take a little time for yourself and curl up with a few good romances? This month, we have four outstanding candidates for you.

Start things off with *Fugitive*, by popular Emilie Richards. An isolated mountain cabin, an escaped convict who is both less and more than he seems, moonshine and memories, and a woman who is just starting to make sense of her life—such are the ingredients that combine in this deliciously romantic brew. You won't want to miss a single word. Ann Williams is a relatively new author; *Haunted by the Past* is only her third book. But what a story it is! A woman on the run from a dangerous past meets up with another sort of danger: a man with revenge in mind and no time for love. But, forced to travel together, they discover that revenge is not always sweet, safety *is* within reach, and a loving future can make up for any past.

Also this month, Linda Shaw returns with *One Sweet Sin*, which will have you on the edge of your seat. There's just something about a man in uniform.... And Nikki Benjamin weaves a tale of romance and suspense in her first book for the line, *A Man To Believe In*.

There's always something going on at Silhouette Intimate Moments, so sit back, open a book and *enjoy!*

Yours,

Leslie Wainger
Senior Editor and Editorial Coordinator

NIKKI BENJAMIN

A Man To Believe In

SILHOUETTE·INTIMATE·MOMENTS®

Published by Silhouette Books New York

America's Publisher of Contemporary Romance

 SILHOUETTE BOOKS
300 East 42nd St., New York, N.Y. 10017

ISBN: 0-373-07359-3

First Silhouette Books printing November 1990

Printed in the U.S.A.

Books by Nikki Benjamin

Silhouette Intimate Moments
A Man To Believe In #359

Silhouette Special Edition
Emily's House #539

NIKKI BENJAMIN

was born and raised in the Midwest, but after years in the Houston area, she considers herself a true Texan.

Nikki says she's always been an avid reader—her earliest literary heroines were Nancy Drew, Trixie Belden and Beany Malone. Her writing experience was limited, however, until a friend started penning a novel and encouraged Nikki to do the same. One scene led to another, and soon she was hooked.

When not reading or writing, the author enjoys spending time with her husband and son, needlepoint, hiking, biking, horseback riding and sailing.

For my mother, Marcella Kuda Wolff,
and in memory of my father, Kenneth F. Wolff—
with my love and admiration always

Prologue

He stood in the doorway of his office, head up, heart pounding, his fingers curled into fists. His loosely knotted tie, rumpled shirt, unbuttoned at the neck, and his weary eyes spoke of a long day edging into a longer night. Yet every muscle in his slender body was taut with tension as he surveyed the dimly lit gallery.

His gaze swept from one side of the long, wide room to the other, as he studied row after row of expensive, antique furniture. Nothing moved among the shadows. Only the gentle tick of a mantel clock on a nearby table and the occasional whoosh of a car passing on the narrow, rain-slick street beyond the glittering bay windows broke the stillness of the night.

As one minute became two, then three, David Evans tried to remember what had brought him out of his desk chair and into the office doorway with such urgency. It hadn't been anything specific, no crash of broken glass, no click of a key in a door lock. In fact, it had been nothing more substantial than a subtle shift in the quality of the silence surrounding him.

Must have imagined it.

He loosened the fingers of one hand and raked them through the thatch of dark blond hair falling over his forehead. Except for himself, the place was empty.

Taking a deep breath, he scanned the room one more time as he tried, unsuccessfully, to quell the anxiety eating at his gut. Then he turned and walked back into his office. He had to pull himself together and he had to do it now. But a glance at the scatter of black-and-white photographs in the open briefcase on his desk did nothing to dispel his uneasiness.

He rubbed his face with one hand, but the fear that had been his constant companion for too long couldn't be wiped away. With a barely audible groan, he slid into his leather chair, tipped his head against its wide back and closed his eyes, cursing his curiosity yet again.

If only he had minded his own business. If only he'd been content to do his job, to manage Jonathan Kiley's exclusive gallery and sell antique furniture to his wealthy customers. If only he hadn't been quite so aware of the other customers, the ones Jonathan dealt with behind closed doors, the ones who rarely glanced at what the gallery had to offer, but always seemed to buy. . . something.

Because it had seemed odd, David had begun to keep a record of their visits. Using a simple code, he'd jotted down names and dates and items purchased. After several months he'd realized that the same names appeared at the same time each month. The items purchased were usually small and reasonably inexpensive. And regardless of their condition, the items were always sent to the Galveston warehouse for some sort of restoration work prior to delivery.

Though the pattern had been unusual, it hadn't been enough to stir up any real suspicion in him. Not only was Jonathan Kiley a savvy businessman, he was a wealthy and respected member of Houston society. David liked the man, he enjoyed working for him, and if anyone had accused him of doing anything illegal, David along with many, many others would have defended him loyally.

It wasn't until a piece designated for delivery to one of the special customers was returned to the gallery by mistake that he found out exactly what was going on. With Jonathan out of town for several days, it had been up to him to correct the shipping error. In order to do so, he had to open the crate to check the contents against the packing slip. Inside he had found a lady's small writing desk. He wasn't sure why he'd opened the drawers, but he had. And inside he'd found hundreds of little packets of cocaine.

If he'd had any sense at all, he would have handed in his resignation within a week and walked away without a backward glance. But David couldn't do it. Neither did he confront Jonathan with his discovery. He quietly continued to update his diary, biding his time, waiting for a chance to gather enough solid evidence. Without it, he knew he'd never be able to convince anyone that a wealthy, respected man like Jonathan Kiley was dealing drugs.

A week ago, during a cocktail party at the gallery, he had had an opportunity to photograph Jonathan with several of his special customers. He'd also photographed him with a man he'd never seen before, a man named Diego Garcia. And last night, with Jonathan out of town again, David had gone to Galveston and searched the warehouse. It hadn't taken him long to find and photograph the area where the drugs were stored. He'd been up most of the night developing the film, then hiding the negatives in a safe place.

He had contacted the Drug Enforcement Agency in the afternoon, requesting a meeting with a senior agent, which was scheduled to take place shortly. In his briefcase, along with the photographs, he had a list of names and dates as well as an outline of how Kiley operated. And almost as an afterthought, just to be safe, less than an hour ago he'd sealed the diary in an envelope and dropped it in the mailbox outside the gallery. His sister would get it in a couple of days. If all went as planned he'd retrieve it before she had time to wonder what it was. If not . . .

The code was a simple one they'd used as kids. Kate wouldn't have any trouble with it. At the end, he had added a note about the negatives, where to find them and what to do with them. If anything happened to him . . . But nothing was going to happen to him. He'd been careful, very careful.

The sudden chiming of the mantel clock urged him from his reverie. He opened his eyes, sat forward in his chair and reached for the telephone. As he dialed the numbers, he realized, as if from a great distance, that his hand was shaking.

Easing back in his chair, he focused on the framed photograph of his sister. Kate had guided him through childhood and into adulthood. And now she was his friend, probably his best friend. Maybe he should have confided in her. Maybe he should have warned her about Jonathan Kiley—

"Hello?" Matthew Owen's gruff voice interrupted the buzzing in David's ear on the fourth ring.

"Mr. Owen? This is David Evans. I'm ready whenever you are."

"It's about time, kid. I've been going crazy waiting for your call. Where are you? I'll pick you up."

"I'm at the gallery, but I'd rather meet you someplace else." He couldn't bear to stay at the gallery any longer. "How about the Four Seasons? There's a bar on the second floor. It's small and quiet. You can take a look at what I've got. I hope it will be enough."

"From what you've told me, and with you to testify, it should be. But if anything happens to you, kid—"

"I've left my diary with . . . with someone I trust. And I've hidden the negatives in a safe place. If something happens to me, be patient. You might not be able to put Kiley in jail, but eventually you should have enough information to make it impossible for him to continue his little sideline."

"Who—"

"I can't tell you. Just...trust me." If anything happened to him, David didn't want Matthew Owen or anyone else drawing attention to Kate. She'd need time to decode the diary and find the negatives.

"I trust you, kid. But you're playing one hell of a dangerous game. I don't want you or anybody close to you to get hurt. Get your butt over to the Four Seasons and do it fast, or I'm coming after you."

"I'm on my way, Mr. Owen."

Without waiting for a reply, David cradled the receiver. Moments later, wearing his dark gray suit coat and carrying his briefcase, he moved through the shadows rimming the back wall of the gallery.

As he stepped through the rear door and eased it closed, cold, damp tendrils of air crept up under his jacket and curled around the back of his neck. The heavy rain of late afternoon had turned to a thick mist that clung to his face and hair. A sudden shiver whispered up his spine, but he told himself it was nothing more than the cold and wet.

He walked down the alley, heading toward the lights of the side street where he'd parked his car. A turn to the right, a few more steps, and he'd be in his car. Barely controlling the urge to run, he stepped onto the sidewalk and...stopped.

A large, black Mercedes, headlights extinguished, idled at the curb, its engine purring. The door on the driver's side opened. A man slid out and strode toward him.

"Mr. Kiley wants to see you."

The dark, swarthy man wasn't much taller than David, but he was broader, beefier, and the hand he wrapped around David's upper arm was like a steel band.

"He wasn't too pleased when you opened the crate. Then he heard you were snooping around the warehouse last night." The man wrenched the briefcase from David's fingers as he shoved him toward the waiting car. "So, we're going to ask you some questions, and you're going to give us some answers. And, then . . . well, then, I guess we'll be saying . . . goodbye."

He couldn't get in the car. He wasn't brave enough or strong enough to face what they had in store for him. He'd give it all away. He'd give them Kate and Matthew Owen. He'd rather die first. He was going to die anyway. . . .

Turning slightly into the man, he drove his elbow deep into his belly. The man staggered, swearing, loosening his grip. Jerking free, David spun away. He ran toward the main street up ahead, shouting at the top of his lungs, waving his arms. Behind him he heard Jonathan calling his name, ordering him to halt. Then he heard gunfire echoing in the alley. He felt the bullets slam into his body, felt the cold, wet pavement under his cheek, felt himself floating . . . floating . . . away. . . .

Chapter 1

She wanted to run far and fast, to a safe place where she could hide forever. Considering the events of the past six days, no one would blame her. But then, how could she live with herself? If she ran away, physically or emotionally, who would see to it that her brother's killer was caught? It was her responsibility, hers and hers alone.

Since she couldn't run and she couldn't hide, she sat at the downtown Houston Public Library's information desk as she did every Thursday morning. As a senior reference librarian, Kate Evans didn't have to do that job. But she enjoyed the public contact once a week, and Thursday mornings were usually so slow that she had time to catch up on odds and ends of paperwork.

The morning *had* been slow, Kate conceded, and after almost a week away she had more than enough paperwork to complete. Yet she was getting nowhere fast with the list of new books she was supposed to order for the library. The peace and quiet of the sunlit lobby, as well as the soft murmurings of friends and acquaintances, helped to ease her pain, but her loss was too new, too real, too raw to be denied for any length of time.

Horrifying memories of the past few days clawed at her concentration like fingernails on a blackboard, while fear and frustration gnawed at her gut. Her head ached and her eyes itched. She had shed too many tears and she had had too little sleep. Thus the simple task of copying information onto forms had become almost impossible to do.

How could she ever forget the early-morning phone call from the police or the trip to the morgue to identify her brother's body? If only that had been the end of it. But later in the day she'd found his car stripped and his apartment ransacked. The officer in charge of the case had asked her dozens of questions, but he hadn't had any answers for *her*. And despite the destruction to David's car and apartment, he'd seemed quite willing to believe that David had been nothing more than the unfortunate victim of a violent mugging.

Such a simple explanation for the brutal end of a young man's life, but under the circumstances, an explanation she had to accept. His briefcase, wallet, watch and keys had been missing. And with his keys, the mugger or muggers would have had easy access to his car and apartment. But then, late Tuesday night she'd returned from the funeral in St. Louis and she'd walked into another kind of chaos.

Her town house had been torn apart, every drawer and closet emptied, furniture overturned, pictures pulled off the walls. Yet despite the destruction, nothing had been missing. As she'd called the police, fear had washed over her with the intensity of a storm-tossed ocean wave. And suddenly there were no simple answers.

If only I'd asked him what was bothering him.... If only I hadn't ignored the changes in him, the deep silences, the unnatural edginess....

"It's been a long time, little girl, a very long time."

The dark voice growling softly, almost intimately, above her head sounded ... familiar. Odd, because the accent was flat midwestern, not the Texas twang she was accustomed to hearing after living in Houston for twelve years. But, then, her mind had been so far away...

Staring at the papers in front of her, she searched her memory for a face to match the voice. An image wavered on the edge of her mind. Only one man had ever called her *little girl*. Her fingers tightened around the pen in her hand. Impossible.... It was...impossible.... Yet, suddenly, every nerve ending in her body was aware of the man standing in front of her desk.

She could feel his eyes on her, watching her, waiting. He hovered over her, blocking out the sunlight pouring through the three-story high windows, muffling the sounds of the people milling around the modern, wide-open lobby. His shadow fell across her hands where they rested atop the papers on her desk. And his voice echoed in her ears ... *little girl ... little girl ...*

Look at him, Kathryn Elizabeth Evans. Look...at...him.

Recapping her pen and setting it aside, Kate eased back in her chair. Lifting the corners of her mouth in a polite, professional smile, she tipped her chin up, raising her eyes. Slowly, very slowly, she studied his features one after another. Then she forced herself to meet his gaze.

Something slipped and slid inside her head. Her stomach lurched with sickening intensity and her heart slammed against her ribs, as if she'd accidentally stepped off the edge of a cliff. She couldn't breathe, couldn't think, and for just a moment, she couldn't see anything but stars sparkling in a black void. Instinctively, she wrapped her fingers around the edge of her desk, trying to steady herself, physically as well as emotionally.

God, no...please, no... Not after so many years. Not now...not today....

She had to be mistaken. It couldn't be him. There had to be dozens of men in Houston with thick, straight black hair, with eyes a pale shade of silvery green, with high cheekbones and a long, hard jaw curving into a defiantly square chin.

But as she sat and stared at him with all the animation of a stone statue, he smiled. With that simple gesture he banished all hope of mistaken identity. That wolfish grin could be claimed by only one man, and long ago he had used it unmercifully, luring her into love.

All the better to eat you with, my dear....

Suddenly, it wasn't only in her head that Kate Evans felt a slipping, sliding sensation.

"Lucas? Lucas Hunter." Her stammered question became a statement. She didn't have to ask. She knew who he was.

"Katie, I thought it was you. I didn't expect to find anything in here more interesting than old newspapers and information on zoning laws." Smile still in place, he settled a hip and length of thigh along the edge of her desk. "It's been a long time, but I'd recognize you anywhere, sweetheart."

Seconds ticked into a minute, then two, but even if her life had depended on it, she couldn't have uttered another word. The reality of Lucas Hunter sitting on the edge of her desk was too much for her. She could do nothing but stare at him. For so many years she had imagined meeting him again, face-to-face, but never had she imagined it would deal her such a stunning blow.

He had changed in the fifteen years since she had watched him board a plane bound for San Francisco—the first leg of a journey that had ended in Vietnam—but the changes were minimal. Although a black polo shirt, sleek and expensive, had replaced the oversize, ragged black T-shirts he had once favored, and his black leather bomber jacket was more new than old, his jeans were just as worn and faded as he'd always preferred. And though he was still as tall and lean as he had been, age had added to the depth and breadth of his chest and shoulders. The brawniness of youth had been harnessed into a strength and power he had obviously learned to control.

He wore his hair brushed away from his face, but now it was styled rather than shaggy, the sides short, the back long enough to graze his collar. Age had added more than a few gray hairs. Age, too, had etched deep lines at the corners of his eyes and mouth.

But age hadn't dimmed his smile, nor dulled the glitter of his green eyes. When he smiled, his eyes flashed fire. When he smiled, he was as rakish as a pirate, as charming as a con man, daring her, as he had done so long ago, to come and play.

But she had played with Lucas Hunter once, and once was enough. She had played with fire, and she had been badly burned. Fortunately, the memory of the pain that had seared her heart and soul hadn't faded over the years. It was as sharp and stark as a slap in the face, a non-too-gentle reminder that loving him had been a very foolish mistake. And like a slap in the face, it was all she needed to pull herself together.

Katie... He had called her Katie, he had called her sweetheart....

"It *has* been a long time, Lucas, but not nearly long enough." By sheer force of will she kept her voice under control, her cool, calm tone masking the outrage building inside of her. How could he have the gall, the unmitigated gall to sit there with a smile on his face?

Maintaining her air of indifference, she turned away from him and began to gather up the lists and forms covering her desk. When he neither moved from his perch on her desk nor spoke, she glanced up at him, arching an eyebrow. The wicked grin had vanished, replaced by an angry frown that almost made her smile. Apparently Lucas Hunter wasn't any more accustomed to dismissals than he'd been in the past. But what did he expect after the way he'd treated her? Surely he hadn't expected her to greet him with open arms?

His eyes holding hers, Lucas barely resisted the urge to grab her by the shoulders and shake her. At a distance she had appeared soft and fragile in her cream silk shirt, her dark brown hair swinging straight and smooth against her shoulders. She had seemed so...vulnerable. He'd been sure that she wouldn't cause a scene, especially in the wide-open lobby. If he'd tried, he couldn't have planned a more perfect time and place to begin his campaign. Or so he'd thought.

But the look in her eyes, the tone of her voice, had all the softness, all the fragility, of an iron fist in a velvet glove. And suddenly he had no doubt that if he pushed her too far, she just might take a swing at him, lobby full of people or not.

"Kate, please, I want to talk to you. I don't blame you for being angry. But seeing you again made me realize..." Injecting a full measure of quiet concern into his voice, Lucas leaned toward her, his gaze unwavering. "It's like a second chance."

Tilting her head to one side, Kate considered his words for a moment, then smiled slightly. "Oh, really? Just like that, huh?" She snapped her fingers to emphasize her point, then continued, each word dripping with sarcasm. "Some enchanted morning you see a familiar face across a crowded lobby, and suddenly you *know* that after years of silence, you *have* to talk to me. Come on, Lucas, give me a break. There is nothing, *nothing* you have to say that would interest me in the least, and I have no intention of giving you another crack at making my life miserable."

And, thank God, I'm not Pinnochio, she added to herself, as she shuffled the papers on her desk. *My nose would reach across the room by now.*

Years ago she had schooled herself to accept the fact that she would never see him again, that she never *wanted* to see him again. But, honest person that she was, she couldn't deny that she was curious about his reasons for trying to renew their acquaintance. Most men would have walked away after the first brush-off. Lucas had endured two ego-bruisers without flinching. *Why?*

Better not to know, she warned herself, her hands crushing the papers she held. Better to be as rude and nasty to him as possible. Sooner or later he would give up, go away and leave her alone. And right now she was better off alone. She had to use every ounce of strength and determination she possessed to find out why David had been murdered. If she had to deal with Lucas Hunter as well, it would be debilitating in the worst way imaginable.

She had trusted him once, loved him once, and he had taught her all she needed to know about misplaced love and trust. If she prided herself on anything, it was on her ability to learn life's lessons well.

But this wasn't the time nor the place to contemplate past mistakes. Not with Lucas sitting, solid as a cement block, on the edge of her desk. He was close, much too close, and he was studying her face, feature by feature, his gaze lingering too long on her eyes, her lips....

Why am I looking at him again?

Kate tried to will away the hot blush rising up her neck, but its heat continued to climb until she knew her cheeks were bright with it. She tried to look away but couldn't. And she had the awful feeling that if she didn't listen to what he had to say now, he would haunt her, his constant presence weighing on her like a ball and chain, until she did. If she remembered anything about him, it was his persistence. Much as she hated to give in to him, even for a few moments, she did.

"All right, you win. It's nice to see you again, Lucas. What have you been doing for the past *fifteen* years? And what, pray tell, brings you to Houston besides old newspapers and zoning laws?" She rattled off the questions in a low, cold voice that made them more insult than interest.

"You've changed a lot, Kate. Or should I say Ms. Evans? You used to be so soft, so sweet." He made no effort to mask the touch of irony in his deep, rich voice.

"What did you expect?" she demanded, her cold tone ignited by a sudden surge of anger. "I used to be a naive eighteen-year-old girl. But even naive eighteen-year-old girls grow up. Eventually."

Her flare of temper caught him off guard. His eyes wavered for an instant. What *had* he expected? Years ago he'd been drawn to her inner strength and determination as well as to her rigid sense of right and wrong, her honesty, her integrity. And although he'd walked away from her for what he'd believed were all the right reasons, what he'd done to her had been wrong. He couldn't deny that he'd given her good reason to be angry. But he had to get her past it. He had to convince her to give him another chance. Too much was at stake. Her life was at stake.

He forced himself to meet her gaze again, not saying a word, knowing his silent scrutiny was having a disturbing effect on her. *Get it out, baby, get it all out. Then let me help you. Please, let me help you.*

"Did you think I'd throw myself into your arms?" She made an effort to remain cool and calm, not allowing her rage full rein while she forced herself to ignore the tears that suddenly scratched at the back of her eyes. She'd cried enough over Lucas Hunter to last a lifetime. She refused to cry over him again, especially when he was watching.

"Well, sorry to disappoint you," Kate continued, her voice low and steady. "But if memory serves, *you* were the one who dumped *me* fifteen years ago. You stopped writing to me, you didn't call me when you came home from Vietnam, you didn't answer the letters I sent to your parents' house, and you didn't have the decency to tell me why. I waited for you." She paused for a moment, drawing in a deep breath, her lips twisting bitterly. "If you had any sensitivity at all, you'd realize you are the last person on the face of this earth that I want to see."

"Maybe I'm just the person you *need* to see, Katie. If you're still so upset over a...a...misunderstanding, it might help to talk about it," he suggested, challenging her with quiet intensity.

Gazing up at him, Kate felt as if the breath had been knocked from her body. Upset? A misunderstanding? The urge to laugh clutched at her as hysteria threatened to over-throw the relatively calm composure she'd maintained so far.

"You did *not* write, you did *not* call, you cut me out of your life without any explanation. Fine. So be it." Her voice quivered slightly as she stated the facts, then sailed away on a dangerously high note. "But there was no *misunder-standing*, Lucas, none whatsoever."

As suddenly as she'd wanted to laugh, she wanted to scream. And then she wanted to strike him. Her rage reached its zenith, shooting through her like lightning across a cloud-shrouded sky, and then it was gone. All the wasted years, she thought bitterly, years they could have shared.

Or at the very least, years when she could have been free of the dull aching pain of self-doubt, free of the uncer-tainty that had scarred her as surely as the slash of a knife across her pale skin. Maybe then her short-lived marriage to Alan Stevens would have had a chance. Maybe she would have been able to love him, to trust him as a woman was meant to love and trust her husband.

She couldn't look at Lucas, couldn't bear to see the smug certainty in his silvery green eyes. He was so sure of him-self, so damned sure, while she had never been more con-fused. Propping her elbows on the desktop, she dropped her face in her hands. In the past six days she had buried her brother, then witnessed the resurrection of Lucas Hunter. It was too much to bear in less than a week.

"I'm going crazy," she murmured, as she massaged her throbbing temples. "Finally, totally and completely crazy."

Hard, warm fingers wrapped around her wrists and gently tugged at her hands. She stiffened against him, but his strength and tenacity were too much for her. Why didn't he go away? Why didn't he leave her alone? He'd done it so well years ago. Why couldn't he do it now?

"Hey, Katie, it's been a long time. Can't we just put it behind—"

"Stop calling me that," she spat at him, cutting off his words with a glare as she wrenched her wrists free. When he called her Katie in that gentle tone of voice, he turned her name into an endearment. When he put his hands on her, he stoked embers deep inside of her that should have died long ago. She didn't want endearments from him, she didn't want to feel his heat. And the only thing she had any intention of putting behind her was him.

"Okay...Kate." For a moment, his eyes wavered again. "Listen, it's a long story." His gaze met hers again, cool, direct and demanding once more. "It's almost noon. Come and have lunch with me. You do get a lunch hour, don't you? We can go someplace quiet where we can talk. This time, let me explain."

"First a misunderstanding, then a long story. I have to hand it to you. You certainly know how to choose all the right words. But how could you possibly begin to explain? And, why would you want—"

"What's the matter? Afraid your boyfriend might object?" He cut through her words with single-minded determination, throwing her off balance.

"I don't have a boyfriend," Kate snapped before she could stop herself.

"Then there's no reason we can't have lunch together. Unless you're meeting someone else. I heard your little brother lives in Houston, too. But, hey, he wouldn't mind if you had lunch with an old friend, would he?"

He didn't want to use her dead brother to knock her down. But short of throwing her over his shoulder and carrying her out of the library, he was running out of ways to get her to budge from behind her desk. And their increasingly heated exchange was starting to attract too much attention.

She focused on the revolving glass doors across the lobby, trying desperately to beat back the pain that sliced through her as she remembered. How many times had David come sailing through those doors, his handsome face lit by a wide smile, his blond hair a little too long, his brown eyes full of laughter? How many times had they huddled in her office, sharing sandwiches, or splurged on a favorite restaurant? So many times. . . .

"My brother was . . . was killed last week."

"Ah, Kate, I'm sorry, so sorry. I didn't know. He was a nice kid. You were always close, weren't you?"

His voice was soft and sympathetic, and very nearly her undoing. "It's all right. . .really. I. . . He. . ." The tears that blurred her eyes weren't totally unexpected. But she thought she was done with crying—for Lucas, for Alan Stevens, for her parents, for David, for all the doors she'd had to close.

Cursing her sudden weakness, she bent her head and rubbed her forehead. "I don't want to talk about it, Lucas. In fact, I don't want to talk about anything with you, ever."

Why, *why* didn't he leave? The pounding in her head was making it harder and harder to think straight. And any minute now she was going to fly into so many pieces she'd never get herself together again.

But he didn't leave. He shifted his weight on the edge of her desk, leaning forward, his arms braced on either side of her, his body over her, around her, shielding her from the people beginning to crowd the lobby, warding off anyone who might dare to approach them.

"Come with me, Kate."

His breath stirred her hair. His body heat warmed her, his scent surrounded her. The tang of worn leather mixed with a hint of spice whirled her back through time and place to dark nights full of love and laughter. If only she had the strength to push away from the desk, to stand up, to walk across the lobby and into her office. But suddenly the good memories were beating down the bad, robbing her of the will to do anything but sit with her head in her hands.

"Come and have lunch with me, Kate." His long, hard fingers gripped her chin. He tilted it up gently, forcing her to meet his gaze. Slowly, slowly, he bent forward until his face was just inches from hers. "Don't run away again. Not now, when you need someone. Listen to what I have to tell you. This time, give me a chance." Though spoken softly, the words were a command. He wasn't asking for the pleasure of her company. He was telling her what he wanted.

How easy it would be to obey. How tempting to forfeit her will in favor of his. Instinctively she knew that he was a strong, powerful man. If he wanted, he could protect her from the nameless, faceless fear that had lurked in the shadows since she'd returned from St. Louis. He might even be able to help her find the answers to her questions. She *did* need someone.

Unless...unless...somehow, some way, he was a part of it.

Though the thought was crazy, Kate felt the frisson of another kind of fear. The fear of being foolish, fatally foolish, skipped up her spine. Until she found out who had murdered her brother, she'd be wise not to trust anyone, especially anyone as basically untrustworthy as Lucas Hunter had proven to be.

With a strength she didn't know she possessed, she wrapped her fingers around his wrist and pulled his hand from her face, freeing herself from his hold. "I'm not having lunch with you, Lucas. Not now, not ever, because we don't have anything to say to each other." Before he could stop her, she pushed away from the desk and stood up.

"What happened in the past can't be changed, and I have no desire to experience a repeat performance. So, go away and stay away. It should be easy for you. It won't be the first time you've done it."

Without waiting for a reply, she spun away from him and strode across the busy lobby. Not once did she glance back.

As she disappeared into the crowd, Lucas stood up. Fingers clenched into fists at his sides, he took a step after her.

Then drawing on years of training, and what seemed to be his last shred of self-control, he halted. Going after her wouldn't help. He had pushed her very near the edge. He couldn't risk pushing her over. He needed her cool and calm and together. And most of all, he had to have her trust. He'd bet his life she had David Evans's diary. He probably *was* betting his life.

At the moment, however, gaining her trust seemed just about as possible as flying to the moon by flapping his arms. Frustration clawed at him. He had overestimated his ability to control her. Equally deadly, he'd underestimated the depth of the pain he'd caused her in the past. And he'd underestimated the effect she would have on him.

She had changed a lot over the years, much more than he'd expected. When he had thought of her, as he'd done far too often, he had thought of a shy, innocent young girl, sparkling with love and laughter. Had he really been foolish enough to believe she'd remained the same, especially after what he'd done to her? Innocence had died in her as surely as it had died in him. Had love and laughter gone, too?

The woman who had sat across from him, pain and anger in her eyes and voice, was just that—a woman. She was marked by the changes of every year they'd been apart, by every experience she'd faced without him. To really know her again would take time and patience, and he'd never had much of either. Yet he wanted to know her, in every sense of the word. Even if there was no future for them, he wanted to know if she was the missing puzzle piece that would make his life complete. And, more than anything, he didn't want to hurt her again.

But Kate Evans was business, not personal, and he'd learned to separate one from the other years ago. It was his duty, his responsibility to protect her any way he could, without regard to the emotional toll they might have to pay. He had to be prepared to sacrifice her mental well-being as well as his own, if that was what it took to get the job done.

He had spent most of his adult life fighting one kind of war or another, and like all wars, the one he was currently waging had too many casualties. But he didn't like the thought of Kate becoming one of them.

After what he'd done to her fifteen years ago, not to mention all she'd been through the past few days, she deserved better. She deserved one hell of a lot better than the lies, the deceit, the danger he had to offer. Given a choice, he'd walk away.

Or would he?

Touching her had triggered an overpowering onslaught of memories, tapping a hidden wellspring of desire. She was a beautiful, vibrant woman. Unfortunately, she was also out-of-bounds. He was wise enough to know he should block out his memories as well as his newly kindled desire, and find someone else to service his physical needs until the job was done. He should, but he didn't think he could.

"Wisdom be damned," he muttered, his lips twisting in a bitter travesty of a smile. He took another step after her, oblivious to the people milling around.

He wanted to touch her again...and again. He wanted to brush his lips against her cheek. He wanted to smooth his hand over her dark hair in a gentle caress, and the desire astonished him because he wasn't a gentle man. He wanted the weight of her body against him, wanted to soothe her with his fingers and mouth. He could almost feel the satin smoothness of her skin. He could almost taste her lips opening under his. A sharp, searing pain shot through him as his soul beat against the bars of its cage.

He cursed.

"Pardon me, sir? May I help you?"

Lucas turned to face the short, blond woman standing behind Kate's desk. For a moment, he studied the name tag she wore, then flashed a wicked grin. "No, thanks, Mary. I found what I was looking for." Tucking his hands in his jacket pockets, he sauntered toward the revolving doors.

Only the slam of his fists against the glass gave away the real state of his emotions as he spun himself around and out into the warmth and sunshine of the March afternoon. On the pavement in front of the library, he stopped to stare at a fuzzy lump of cloud in the bright, blue sky, studying it as if it held the answers to all the questions he had to ask.

How was he going to get close to her? What was he willing to say and do to regain her trust?

Moments later, he moved down the sidewalk, the bitter smile twisting his mouth once again. He didn't have to search the sky for answers to his questions. He knew the answers, every last one of them. They were buried deep inside of him, and they weren't pretty, not pretty at all.

Stopping for a moment at the street corner, he turned slightly, glancing behind him. The swarthy, heavyset man studying the bus schedule half a block back had been in the library when he'd entered. He had also been very interested in his conversation with Kate. Now Lucas had a good idea why. Someone was keeping tabs on her, someone who obviously considered him worth a little extra attention. Just how much extra attention, he planned to find out.

"Time to have some fun," he muttered, still smiling.

Then, refocusing his thoughts on how best to handle his next meeting with Kate, he started across the street.

In her office, with the door locked, Kate sagged against her desk. She grabbed a handful of tissues from the box atop it, and pressed them to her eyes, forcing back the tears that continued to threaten despite her best efforts to will them away. She would not cry.

But damn Lucas Hunter for bringing on the urge to bury her face in her hands and sob her heart out when she thought she'd never feel that way again. Damn his awesome nerve, damn his charming smile, damn his sick interpretation of a misunderstanding. Damn, damn, damn....

For some strange reason, the silent swearing seemed to help. Kate blotted her eyes one last time, blew her nose and tossed the tissues into the wastebasket beside her desk. She was going to be all right. She had to. There was nothing she could do to change the past. What was done was done. And as painful as his reappearance had been, Lucas was a minor problem she'd dealt with successfully. Her major problem was finding the answers to some very scary questions.

David had died a violent death. Initially it had been easy to accept the possibility that it hadn't been intentional, but not anymore. Even the officer in charge of the case had admitted there was more to it. However, in typical, authoritarian style, he'd given her a verbal pat on the head coupled with vague assurances that they were working on it.

Of course the police were working on it, along with several hundred other cases. It could take weeks, months, for them to figure out what had happened and why. And in the meantime, she'd be left to wonder when and how she'd be approached again.

She and David had been very close. Because she was several years older, she had been as much mother as sister to him while they were growing up. And when their parents had died within months of each other, shortly after her divorce, it had seemed right for him to move to Houston.

He had finished college and gone to work in the accounting department of a major oil company. Within a few years he'd passed the CPA examination. And then, through his love of antiques, he had met Jonathan Kiley. When Jonathan had asked him to manage the gallery, David hadn't hesitated a moment.

He had enjoyed his work, and he had liked and admired his employer. And though he was a quiet man, he had made several friends, male and female. Friends he had seen less and less over the past few months, something she'd discovered when she'd called several of them yesterday.

Why had he cut himself off from his friends without telling her? Come to think of it, he hadn't talked about much of anything the last few times they'd been together. And he'd been nervous as a cat in a dog kennel. Why?

In the silent solitude of her office, Kate wrapped her arms around herself, attempting to ward off the chill that threatened to settle deep in her soul. Had he been involved in something deadly dangerous? And if he had, was she unknowingly involved in some way, too? She had to find out, and she had to find out fast. Now all she had to do was figure out how.

As if she didn't have enough to worry about, her thoughts skipped back to Lucas Hunter. He'd been so cool, so calm, so *determined* to talk to her. Why? Under normal circumstances, she wouldn't be so suspicious. But the past few days had been anything but normal. And after fifteen years, Lucas was an unknown . . .

In any case, known or unknown, he could take his cool, his calm, his almighty *determination* for a long walk off a short pier. He'd caught her with her guard down once, and he'd used her pain, her anger and confusion against her. However, she had no intention of letting him get that close to her again, either physically or emotionally. If she did, it wouldn't take him long to realize that she'd never stopped loving him.

She was smart, and over the years she'd learned to be tough, but she wasn't much of an actress. She had never been able to deceive anyone. Even David had teased her about being too honest. She hadn't been able to mask her anger and pain earlier. Neither would she be able to hide the love and longing she'd beaten down but never quite destroyed.

Allowing Lucas entry into her life, even for a short time, was something she simply could not do. It would be so easy, especially now that she was truly alone and frightened. But it would also be a very stupid thing to do. Even the smartest, toughest woman in the world couldn't play with fire without the risk of being burned. And she refused to be burned again.

Chapter 2

"The conversation was intense."

"Hmm, that's interesting. Was the intensity laced with pleasure or . . . pain?"

"She wasn't happy to see him, but he was persistent. He's an old boyfriend. There are pictures of him in a photo album I found when I tossed the house. I got a name—Lucas Hunter."

"Never heard of him. Call my friend at the Houston Police Department. Find out all you can about Mr. Hunter, and do it fast."

"Yes, sir, Mr. Kiley. Anything else, sir?"

"I want you outside Kate Evans's front door early tomorrow morning, and I want you to stay with her all day. If you see or hear anything unusual, I want you to call me."

"Yes, sir, I will."

"Oh, and Jackson, watch yourself. There have been too many mistakes lately, and I don't like mistakes. It was your job to get rid of Evans, not mine. Do you understand?"

"I understand, sir."

"I hope so. I certainly hope so."

"Lucas, Lucas, Lucas. What's the world coming to when one of the agency's best and brightest can't handle a dame? Losing your touch, kiddo?"

"Shut up, Owen. She's *not* a dame, and I'm not losing my touch."

Resting a shoulder against the floor-to-ceiling window that served as one wall of the elegant hotel room, Lucas tried to concentrate on the activity on the streets below as he kept his back to the man lounging comfortably across the king-size bed. It was early evening. Houston's infamous rush hour was in full swing. Cars crept along at a snail's pace while people hustled up and down the same sidewalks Lucas had wandered during the afternoon.

He had stopped at several bars, too. Some had been seedy, some had been surreal, each one offering the liquid comfort he rarely wanted or needed but had wanted and needed that day. He might have told himself he was indulging only for the benefit of the bozo on his tail, but each time he'd swallowed a mouthful of bourbon, somewhere deep inside himself he'd known the real reason why. It had been just past six when he'd left his last stop, the hotel bar. Sick of himself and the drift of one love song after another over the sound system, he'd picked up his key and headed for his room. Matthew Owen had been waiting for him there.

In his present frame of mind, the last thing he needed was a confrontation with his boss, but he was smart enough to know when one was unavoidable. Pudgy, balding and prone to wearing plaid sports coats, Matt looked like a dime-novel detective. But in reality, he was one of the DEA's most valued agents.

He was smart and tough, and nobody's fool. If he appeared soft or stupid, he did so only because it was to his advantage. Beneath the facade Matthew was hard as nails, and he had a mind like a steel trap. Nothing, no one, got past him. He had solved more than one case because of his dog-with-a-bone mode of operation.

"Sensitive, aren't you?" Matt goaded. "Sure you're up to this one? It's not too late to change the game plan. I can pay Ms. Evans a visit, ask her about her brother's diary and the photo negatives. See what she says, see what she does. Of course, I'd have to identify myself, and there's no guarantee she'd understand our caution about working with the police department."

Tipping his forehead against the cool glass, Lucas tried to focus on what his boss was saying, but he was a bourbon or three past keeping his mind on business. Stupid thing to do, drinking in the afternoon. He should have known Matt would show up with nothing better to do than gnaw on him.

But he'd kept seeing her face, he'd kept hearing her voice, and the thought of how much she'd changed had haunted him. She had been so young, so innocent, so full of joy. And she had completely, unconditionally, offered him her love and trust—the love and trust he'd taken, then tossed away. The pain he'd begun to feel each time he acknowledged her right to hate him clutched at his gut yet again.

No matter how often he told himself that he'd been forced to let her go, in all honesty he knew the final decision had been his and his alone. And though he'd spent years trying to convince himself that he'd done the right thing, he could no longer deny the truth. She had been attractive, and she had never lacked admirers, but she had loved *him*. And she had waited for him until she no longer had any reason to wait.

Somewhere along the way, sometime after he'd joined the DEA, he had heard that she'd married. It was then that he'd tried to accept the fact that they were better off apart. She was the kind of woman who deserved a husband and a house full of kids, and the kind of life he'd chosen to lead left little room for a wife and family.

Yet he'd jumped at the chance to charm his way back into her life. He hadn't hesitated a moment when Matt asked for his help. In fact, he had banked on his ability to gain her trust not only as a means to get Kiley, but to protect her, as well. However, if he lost his cool where she was concerned, or if he couldn't play his ace, if he couldn't get her to cooperate with him, Matt would pull him out so fast his head would spin.

Running a hand through his hair, he turned away from the window, sagged into a chair and leveled his eyes at his boss. "No changes." He broke the long silence as he stretched his legs out in front of him. "Evans warned you that Kiley has a friend at the police department the first time he contacted you. If anyone on the force finds out she's talked to the DEA, word will get around that we're interested, and she'll end up like her brother.

"We have to find out if she has his diary without arousing her suspicions or Kiley's. We also have to protect her. We owe it to her brother. Once I gain her trust, I can do both. And I can gain her trust a hell of a lot faster than a stranger."

Despite the alcohol haze, Lucas knew he was making sense. He *had* to make sense. He'd gone to hell and back on Matt's orders in the past, but he wasn't going to walk away from Kate Evans as long as Jonathan Kiley was on the loose.

"You think so, huh?" Though he was posed casually on the bed, Matt's eyes had narrowed considerably.

"I *know* so. We're not the only ones who think she's the missing link. Somebody trashed her town house while she was burying her brother. And today somebody was keeping an eye on her at the library, somebody who was very interested in our conversation, so interested he followed me in and out of bars all afternoon. Last I saw of him, he was in a telephone booth in the hotel lobby."

"You think he's Kiley's man?"

"Damn right I do. David Evans wasn't the victim of a violent mugging, and the break-in at Kate's town house was no ordinary burglary. You know as well as I do that Kiley is responsible. He got his hands on whatever Evans intended to give you, and he isn't going to rest until he's sure no other evidence against him exists."

"He doesn't know about the diary."

"No, but Evans said he had a list of names and several photographs for you. Kiley's got to be wondering if there's only one copy of that list, and he's got to be wondering where the negatives are. If he's found them, why is somebody keeping tabs on Kate? So far, he's been biding his time, watching and waiting. But I don't think he's going to be patient much longer. He's going to go after her. And once he's knocked as much information out of her as possible, he's going to get rid of her the same way he got rid of her brother."

Shifting forward in his chair, his hands clasped between his knees, Lucas held his boss's gaze. His voice was clear and cold.

"Damn it, Matt. Her brother died trying to stop Jonathan Kiley. We owe her one hell of a lot more than protection. We owe her Kiley's head on a platter, but the only way we can give it to her is with her trust and cooperation. She's spooked, really spooked, and she's barely holding herself together. But I can handle her. I can and I *will*."

"I'm beginning to wonder, kid." Matthew Owen sat up, swinging his legs over the side of the bed. He pulled a cigar from his jacket pocket and rolled it slowly between his palms, giving every indication that he was deep in thought.

"We have a lot riding on your ability to gain Kate Evans's confidence. I brought you in because of your past association. I thought you'd be able to gain her trust without a problem. But the fact that you spent the afternoon boozing leads me to believe Ms. Evans wasn't overjoyed to see the ghost of Christmas past."

"I didn't spend the afternoon *boozing*," Lucas retorted, his voice harsh and angry. After throwing himself out of the chair, he began to pace along the windowed wall.

"Face it, Matt. She's our only solid link to the evidence her brother had on Kiley's drug-dealing operation." Trying valiantly to pull himself together, he turned to face his boss, and continued in a calmer, quieter tone. "If anybody knows where his diary and the negatives are, she's the one. I've got as good a chance as anybody to gain her trust, and I can do it without arousing suspicion. If Kiley gets suspicious, he'll kill her."

"I don't know, Lucas. I just don't like it. Whether you're willing to admit it or not, you're emotionally involved. You've been drinking all afternoon, and all you've done is talk to her. I know the signs, kid, and I repeat, I don't like it. Are you going to be able to do your job? If it comes down to it, will you be able to use her if we have to bait a trap to catch Kiley?"

"Don't worry about me," Lucas muttered, as he started pacing again. Rubbing a hand over the back of his neck, he tried to relax muscles strung too tight, as he sought to inject some measure of authority and control into his voice. "I'll do whatever it takes to get the job done." He glanced over his shoulder, meeting the weary eyes of his friend and mentor. "Haven't you heard the rumors about what a heartless bastard I am? Hell, I'm a real son of a bitch."

"You'd better be. Kiley's a dangerous man. If you're right about his goon, he's probably got somebody at HPD checking on you already."

"Fine with me. I'm in Houston on business, legitimate business he can verify if he wants. You know as well as I do that there's no way he can connect me to the DEA. In fact, if he gets his hands on the background information we've plugged into the computer, I wouldn't be surprised if he offered me a job."

"I think you're starting to believe your bio, Lucas. That's one sure way to end up in a rubber room. Or an early grave. You've been courting death, putting yourself in the line of fire more and more. What's it going to take to convince you that you deserved to live fifteen years ago?"

"Shut up, Matt. Just . . . shut . . . up." He stood very still, his spine stiff, his jaw tight.

"You climbed out of hell when you came home from Vietnam. *You* pulled yourself out of the muck. Whatever debt you feel you owed, believe me, son, you've paid it."

"It's none of your business, Matt."

"It is if you throw your life away attempting to be some version of a hero. Just . . . watch yourself, will you?"

"Yeah, sure. And you'd better watch yourself, too." Lucas turned, flashing a false grin Matt's way. God, he wanted the man out of the room, wanted to crawl into bed, wanted to sleep for a week. "We've got to stop meeting like this."

The older man obviously wasn't deceived. Sometime during the past eight hours Lucas Hunter had come face-to-face with who and what he was, where he'd been and where he was going. He was too close to this case and had allowed his control to slip. He'd sought comfort in a bottle of bourbon, something he never did. But despite the warning signs, Lucas was right. Whole, or in pieces, he was the only one who had a chance of getting the job done, and keeping Kate Evans alive in the process.

"Do what you have to do, Lucas. But don't let it get too personal. In this business, when you start thinking with your heart instead of your head, you can end up hurt, or dead. I know you agreed to this assignment because of Kate Evans. But you're going to have to use her, too. Are you sure you're up to it?"

Lucas nodded imperceptibly.

"We've got a lot riding on this one. If we get Kiley, we'll be able to close down a major operation. A lot of people will go to prison for a long time. We want him any way we can get him."

Without waiting for a reply, Matthew Owen slipped out of the room.

"Don't worry, Matt," Lucas muttered, turning away from the closing door to rest his forehead against the window once more. "We'll get him. Any way we can."

On the street below a stoplight changed from red to green, and the mass of cars crept forward on their journeys home.

For the first time in a long while he wondered what it would be like to live a normal life, to sit at a desk in an office eight hours a day, five days a week.

There were many ways to fight the war. Maybe he'd been at the front long enough. He had been offered other positions and promotions within the agency, but he had always chosen to continue working undercover, often volunteering for the most dangerous assignments without hesitation.

Compared to where he'd been and what he'd done, fighting rush-hour traffic would be a breeze, especially if he had a wife and kids to come home to every night. He closed his eyes and saw her again, sitting at the desk in the busy lobby of the library, head bowed, hurting because of him.

"What am I going to do?" he muttered, as he rolled his forehead against the cold glass of the window. "What the hell am I going to do?"

You're going to do your job, and you're not going to screw up. Otherwise both of you will end up dead.

Straightening his shoulders, he moved away from the window. He shrugged out of his black leather jacket and tossed it on a chair, then reached behind him to unclip the holstered automatic he wore at the small of his back. He set it on the nightstand and sat on the edge of the bed, staring at the telephone for a moment before lifting the receiver. He punched in three numbers without hesitation, stopped, hung up. He lifted it again, held it for several seconds, then slammed it down.

What, exactly, was he going to say to her? And what did he expect her to say to him? If her behavior in the library was any indication, he'd end up with a broken eardrum. But it might be worth it if he could hear the sound of her voice again before he tried to sleep. He couldn't see her, touch her, hold her in his arms, but he could let her know he was thinking of her. And then she could tell him where he could go and what he could do with his thoughts....

Uttering a few choice words that aptly described the situation in general and himself in particular, Lucas stretched

out on the bed, folded his hands behind his head and settled in for a long night of staring at the ceiling.

"Will this day never end?" Kate murmured as she eased
her foot off the brake, allowing her car to creep forward a
foot or two.

Somehow she had managed to get through the afternoon. She had eaten part of the sandwich she'd brought for
lunch, sitting with friends in the employees' lounge. She had
spent several hours in her office, catching up on paperwork. Then she had contributed her fair share of solutions
to the problems discussed at the weekly staff meeting.

Yet off and on all afternoon silvery green eyes and a
wicked grin had invaded her thoughts, along with a single
question. *Why?* Now, alone in her car, inching along the
freeway, with twilight fading into darkness, she gave in to
the inevitable and allowed herself to dwell on Lucas Hunter's sudden reappearance.

He had taken her by surprise. He had been so smooth, so
cool, while she had been rattled to her toes. Gripping the
steering wheel, Kate shifted uncomfortably as the heat of a
blush stained her cheeks. If only she had been as cool about
the meeting as Lucas, instead of letting her emotions get the
better of her.

She had been hurt and angry all over again, and he had
seen it in her eyes and on her face. He had heard it in her
voice. Had he also seen and heard the longing that had
stirred deep inside of her just as it always had whenever he
was near? Probably, she thought, mentally cursing her in-
ability to hide her emotions, especially those that should
have died long ago.

How was it possible to feel even a shred of desire for him
after the way he'd hurt her? He was dangerous—heart and
soul dangerous—and she knew it. Only some sort of closet
masochist would want anything to do with him. Thank God,
she didn't. Or did she?

"If you had to barge into my life again, Lucas, why couldn't you look and act like the dirty, rotten scoundrel you are?" Kate muttered.

If he weren't such a strong, powerful, attractive man, dealing with him might have been easier. And it might have been easier to ignore the questions he raised, easier to convince herself that she didn't care about the answers. But then, easy had never been Lucas's style.

"So, Katie, my dear, now that you've chased him away, I guess you'll go to your grave wondering what happened to him fifteen years ago," she taunted herself, as she stepped on the gas pedal, then braked yet again. With a sigh, she squeezed her eyes shut and shook her head.

There was a time when knowing what had happened might have helped. It might have allowed her to love another man the way she'd loved him. But what good would it do now? It was impossible to go back and relive the past. And there was nothing he could say to ease the pain that had settled in her soul like a living, breathing thing. Rather than wasting her time and energy on him, she should be searching for the reason why her brother had been killed.

The blare of a horn brought her back from the edge of another kind of pain. She opened her eyes to find the cars in front of her picking up speed as a break in the traffic came at last.

"Finally," she breathed as she stepped on the accelerator, forcing herself to concentrate on her driving for the remainder of the ride home.

It was almost seven o'clock when she pulled into the garage tucked behind the two-story town house nestled into a corner of West University. She slipped out of the car, locked it and the garage, then walked quickly across the walled courtyard brightly lit with newly installed floodlights. Dealing with the intricacies of the electronic security system, also newly installed, took a few more seconds. Then, she opened the French door and stepped into her living room.

Just inside the doorway, she stopped. Standing perfectly still, she scanned the living room, her ears straining to catch any unusual sounds as uncertainty swept over her in a long, slow wave. The house had once been a warm, welcoming haven. Now, despite the bright lights, the security system and the small revolver stashed inside her purse, she was afraid.

Though everything was as neat and tidy as she'd left it that morning, she couldn't quite banish the memory of open drawers, emptied closets, books and chair cushions strewn across the floor. Once again she imagined some horrid, dirty being defiling her home, pawing through her most cherished possessions. And once again she felt the violation deep inside herself. Its rending, twisting grasp held her like a claw at the back of her neck while her heart pounded and her palms grew damp.

It was then that he hit her, flying out of the darkness in a silent swoop, slamming into her chest, knocking her back and sideways into the door frame. Her scream was short and sharp, and followed by a vicious curse as she wrapped her arms around her attacker.

"Damn you, Caesar," she groaned, her heart beating double-time. "If you rip my blouse, you're going to the dog-food factory first thing in the morning."

Reassured by her gentle hold and the tone, if not the meaning, of her words, the huge, black cat released her, closed his silvery green eyes and began to purr. Balancing him in one arm, rubbing a cheek against his thick, soft fur, murmuring vile threats in a velvet voice, she closed and locked the door. The poor cat was as scared as she was since the break-in, she thought, as she reached for the light switch.

She had taken three steps toward the kitchen when the telephone began to ring. Changing course, she crossed the living room, perched on one arm of a pale green-and-beige striped love seat, and reached for the receiver.

"Well, it's about time, Kathryn. I've been dialing your number and listening to the damn thing ring and ring for over an hour. Enough to drive a woman to drink."

"Grace, when did you need an excuse to have a drink?" Kate teased lightly, smiling at the welcome familiarity of the gravelly voice, steeped in a West Texas accent so strong only a native could, or would, claim it. At the same time, she refused to acknowledge the tiny pang of disappointment she felt. Of course it wouldn't be Lucas. She didn't *want* it to be Lucas.

"Now, listen, girlie, don't get smart with me. I've been worried about you."

"I'm fine," Kate replied, trying hard to convince herself as well as her friend. "The staff meeting ran later than usual and the traffic on the freeway was a mess." Suddenly the smile disappeared from her face and voice. Her last words trailed out along with a weary sigh as she sagged onto the love seat, tipped her head against its cushiony softness and settled Caesar in her lap.

"What's the matter, honey?" Grace's voice softened with concern. "You don't sound all that fine to me."

"I am...really," Kate murmured, closing her eyes.

"Kathryn, talk to me."

If only I could, she thought, gripping the telephone as if it were a strong, sturdy lifeline. But she wasn't ready to discuss her growing suspicions concerning David's death. Nor was she ready to discuss Lucas Hunter, not even with Grace Stone, her best and dearest friend.

She would never forget the day ten years ago when she'd wandered into the old bookstore tucked in among the fashionable boutiques and gourmet shops of Rice Village. Despite their twenty-year age difference Kate had liked the tall, thin redheaded owner almost at once, and she'd been pleased to discover the feeling was mutual. Since then Kate had shared the very best and the very worst with Grace. But she couldn't share her current problems just yet.

"Listen, honey, stay put. I'm on my way over."

"No, Grace, please don't." Kate spoke quickly. "I just had a bad day. Honest. It's nothing a hot shower and an early night can't cure. And I've got Caesar to keep me company."

"That damn cat is no substitute for the husband and children you deserve." Grace paused for a moment, then continued in a softer tone of voice. "Well, if you're sure you don't need me—"

"I'm sure," she responded immediately, brushing a hand across her eyes, surprised by the trace of moisture on her fingertips. "And, Grace . . . thanks."

"For what? Listen, go on and get yourself to bed. I'm going out for a while, but if you need me for anything, anything at all, call and leave a message, and the answering service will find me. All right?"

"All right," Kate agreed, glad that her friend had plans for the evening. At least she wouldn't be tempted to drop by. If she wanted anything tonight, Kate thought, it was to be alone. "Got a hot date?"

"Just an old boyfriend, someone from my lurid past. He's in town on business, or so he says."

"Are you going to behave yourself?" Kate asked, a hint of laughter edging into her voice. Apparently she wasn't the only one with a past intent on catching up with her.

"Hell, no." Grace laughed, too. "But I promise to tell you all about it if you'll have lunch with me on Saturday."

"Every gory detail?"

"And then some."

"About twelve-thirty?"

"I'll pick you up then. Now get some rest, darlin'."

"I will. See you on Saturday."

Kate dropped the receiver into its cradle, then sat on the love seat for a few moments while scratching the big cat's belly. She was tempted to kick off her shoes, curl up, cuddle Caesar close and sleep in her clothes. However, she knew if she did that, she'd end up waking at one or two in the morning, stiff and sore, with the balance of a sleepless night ahead of her. So, shifting her furry friend off her lap, she stood up and headed for the staircase.

As she entered the front hall, she paused for a moment. The floor beneath the slot in the front door was littered with mail. She'd called the post office yesterday afternoon to re-start delivery—she'd had it stopped while she'd been in St. Louis—and they'd done so with a vengeance. Later, she promised herself as she started up the stairs. She'd sort through the mess later.

In her bedroom she dropped her purse in its usual place on her dresser, then headed straight for the bathroom.

The pounding spray of the hot shower eased her weari-ness instead of increasing it. And as she rubbed a thick, fresh towel over her body, she realized she was hungry. Slipping into an ancient, blue terry-cloth robe, she re-turned to the kitchen to find something to eat.

The freezer yielded a classic dinner. Fabulous food on a plastic plate in a matter of minutes, she thought, as she popped it into the microwave oven. Then, to appease the grumpy lump winding around her ankles, she opened a pouch of cat food and poured it into a bowl. While Caesar picked and nibbled, Kate stood at the counter, eating quickly. When she finished, she rinsed the plate and tossed it into the trash can.

After checking the door locks and assuring herself that the alarms were set, she retrieved her reading glasses from the coffee table in the living room, gathered the mail off the hall floor, and returned to her bedroom. She wasn't sure whether she wanted to tackle the assortment of envelopes, magazines and catalogs, or read, or sleep.

None of the above, she thought, with a bitter smile as she dumped the mail on the bed. She strode across the room to the large, mahogany dresser standing against one wall, dropped to her knees in front of it, and pulled open the bottom drawer.

She had been moving slowly but surely toward this mo-ment since she'd walked away from Lucas at the library.

Carefully she shifted a pile of frothy silk and lace lingerie to one side, revealing an old stationery box. Lifting it from the drawer, she stood up and returned to the bed where she settled back against a pile of pillows. Her glasses perched on her nose, she opened the box and removed the small photograph album.

She hadn't looked at the photographs for years, not even when she'd found the album, along with her lingerie, on the bedroom floor Tuesday night after the break-in. She had simply picked it up and put it away. Looking at the pictures now made about as much sense as worrying a sore tooth with your tongue. It was an unproductive act that would result in nothing but more pain. Yet she opened the soft leather cover and began to turn the pages.

Lucas, so young, so long and lean, laughing as he stood poised on the edge of the neighborhood swimming pool, surrounded by the other lifeguards . . .

She had known him forever, the boy down the street, just two years older, but part of another world. He'd gone to public school while her parents had sent her to a private school for girls. He'd run wild in the neighborhood while she'd rarely ventured more than a block or two from home, and only then with several friends. Yet through grade school and high school, on the rare occasions when they'd met, they had always smiled and said hello, the rowdy boy and the shy, quiet girl. *Hey, little girl . . .*

The summer before her freshman year at college her parents had allowed her to spend one lazy day after another with her girlfriends at the neighborhood swimming pool, her reward for graduating at the top of her class and winning a scholarship. Lucas and the other lifeguards had teased and flirted with them unmercifully. By midsummer the two groups had paired off. And though it had seemed odd to everyone else, Lucas and Kate had been drawn to each other as if their coupling had always been meant to be.

The two of them, sitting on an old quilt under a tree in the park, arms around each other . . .

Who had taken the photograph? Who had captured the warmth of their embrace, the love in their eyes? Kate couldn't remember.

Lucas, his face cold and angry, glaring at the camera, as he sat beside his parents and his older sister at a backyard barbecue at his home...

Even Kate's gentle teasing hadn't been enough to elicit a smile. He'd argued with his father about returning to college, their harsh, angry words echoing through the house. They hadn't spoken to each other the rest of the day, or for a long time thereafter.

Lucas in his army uniform, proud and handsome, even with his hair clipped short...

She closed her fingers around a memory of the spiky feel of it, recalling how she had run her hands over it in wonder the first time he'd come home on leave.

Lucas in Vietnam during his first tour of duty, and his second...

What demon had driven him to join the army when most young men had avoided military service like the plague? And why had he volunteered for a second tour of duty? Kate studied the photographs of him with his buddies outside a tent, standing beside a tank, talking to a small, sad child, as if these shots held an answer to her question.

He had been home for a month between tours. His family had moved to Columbus, Ohio, by then, so he'd gone there first to spend a few days with them. Then he had flown to St. Louis, and for the remainder of his leave he and Kate had been inseparable. She would never forget their last night together. They had vowed to love each other always, but when she'd begged him to make love with her, he'd refused.

I love you, Katie. No matter what, I will always love you. But I want us to wait until we can be together always, until we can be married.

And she had believed him.

As she turned the final page of the old album, a single sheet of paper, folded once, fell into her lap. Curious, she opened it and began to read.

September 15, 1972
Katie,
I can't wait to get out of this hellhole. I've got less than six months left, but it seems like forever. Your letters help a lot. Glad you're enjoying school, but you better not be enjoying it too much. No guys, right?

God, I can't wait to get my hands on you, little girl. I'm going to love you till we're weak.

In the meantime, don't get upset if you don't hear from me quite as much. We're moving around a lot, getting ready for some sort of special assignment. Don't worry—no danger involved, but I'll be busy. Should help to pass the time, and I might get out a few months early if everything goes as planned. Just remember I love you.

                                                    Lucas

It was the last letter she had received from him, and she had spoken to him once after that, for less than a minute. Exhibiting excellent timing, he had called almost two years after he'd returned from Vietnam, on the night of her engagement party. He had wanted to see her, to talk to her, but as she'd done today, she had refused.

Not for the first time she wondered what would have happened if she'd slipped away from the party and met him as he'd suggested. She could have talked to him then. She *should* have talked to him then. She would have spared herself so much if she had. Shoulda, woulda, coulda.... Words, like the afterthoughts they represented, that were too little, too late.

"You're spinning your wheels again," she chided herself, as she folded the letter and slipped it into the album. The past was over and done. Nothing could change it.

She put the album back in the box and replaced the lid. Tossing it to the side, she bent forward and scooped up her mail. But as she settled back again the telephone on the nightstand began to ring. Her mind on the assortment of envelopes, catalogs and fliers in her lap, she lifted the receiver with one hand and offered a quiet, almost absent-minded greeting.

"Hello, Kate."

His voice was deep and low. The sound of it set her heart racing. She tightened her hold on the receiver, closed her eyes and drew in a ragged breath.

"Lucas." She half sighed, half groaned his name. Why did he have to be so damned persistent? And why did she feel so...so *pleased* that he was? "How did you get my telephone number?"

"Telephone directory. K. E. Evans—Kathryn Elizabeth Evans. I've got your address, too. I can be there in twenty minutes if you're ready to talk."

"Didn't you hear a word I said this afternoon?" she demanded, making no effort to hide her exasperation. He had to be the most infuriating man on the face of the earth.

"I heard every word."

"Then why are you calling me?"

"You wouldn't believe me if I told you," he muttered, his voice suddenly harsh and weary.

Try me, she thought, but she didn't say the words aloud. If she gave him an inch, he'd take more than a mile. He'd tell her exactly what he thought she wanted to hear, and he'd end up convincing her that he meant it. "Probably not, Lucas, so why waste your breath?"

"Yeah, right." He paused for a moment, then continued in a lighter, teasing tone. "So, how about lunch tomorrow? I'll pick you up at the library at twelve-thirty. I thought we'd go to Harry's? It's just a couple of blocks away. If I make reservations you can be back at work within an hour."

"Lucas, please, listen to me. Stop wasting your time and mine. I am not, repeat *not* having lunch with you tomorrow—"

"And I'm not taking no for an answer," he snapped, cutting her off, first with words, and then with a decisive click as he hung up on her.

"Why, you . . . you dirty . . . rotten . . ." Kate stared at the buzzing receiver for several seconds before slamming it into the cradle.

"If you think you're going to coerce me into having lunch with you and listening to your lies, you have another think coming, Lucas Hunter." She tossed catalogs in one pile, bills in a second, and junk mail in a third. "When I say no, I mean *no*—"

As her fingers closed around a small, padded envelope, and she focused on the handwriting that spelled out her name and address, her ramblings came to an abrupt halt.

"David? Oh, Davey. . . ." she whispered, tearing into the package.

Her heart racing, her hands shaking, she pulled a small, black, leather-bound book from the envelope. She realized it was a daily diary when she opened it. As she flipped through the pages, she saw that each day and date were written in her brother's flowing script, but each entry consisted of a series of numbers.

"What in the world..." she murmured, going back to the beginning of the book. There was no letter or any instructions, just a small diary with page after page of coded entries, some short, some long.

As a young boy he had been fascinated with codes of all kinds, especially after she had read him a book by Peggy Parish called *Key to the Treasure*. After that, they'd spent days making up codes of their own, using numbers to represent letters of the alphabet. The number-letter combinations had varied greatly depending on what they were coding.

But what kind of information had David been recording, and why had he done it in code? What number-letter combination had he chosen to use? And, most important of all, when and why had he sent her the diary?

The when was easy enough to discover. Setting the book aside, she picked up the envelope and checked the postmark. It was dated in the a.m. the day after he'd been killed, so he must have mailed it the previous afternoon or evening. The why would be much harder to determine. In fact, if she had trouble cracking his code, it could take days. And since the break-in, she hadn't felt as if she had a lot of time.

She dumped the rest of the mail out of her lap and slipped off the bed. Diary in hand, she headed for the kitchen. What she needed was a pot of coffee, a pad of paper, a pencil and a little bit of luck. She knew she would find three of the four downstairs. As for the luck, well . . . She thought of Grace's favorite line. *Cross everything but your knees, and hope for the best, darlin'.*

"Exactly," Kate murmured, switching on the kitchen light. "Hope for the best."

Chapter 3

"Francis? Francis, where are you?" Kate murmured, balancing on the balls of her feet so she could scan the top shelf of books. It was just past noon, and *Nerve* was the last title on her list.

Though she'd stayed up until almost two in the morning working on David's diary, she had awakened as usual at seven. Fortified with fresh coffee, she had dressed with care, determined to mask her weariness and uncertainty. She couldn't afford to miss another day of work, and if she had to face Lucas Hunter again, then she would do so with an appearance of dignity and control.

She'd coupled her suit—a slim, navy blue skirt and tailored jacket—with a plain white silk blouse, then knotted a dark red scarf under the collar. Her low-heeled navy pumps were nothing if not sensible. She'd twisted and pinned her long brown hair into a neat coil at the nape of her neck, and blotted out the shadows beneath her eyes with a light touch of makeup. Thus armored, she had left for work feeling sure that she could handle Lucas when he appeared at the library.

Not if—when. But she didn't have to wait for him like a sitting duck, did she? Not when she could spend the morning looking for lost books in an area of the library closed to the general public. The idea had hit her as she'd sat in her office, eyeing the clock on her desk, waiting for the library to open. After a word with her supervisor, she'd acted on it immediately, spending almost three hours in the closed stacks.

She wasn't hiding, not really. But considering her last conversation with Lucas, it did seem like the safest place to be. And working alone in the solitary peace and quiet of the fifth floor at a job that required little concentration *had* allowed her ample time to review the information she'd decoded before she'd fallen asleep.

It had taken her awhile to figure out the pattern of David's letter-number combinations, but once she had, the actual decoding had gone quickly. She had gotten through about a third of the book, and although the entries hadn't made a lot of sense to her, she had noticed certain similarities. Each of the relatively short notes had begun with the words "met with," followed by the name of one of eight different people. An item purchased at the gallery had been coupled with each name. Each item had been sent to the warehouse for restoration, then delivered.

For example, Suzanne Cooper, a tennis pro at the River Road Country Club, had purchased a late-nineteenth-century Chinese Chippendale dresser on December 10. It had been sent to the warehouse for refinishing, then delivered to her home on December 15. On January 9 she had purchased a matching bureau, also sent for refinishing, and delivery on January 14.

But who was Suzanne Cooper? In fact, who were the other seven people David had met with over the past several months? If they had been friends of his, surely he would have told her about them. But if they were business associates or customers, then why had he kept a coded record of their dealings with the gallery? And why had he sent the record to her shortly before he was killed?

There was only one way to find out. She would have to finish decoding the entries. And in the meantime, she could contact some of the people listed in the diary. If they had met with her brother, then they knew him. And if they knew him . . . She knew that it was a risky thing to do considering one of them might be her brother's murderer, but she didn't have much choice. She had to start somewhere, and if it meant using herself as bait to draw out his killer, she was ready, willing and able.

With a mental shake, Kate forced herself to focus on the task at hand. The sooner she found the last book on her list, the sooner she could return to her office and start making telephone calls. Peering through the small, rectangular, wire-rimmed reading glasses perched on her nose, she checked the card she was holding one more time.

Yes, the library owned a copy of *Nerve* by Dick Francis, but no, the book was not in circulation. It had to be here somewhere. Her gaze traveled down to the second shelf, then the third. Ah, there it was, stuck in among the Franks. How in the world had it ended up so thoroughly misplaced? Smiling slightly, she reached out to claim the missing book.

"What in God's name have you done to yourself, woman?"

The deep, demanding voice shattered the silence surrounding her with the shock value of a shotgun blast. Startled, Kate spun around, book and card flying from her fingers. Forgetting the small stack of books piled at her feet, she took a step back straight into them, stumbled and fell flat on her fanny. Her mouth opened in surprise at her sudden change of position. Her cheeks blazed bright red as she remembered she had an audience. But then, as she focused on the tall, masculine figure lounging against the end of the bookcase, embarrassment ignited into indignation.

"You!" she snapped, glaring at Lucas Hunter over the rim of her glasses.

He was dressed in a dark gray suit, pale blue shirt, gray striped tie and sleek, black loafers. Slumped against the bookcase, he radiated a combination of casual elegance, power and authority. Any trace of the boy she'd known was blotted out by the man she was not familiar with. And though, for just a moment, something vaguely resembling honest emotion flickered across his face, Kate sensed that he was watching her as if from a great distance. His question had been playful and his smile was teasingly familiar, but he *was* a stranger, a fact she'd be wise not to forget.

With no amount of grace, she pulled herself to her feet, brushing the seat of her skirt with one hand, tucking a loose strand of hair behind her ear with the other. Then, straightening her spine and lifting her chin in an attempt to regain her lost composure, she faced him with what she hoped was a haughty expression.

"Wipe that false, silly smile off your face, Lucas, and tell me what you're doing up here. This floor of the library is closed to the public," she informed him in an even tone of voice.

"Why, I'm looking for Miz Kathryn Elizabeth Evans." He drawled her name in a phony Texas accent that set her teeth on edge.

Still smiling, hands in his pockets, he pushed away from the bookcase and strolled toward her. When he finally stopped just inches from her, she had to fight the urge to back away from him. Her body rigid, she concentrated on counting the narrow stripes in his tie. She made it to three before he caught her chin in his hand and tipped her face up, forcing her to meet his eyes.

"I know she's here somewhere," he murmured.

Mesmerized by his voice, the heat of his hand on her face and his glittering green eyes, Kate stood still, unable, almost unwilling to move as he eased her glasses off with his free hand. When he folded them deftly and slipped them into his jacket pocket, she started to protest, but he placed a finger across her lips, silencing her with a shake of his head.

"Don't talk, and don't move," he commanded, his voice gruff, his hand on her chin tightening for an instant, as if in warning, before he released her.

Unable to do anything but obey, she fixed her eyes on the striped tie again as Lucas quickly and carefully removed the pins securing her hair. One by one he dropped them on the floor until the coil came free. Running his fingers through the dark, silken strands again and again, he fanned her hair out and over her shoulders until she closed her eyes against the pleasure of his touch. She wanted to remember he was a stranger, a dangerous stranger, and that somehow, in some way, he threatened her existence, yet her body tipped toward him as if seeking shelter.

His hands left her hair and settled on her shoulders, holding her away. She opened her eyes and gazed into his, wanting to speak, but again he silenced her with a shake of his head.

Dear God in heaven, it was one thing to take control of a situation in your mind, but quite another in reality. In reality, she had absolutely no defense against the power of Lucas's presence, nor any control over the reaction of her body to the sound of his voice or the touch of his hand. And when he was so close to her, caressing her with such tenderness, it was impossible to believe that he would hurt her again, either physically or emotionally.

Lowering his gaze, Lucas bent slightly, undoing the scarf fastened under the collar of her white silk blouse and pulling it loose. He dropped it on the floor, then started on the top button of her blouse. As he released first one button, then another and another, the backs of his fingers brushed against her skin. A shiver raced through her as she felt the strange, slight tremor in his hands. He wasn't quite as aloof as he pretended to be. The realization gave her some small measure of satisfaction.

He stopped at the third button. Then hesitating only a moment, he traced the line of the open shirt with the fingers of one hand, outlining the swell of her breast, the edge of her collarbone, the slim column of her neck. She shivered again and tried to back away from him. Satisfying or not, she wanted him to stop. But before she could move, he wrapped his fingers around the back of her neck, holding her, grazing the edge of her jaw with his thumb. Tipping her face up, he held her eyes in a long, steady gaze.

"Don't fight me. Please, don't fight me," he whispered. Then he pulled her into his arms and rested his cheek against her soft, dark hair.

Don't fight you? Kate barely managed to choke down the hysterical laughter breaking at the back of her throat. Not hardly. Not when he was so close. Not when he was holding her against the lean, hard lines of his body with a grip so tight she could barely breathe. No, she couldn't, wouldn't fight him now.

But eventually he'd let her go. That was when she would regain her wits and fight him with everything she had. In the meantime, however, it felt so good, so safe, so secure, to be in his arms again. She held on to the lapels of his jacket, rested her head on his shoulder, closed her eyes and whirled back to a time when all she'd wanted, all she'd needed was his love.

As suddenly as he'd pulled her into his arms, he released her. Cursing herself for letting her guard down, she squared her shoulders, tipping her chin up in a defiant gesture. Her fingers clenched into fists as he stepped back to survey his handiwork, his eyes roving over her from head to toe.

"Unfortunately, I can't do anything about the rest of it," he muttered, indicating his disapproval of her tailored clothing and her plain, low-heeled pumps with a mocking frown. "At least, not here," he amended, pushing back his jacket so he could slip his hands into his pants pockets.

He raked her with his eyes once more, then turned on his heel and sauntered to the end of the bookcase. "Come on. Let's go."

"Lucas, what are you doing here?" Kate repeated her question in a surprisingly steady tone of voice, all things considered. Choosing to ignore the melting sensation that lingered in the pit of her stomach, she stood her ground against his command to come. Amazing how quickly she could pull herself together once he moved away from her.

"I told you," he replied, resting a shoulder against the edge of the bookcase. "I was looking for Miz Evans. Now that I've found her inside that obnoxious Pure Prudence outfit, I'm taking her to lunch. Harry's. We have reservations for twelve-thirty. So, come on. Let's go."

"I declined your invitation last night, Lucas," she retorted, jamming her clenched fists into her jacket pockets. *Pure Prudence outfit?* "What makes you think I changed my mind?"

He didn't respond. He simply stood there, blocking her only possible escape route, patiently watching her.

"How did you get up here anyway?" she asked, veering off on a new tack. Although, if she remembered correctly, Lucas had never been one to obey rules, she was willing to try anything to get rid of him. "This area *is* closed to the public."

"Mrs. Hughes unlocked the elevator for me."

"Mrs. Hughes?" She couldn't contain her astonishment. What could have induced her prim and proper supervisor to allow Lucas Hunter access to this part of the library? *"Mrs. Hughes?"*

"I told her I was with the district attorney's office and we had some personal...business to discuss. She was more than happy to cooperate."

"Lucas, you didn't."

"I did," he assured her, his eyes glinting with pride. "Now get your cute little butt in gear. It's nearly twelve-thirty." Bending at the waist, he picked up her navy blue purse, which she'd left on the floor beside the bookcase, and slung the strap over his shoulder.

"Lucas, give me my purse and my glasses *now*," she demanded, taking two steps in his direction, then stopping. She was so angry with him, and with herself, she could have chewed nails. He was much too adept at getting what he wanted, and she was much too easily manipulated. Suddenly, she wasn't sure who she despised more.

"Not until after lunch. I told you I don't take no for an answer. We're going to talk, Kate, one way or another. This time you are going to listen to what I have to say." He strode toward the elevator and punched the Down button.

"Why, Lucas? Why, all of a sudden, do you want to talk about the past?"

"Because I've spent too many years wondering what might have happened if I'd gone after you and forced you to listen to me the night you hung up on me," he shot back, rounding on her, his eyes shooting sparks.

"You can't change the—"

"No, I can't," he ground out, his voice harsh and unyielding. "But I can damn well do something about the future. And," he added, his tone softening, "maybe I can find out why it still feels so good to hold you in my arms."

Stunned by his admission, she stared at him for one long moment. Then, as the elevator door slid open, she moved down the aisle between the bookcases.

She didn't want to go with him, she didn't want to hear what he had to say. But, she reasoned, if she didn't, she'd be stuck at the library without her purse. No car keys, no house key, no money, no...protection. And most important of all, David's diary was in her purse and her decoding notes were in the outside zippered pocket. If she had lunch with him, if she listened to him talk, then she could reclaim her purse, and say goodbye. Easy.

"All right, you win. We'll have lunch, and you can talk until you're blue in the face. But that's it," she muttered, refusing to meet his eyes.

She stepped into the elevator, Lucas following close behind her. Moving as far away from him as possible, she edged into a corner, her spine stiff, her jaw clenched, her eyes looking straight ahead. If he wanted to talk, he could talk. But there was nothing he could say that would change how she felt about him. There was nothing he could say that would rekindle her love and trust. He might have bullied her into having lunch with him, but he was about to discover that Kate Evans wasn't an impressionable young girl, not anymore.

As the elevator door closed, some of Lucas's tension eased. So far, so good, he thought, watching her out of the corner of his eye. He had returned to the library intent on forcing her into a corner, literally as well as figuratively, but he hadn't been quite sure how to do it. Because he wanted her trust almost as much as he needed it, he had planned to work on her, to whittle away at her defenses until she agreed to talk to him.

Confronting her in the most secluded part of the library had given him just the edge he needed. He had caught her off guard and he had pressed the advantage. In fact, if he had wanted to strip her naked as they faced each other among the bookcases on the fifth floor, he probably could have done it. He ought to be proud of himself for being so good at his chosen profession, but pride wasn't exactly what he was feeling. What he was feeling was sick—sick of himself and of what he was willing to do in order to get the job done. He was willing to allow her to believe he *was* pursuing her because he wanted her.

Of course, since he was being so honest with himself, he'd have to admit that he was pursuing her because he wanted her. It wasn't the original reason, nor was it the only reason, but damn it, he had pulled her into his arms as much out of desire as duty. The weight of her body pressed against him had felt good, too good. The sudden, intense pleasure had been as stunning as a blow.

He shouldn't have done it, shouldn't have wanted her in his arms, shouldn't have felt so warm and so... so peaceful while she was there. And he *never* should have been so honest about his thoughts and feelings. He had to remain detached. He had to remember that he'd hurt her once and that it was almost certain he'd hurt her again before he was done.

As the elevator slowed to a stop and the door eased open, he forced himself to concentrate on the confrontation ahead. Though he didn't want to do it, he had a feeling he was going to have to tell her the ugly truth about why he hadn't contacted her when he returned from Vietnam. He had hoped to put her off with sweet talk and nonsense. But she was already suspicious, not to mention mad as hell.

He could sense her anger, simmering slow and steady, as they crossed the busy lobby and spun out through the revolving glass doors. Even the warm, sunny March day did little to lighten her mood. She could have been a stranger striding along beside him, her face set, her eyes fixed on something off in the distance. Tightening his hold on her neat, navy blue purse, he draped an arm around her shoulders.

"Don't push it, Lucas," she warned, turning the full force of a furious scowl on him as she wrenched away.

Smiling slightly, he settled his arm around her again, this time clamping his hand on her upper arm with a viselike grip. His eyes dared her to fight him in the middle of the busy sidewalk. She was really tempted, he thought, as he felt her body stiffen. He winced in anticipation of the elbow he expected her to jab into his ribs. Instead, she surprised him by drawing in a deep breath and relaxing.

"What's the matter? Afraid I'm going to run away?" she prodded, sarcasm dripping off every word. As they stopped at a street corner to wait for the light to change, she glanced up at him, her eyes challenging.

"Now that I've got you this far, I'm not taking any chances," he replied with utter honesty. "Anyway, this feels nice, doesn't it?"

"Oh, yes. Being mauled by a big, overgrown bully is really quite wonderful." She held his gaze a moment longer to emphasize her point, then turned her face away.

"Don't fight it, Katie," he cautioned softly, resting his chin atop her head for an instant. "Don't fight me."

His words, almost pleading in their intensity, surprised him as much as they surprised her. When she tilted her face up to look at him again, her eyes full of questions, he turned away.

Focusing on a huge glass-and-steel office building on the next corner, he tightened his lips. Matt was right. He was too close to her. And getting closer by the minute wasn't going to help. He had to distance himself from her, and he had to maintain the distance despite his personal feelings and desires.

No matter how much he wanted their growing relationship to be real, he had to remember it was being built on something other than absolute truth. It was being built on lies and deceit. With that kind of unstable foundation, it was temporary at best. He couldn't forget that fact for a moment. If he did, he might say or do something that would scar both of them for the rest of their lives.

As the light changed, and they started across the street, Lucas released her shoulder. Dropping his hand to the small of her back, he guided her toward the restaurant, his eyes blank, his touch impersonal, his heart aching.

Confused by his sudden change of mood, Kate walked through the tall, molded-brass doors of Harry's, her mind whirling with questions. What was going on? What kind of game was he playing? One minute he was warm and playful, the next he was cold and distant. Why? At odd moments she thought she knew him, only to realize she didn't really know him at all. He was as much a stranger today as he'd been yesterday, she mused.

Slipping away from him, she moved ahead up a short flight of steps, her eyes scanning the entryway and the bar off to one side for familiar faces. The restaurant's cool, quiet elegance wrapped around her, easing her turmoil. Thank God he'd chosen Harry's. If she had to talk to him, it was just as well she was doing it in a place where she felt so at home. Since the restaurant had been one of David's favorites, they'd come here often to celebrate special occasions.

For just a moment, she hesitated at the top of the steps, the reality of her loss weighing on her with renewed intensity. Then, as a tall, elderly man in a black tuxedo strode toward her, she smiled.

"Gerard, it's so good to see you again. How are you?"

"Ms. Evans, it's good to see you, too. It's been a long time." The maitre d' took her outstretched hand, dropped a gallant kiss upon it, then straightened, his eyes full of sympathy and concern. "I was so sorry to hear about Mr. Evans."

"Thank you, Gerard. He was a good man. I loved him very much." Kate held onto his hand a moment longer. "And thank you for the flowers. They were lovely. You received my note?"

"Yes." He paused for an instant, then released her hand. "So..." He nodded his head once. "Are you meeting—"

"She's with me," Lucas cut in, resting his arm across her shoulders. "Hunter. Lucas Hunter. I have a reservation for twelve-thirty."

"Ah, yes, Mr. Hunter. Your table is ready." Though his reply was directed toward Lucas, his eyes questioned Kate. At her slight nod, he turned on his heel, reaching for menus as he passed the podium at the doorway to the dining room. "If you will follow me, please."

The dining room was actually a series of small rooms, the walls covered in deep green, watered silk and hung with jungle prints and trophies from African safaris. Soft, glowing light radiated from brass and glass fixtures. The tables, stationed discreetly far apart, were covered with white linen and set with china, crystal and heavy silverware. Huge silver bowls of bright red and yellow tulips and pale baby's breath covered the sideboards, while identical arrangements in smaller silver bowls served as centerpieces.

Gerard led them into the farthest room, seating them at a corner table for two. His eyes questioned Kate once more as Lucas tucked her purse against the wall on the floor beside his chair. Again, she nodded slightly and gave Gerard a reassuring smile as she accepted a menu. Glancing up, she saw Lucas frowning at her.

"Would you care to see the wine list, sir?" Gerard offered, as he handed him a menu.

"No," he muttered, shifting his frown to the maitre d' as he dropped his menu on the table.

Nodding curtly, the maitre d' murmured something about sending a waiter to take their orders in a few minutes, turned and walked away.

"You didn't have to be so rude," Kate chided, her eyes steady as she gazed at Lucas over the top of her menu.

"Oh, really? Is he a *friend* of yours?" he asked, a hint of sarcasm in his voice.

"Yes, he is." She paused, holding his gaze for several seconds. When he remained silent, she challenged him with a question of her own. "Are you jealous?"

"Of course not. I'm just curious," he admitted in a calmer tone of voice. If he didn't dispense with his rotten mood, they'd end up spending the next hour snapping at each other, and that definitely wouldn't further his cause. "Seems like you're pretty familiar with this place."

"It was one of David's favorite restaurants. We came here often. Gerard adopted us somewhere along the way." Kate flipped open her menu and pretended to study it, no longer willing to meet his probing gaze.

"I'm sorry. I didn't know. Would you like to go somewhere else?"

"There's a lot you don't know, Lucas." She glanced at him, then returned her attention to the menu. "But this is fine. If I have to have lunch with you, it might as well be here."

He couldn't blame her for her attitude, but he didn't have to like it. In fact, he didn't like it at all. He had coerced her into having lunch with him, but she didn't have to rub his nose in it.

"Well, since you're practically a member of the family around here, what would you recommend?"

Lucas's taunting question cut into Kate's memories of happier days, reminding her that she had too many problems to solve to waste time daydreaming. And if she wanted to solve the problem sitting across from her, she'd have to have all her wits about her.

"Scallops," she replied, without hesitation, ignoring his glare and the tap, tap, tap of his fingers against the menu he had yet to open.

She was sure that he wasn't pleased with his choice of restaurant. He hadn't expected to end up on her turf, but she had no intention of leaving. In fact, she intended to use Harry's to her advantage.

"They're very good," she continued, feeling a smile play at the corners of her mouth. "Of course, *you* might prefer the steak tartare, since you obviously haven't had your daily ration of raw meat yet."

For a moment she was afraid she'd pushed him too far. His eyes narrowed, his jaw hardened, and a fine, white line etched its way around his mouth. She had no idea what had been eating at him since their walk to the restaurant, but she had a feeling she was going to find out. He looked as if he'd like to reach across the table, grab her and shake her. Preparing for the worst, she lifted her chin. But suddenly, he was smiling.

"You've grown up, haven't you, little girl? And you've got one hell of a smart mouth. I'm not sure what you need more, spanking or seducing. Maybe a bit of both," he murmured, tracing the line of her jaw with his fingertips, his eyes alight with interest, admiration and more than a hint of anticipation.

"I don't *need* anything from you, Lucas Hunter," she countered in a low, even tone as she jerked away from his touch. His mood swings were frustrating. "If you hadn't forced me—"

"Everything all right here, Ms. Evans? Are you ready to order?" Gerard appeared out of nowhere to stand beside her, his eyes and voice full of quiet concern.

"Yes. Yes, of course," she replied, dredging up yet another reassuring smile as she watched Lucas out of the corner of her eye, uncertain what he might say or do.

Apparently he was as unwilling as she to cause a scene. He, too, agreed that he was ready to order. In a cool, calm voice he requested scallops and iced tea for both of them, then dismissed the maitre d' with a flip of their menus into his outstretched hand.

They sat in silence for several seconds while a busboy filled their crystal water glasses and placed a basket of crusty French bread on the table. Kate lowered her eyes, stiffened her spine and folded her hands in her lap, refusing to meet Lucas's steady stare. In an hour, perhaps less, the ordeal would be over. All she had to do was listen to what he had to say, then tell him she never wanted to see him again.

Sorted out in such a manner, lunch with Lucas was something to get through as gracefully as possible. She could handle it without falling apart. She *would* handle it without falling apart. Smiling slightly, she took a deep breath, lifted her eyes and ended up mentally knocked to her knees all over again by the intensity of his silvery green gaze.

"You're pretty when you're mad."

His teasing tone signaled yet another mood swing. His wolfish grin, infinitely tempting yet subtly threatening reminded her of strangers and candy and Little Red Riding Hood lost in the woods. Lord, if she didn't get tough, *she'd* be lost in the woods. He had brought her here to talk about the past, but he seemed to be avoiding the subject with the same single-minded determination he directed toward driving her crazy. Enough was enough.

"I didn't agree to have lunch with you in order to listen to a lot of false flattery. It's not your style, Lucas, and it's a waste of my time."

"So?" His teasing tone disappeared as did his cocky grin. His eyes narrowed slightly though his gaze didn't waver.

"So, how about the long story you mentioned yesterday? How about our fifteen-year-old *misunderstanding*?" she demanded, her voice low and even.

"Ah, Katie, do you really want to rehash the past? It's been a long time, and we can't change what happened. What we can do is start over." His voice was soft and coaxing, his smile hinting at something naughty. "If you're honest, you'll admit that the attraction between us is as strong as ever. You can pretend to fight it, but, sweetheart, you want me as much as I want you." He was so smooth, and he watched her with eyes like shards of ice, watched her and waited.

"You . . . you . . ." Her voice shook with anger as she gripped the edge of the table. Her knuckles turned white as she forced herself to stay seated. At the back of her mind she knew she should stop speaking before she gave too much of herself away. Unfortunately, it was too late. Words tumbled out as years of pent-up fury and frustration exploded inside of her.

"You...you...piece of crud. You have no idea how you betrayed my trust, do you? I waited for you to fulfill your promise to come home to me. When you didn't, I called your parents. Your mother... she said... she said you had a good reason for not contacting me. She told me not to worry about you, to go on with my life, that maybe one day...one day..." She felt the welling of unshed tears in her eyes as the anger in her voice turned to anguish.

Dear God, how could it possibly hurt so much after so long? And how could she allow herself to come so close to letting him know it? Refusing to meet his gaze, she fixed her eyes on the wall behind him, willing herself not to cry.

"If you didn't want anything to do with me, you should have had the courage to tell me. But not you. You took the easy way out, didn't you? You dumped me without a word, and believe me, I'll never forget it. And I have no intention of making the same mistake twice. I wouldn't want you if you were the last man on earth."

"Katie, I'm sorry...so sorry," he muttered, but as he reached for her, she stiffened and turned her head away.

"Don't Lucas. Just...don't...touch...me."

"Damn it, Kate—" he growled, his hand knotting into a fist atop the white linen tablecloth.

"Your salads, sir."

The waiter served them with quick, efficient movements, his blank face giving no indication of what he might have overheard. Then, assured by Lucas that everything was satisfactory despite the strained silence shrouding the table, he moved away.

Kate lowered her eyes. She picked up her fork, only to set it down again, leaving her food untouched. The hushed murmur of voices swirled around her, the chink of crystal and silver cutting at the edge of her mind. One teardrop slid down her cheek, defying her attempt at self-control.

Lucas wanted to touch her, but he kept his clenched fingers atop the table. His eyes were riveted to the glistening drop of moisture marring the soft, smooth surface of her skin. He wanted to hold her in his arms, to comfort her with quiet words, to soothe her with his hands and his lips. But as surely as he knew his name, he knew she wouldn't allow it. She didn't trust him, and he didn't blame her. He had played games with her once too often. If he had any hope of hanging on to her, he would have to tell her the truth, and he would have to do it now.

"There are enough books and movies about the war in Vietnam to give you a good idea of what it was like, but unless you were a part of it, a part of the relentless heat and humidity, the death and destruction, the absolute horror...'' He spoke in a flat, cold, quiet voice, faltered and began again.

"Volunteering for a second tour of duty was one of the dumbest things I've ever done. I'm not sure why I did it—to serve my country, to defy my father, to prove... what? Damned if I know. I was scared of dying, or worse, being maimed for life, but it was something I *had* to do," he confessed in a bitter whisper.

Raising her head, Kate wiped her cheek. She met his gaze, and in his eyes she saw a mixture of pain, anger and uncertainty spiced with a heavy dose of self-disgust, emotions as honest and intense as her own. As suddenly as if he'd been swept away by a strong wind, the stranger had disappeared. In his place was the man she had known and loved so long ago, the man who had wanted her, needed her as much as she had wanted and needed him. She was filled with an overwhelming desire to touch him, to wrap her arms around him and hold him, but she stayed as she was—still and silent.

"In my last letter I mentioned a special mission, didn't I?'' Lucas glanced down at the table, picked up a fork and began rolling it between his fingers. He remembered writing the letter as if he'd done it yesterday. It had been one of the hardest things he had ever done, saying goodbye without saying goodbye, sharing his hopes for the future when he hadn't been sure he'd have one.

"Yes," Kate murmured, nodding her head in answer when he looked at her. "But you said it wasn't dangerous."

"Sweetheart, believe me, *every* mission in Vietnam was dangerous," he muttered. "Anyway, this was a search-and-destroy, pretty basic, except that we were blessed with a new lieutenant. He was a West Point grad, but green as grass, scared spitless, and after six weeks in-country, so high most of the time he didn't even know his own name. Just like half the guys in the company. To make a long story short, we went out, but only three of us came back alive. Actually, we were barely alive three days later when a Huey finally came in and pulled us out of the jungle. The VC were waiting for us. They blew us to bits."

"Oh, Lucas," she whispered, her breath catching in her throat. But he didn't seem to hear her. He was far away, in another time, another place.

"I was in and out of consciousness for days . . . weeks. . . . When I finally came around I was in a military hospital in Ohio. My folks were there. They looked like hell, but I guess I looked like hell, too." He tried to smile, but his lips twisted bitterly. "I kept asking them what happened. Nobody would tell me. I kept asking about the other guys, my buddies. When I began to realize what had happened, when I started to remember I . . . I went kind of . . . crazy. I couldn't understand why I had lived when so many of my friends had died. I felt so . . . so unworthy and so . . . angry. There were times when I was so filled with rage that I wanted to smash something . . . anything. And there were times when I . . . wanted to . . . die. . . ."

Stunned, Kate remained still and silent, gazing at him as he stared off into the distance. He had been badly hurt physically and emotionally. Yet he had turned away from her. He had closed in on himself, shutting her out. And he had wanted to die.

"Why didn't your mother tell me you were in the hospital? Why didn't she tell me you were hurt?"

"I made her swear she wouldn't. I didn't want you to know. I didn't want you to feel . . . obligated to me in any way," he admitted, glancing up to meet her wide, sad eyes. She had trusted him, but he hadn't trusted himself. Worst of all, he hadn't trusted her. "I thought it was best to . . . to cut you loose. I knew that if I talked to you or saw you again, I wouldn't be able to let you go. And I *had* to let you go. I wasn't too . . . stable . . . for a while. There was a time when I might have hurt myself, or God help me, when I might have hurt you, physically hurt you, Kate. As it turned out, I hurt you anyway, didn't I?'' Once again he dropped his gaze to the table, but not before she saw the despair deep in his eyes.

"But Lucas, I could have helped you. I *would* have helped you. If I had known the truth, I would have come to you and stayed with you day and night until you were better. I would have waited for you to heal, no matter how long it took." In fact, Kate felt as if she *had* been waiting for him in some small, secret part of her soul.

"Damn it, Kate, that's exactly why I didn't want you to know. You were just a kid, a sweet, innocent kid. You were young, bright, attractive. I didn't want you wasting your time on me. I was in pieces, baby, lots of tiny, jagged pieces. You deserved somebody strong and whole, and there was a chance I'd never be strong and whole again. You deserved better, a hell of a lot better than me. If you had seen me, you would have realized—"

"Did it ever occur to you to allow *me* to decide what I deserved? You could have given me some credit. You make me sound like a bubble-headed bimbo, too weak and silly to be trusted to make it through the hard times. You really had a low opinion of me, didn't you?"

"No, I didn't. I just did what I thought was right at the time. I wanted to set you free so you could have a decent life for yourself."

"Well, thanks a lot, Lucas," Kate countered in a grim tone of voice. "But, unfortunately, your good deed backfired. You see, I don't think I've ever been free of you. And I wanted to be free of you. Lord, but I want to be free of you, once and for all."

"Well, sweetheart, that makes us even. I don't think I've ever been free of you, either." It was a line, just a line to draw her closer. It wasn't part of the truth he'd been telling. It couldn't be, he assured himself as he pasted a charming grin on his face. "Guess that means we've got unfinished business. Since I'll be around for a few days..." He allowed the unspoken suggestion to hang between them.

"Is that why you were so determined to talk to me? So we could finish *business*?" Kate asked, her voice soft and tentative. If what he was saying was true, and she had no reason to doubt him, then what he'd done, he'd done because he had cared for her. Now, perhaps he, too, simply needed to know whether or not what they'd shared in the past was gone forever.

"God, I don't know," Lucas muttered, his smile fading as he tossed the fork he'd been worrying onto the table where it landed with a clatter. How easy it would be to say yes. Because, in a way, it was true. He did want their past put to rest. But it wasn't the only truth, nor was it the primary truth. So how could he let her think that it was?

"I came to Houston to lease some warehouses. I stopped in the library to look at back issues of the local newspapers to get a feel for what's happening here, and to study the zoning laws. I saw you across a crowded lobby, as you put it. What else can I say?"

The truth, Kate thought, *you can tell me the truth.* Amazing how she knew the instant the stranger returned just by the tone of his voice and the look in his eyes. One moment he was the man she had loved and trusted, a man she might love and trust again. The next moment he was something else altogether, something smooth and slick and scary. Her soaring spirits crashed and burned with soul-shattering intensity.

"Something wrong with the salads, Ms. Evans?" Gerard inquired politely from somewhere above her head.

"The salads?" Kate asked, her voice whisper-soft as she stared at the maitre d' in confusion. "The salads are fine, but I don't think I can..." She glanced down at the table, her face full of dismay as the sickening sensation in the pit of her stomach climbed to the base of throat.

With a sudden movement that surprised both men, she scraped back her chair, stood up and walked away. She couldn't think, and suddenly she was having trouble breathing. If she didn't get out of the restaurant, if she didn't get away from Lucas Hunter, she might give in to the urge to start screaming, and never, ever, stop.

Chapter 4

Once again he had pushed her too far. Maybe Matt was right. Maybe he was losing his touch. At other times, in other places, he'd had no trouble telling a woman what she wanted to hear in order to gain her cooperation. But telling Kate what she wanted to hear, telling her that he'd sought her out because he still loved her, would have been a lie, the kind of lie that would wound her in the worst possible way when she finally learned the truth. It had seemed wiser to fall back on the cover story he'd created. Watching her wend her way through the scattered tables, her chin up, her back straight and stiff, Lucas had a good idea of just how wise he'd been.

"Not very wise at all," he muttered, tucking her purse under one arm as he stood up.

"Excuse me, sir?" Gerard looked at him as if he gave off a bad smell.

"Nothing," Lucas replied, reaching for his wallet. Before the maitre d' could stop him, he dropped a fifty-dollar bill on the table, then swept past the man, determined to catch Kate before she got out of the restaurant.

Swiftly, he maneuvered his way around waiters and bus-boys, through the maze of small dining rooms, slowing his steps when he reached the doorway leading into the restaurant's entryway. She was just ahead of him, descending the short flight of steps, one hand already extended toward the handle of the huge, brass doors. Sure that her mood would be less than welcoming, he slowed his pace. Better to catch her just outside the restaurant. On the sidewalk, in the sudden glare of sunlight, with people crowding past, she would be off balance just enough for him to regain control of the situation. And once he regained control, he wouldn't relinquish it again.

As she reached the entryway, Kate, too, slowed her steps. Anger and confusion still roiled around inside her, but the panic that had fueled her flight was receding. She wasn't sure why she'd run from Lucas. Perhaps she had been running from herself, as well, running from her yearning for something that could never be.

Surely after so long a time it had been foolish to allow herself to believe that he still cared for her. As foolish as it was to admit that *she* still cared for him. If he had pursued her simply to satisfy his curiosity, well, that was his right. But now that he had satisfied himself, and now that he'd finally spoken of the past, it would be better for her if she never saw him again. Or would it?

If she believed what Lucas had told her, and she did believe him, then he hadn't betrayed her love and trust in quite the way she'd imagined. He had wanted what was best for her, and he hadn't considered himself to be the best. He had wanted to protect her from himself and the harm he might have done to her. He had freed her from any obligation she might feel toward him in the sharpest, starkest way possible, guaranteeing she wouldn't pursue him and discover the real reason why he hadn't come home to her. And he had done it because he had cared for her. If he had been guilty of anything, he had been guilty of not trusting her, of not trusting in the strength of her love for him.

Was he still guilty of not trusting her? Was that the reason why he'd told the truth about the past, yet lied about the present? Because he had lied about his reason for hounding her. She was sure of it. He had slid into smooth and slick with such infuriating ease, the shutters slamming shut on the man she remembered, leaving behind the stranger she would never know.

"Hang on to that thought," she cautioned herself in an undertone as she reached for the brass door handle. "Leave behind the stranger you'll never know." It was too late, much too late for them. To think otherwise was to think like a fool.

Intent on nothing more than getting away, she wrapped her fingers around the curve of smooth, cool metal only to have it wrenched from her grip by someone pulling the door open from the outside. Startled, she stepped back to one side, moving out of the way of the tall, thin man entering. Glancing at him, she caught her breath, her eyes widening with surprise. When he recognized her, smiled and extended his hand, she had to fight the urge to take another step back.

"Ms. Evans, this is an unexpected pleasure, though I wish we were meeting under happier circumstances. Once again, let me offer you my deepest sympathy. I sorely miss dear David."

"Thank you, Mr. Kiley," she replied, trying not to flinch as the man's long, slender fingers wrapped around her hand.

He was a charming, sophisticated man, wealthy and highly respected, with the outward appearance of an elder statesman. David had admired him and enjoyed working for him. To be thoroughly honest, her brother had been devoted to the man. Unfortunately, Kate had never liked him, a fact she had tried hard to hide over the past few years.

For a long time, she had thought her feelings were the result of petty jealousy. She had seen less and less of David after he'd gone to work for Jonathan. But as she'd gotten to know him, her instincts had warned that he wasn't all he appeared to be. Despite the facade of fine clothing and impeccable manners, there was an aura about him, an instability that she had found more and more disturbing.

"You forgot your purse, darling." Lucas's arm wrapped around her shoulders. Giving her a reassuring squeeze, he smiled into her startled eyes when she tipped her head up to meet his gaze. "And you've run into another friend, haven't you?"

"Yes," she replied, hesitating an instant as she glanced at Jonathan. *You might say that,* she thought.

In reality, she felt as if she were trapped between a rock and a hard place. Clutching at common courtesy as if it were a means of escape, she introduced the two men.

"Jonathan Kiley, Lucas Hunter. My...David worked for Mr. Kiley, Lucas."

Pulling her hand free of Jonathan's grasp, she eased back against Lucas, seeking his protective warmth since she deemed him, by far, the lesser of two evils. Again he squeezed her shoulder. Then, reaching around her, he offered his hand to the older man.

"Nice to meet you, sir." Lucas's handshake was firm, his voice polite and friendly, as he masked an urge to slam the man against a wall. He was slime, the worst possible kind, and he had had the gall to put his hand on Kate. One day soon...

"I don't recall David ever mentioning your name," Kiley probed, sizing him up with cool disdain.

"I'm a friend of Kate's. We knew each other before she moved to Houston. I'm in town on business, and we just happened to meet again for the first time in years."

"What kind of business?"

"Import/export. What about you, sir?"

Kate stood between the two, head swiveling one way, then the other, as they sparred in a way that could only be described as hostile. What the hell was going on? she was about to ask when Jonathan spoke her name.

"Yes, Mr. Kiley?"

"I was saying I've discovered that some notes and...things that David kept for me are missing. You haven't, by any chance, run across anything related to the gallery among his personal papers have you, my dear?"

She hesitated for a long moment, thinking of the coded diary in the purse tucked under Lucas's arm. What she had deciphered *was* related to the gallery, but something about the steely glint in Jonathan's eyes prevented her from trusting the honeyed, coaxing tone of his voice.

"I haven't found anything related to the gallery, and I've gone through most of his things."

"I see. Well, if something should turn up, you will contact me, won't you?"

"Of course," she assured him, matching him false smile for false smile as he brushed past them to greet the waiting maitre d'.

"Come on, sweetheart, let's get out of here," Lucas muttered, his warm breath ruffling the wisps of hair near her ear. Before she could protest or pull away, he led her out of the restaurant.

She walked down the sidewalk with him, head bent, her hands tucked into the side pockets of her skirt. Meeting Jonathan Kiley face-to-face had forced her to refocus her thoughts. For a time, albeit a short time, she had forgotten about her brother, allowing herself to be sidetracked by Lucas Hunter. But why was she wasting time rehashing the past with him when David's murderer was on the loose? She should have spent her lunch hour working on the diary or trying to contact some of the people mentioned in it. If she returned to the library now, she might have time....

Slowing her steps, she raised her head, squinting in the soft, March sunshine as she tried to get her bearings. Realizing they weren't heading toward the library, she stopped.

"I have to go back to work," she said, turning to face Lucas.

"Not yet." He tightened his hand on her shoulder and started walking again, guiding her gently but firmly toward a bench near the reflection pond outside city hall.

"Lucas, please..." She hated to beg, but in the short time since their meeting with Jonathan, she had begun to experience a new and unexpected urgency to find out whatever she could about her brother's death. It was as if a time bomb had begun ticking in her head, and when the bell sounded—

"You don't like him, do you?" Lucas asked, his eyes full of concern as he stopped beside the bench and turned her to face him.

She hesitated only a moment. "No, I don't."

"Why not?"

She shrugged, lowering her gaze to the sidewalk. "I don't know. He's never really said or done anything to warrant it."

"Did you lie to him about the papers he mentioned?" Lucas prodded in a soft voice.

Her head snapped up. Her eyes glittered dangerously. He was treading on territory that was out-of-bounds considering his own avoidance of the truth. "Did you lie to me about why you're in Houston, about why you were so anxious to talk to me?"

Checkmate, he thought.

He sat on the bench, bringing her down beside him with his hands on her shoulders. His green eyes drilled into her with sudden intensity. "You don't trust me, do you?"

"And you don't trust me. But then you didn't trust me fifteen years ago, did you?" Again she shrugged, freeing herself from his hold. "We've managed without trusting each other for a long time, Lucas. Why start now? Why not just give me my purse so I can go back to work?"

Because I need your trust if I'm going to keep you alive.

He came so close to saying the words aloud, as the urge to dispense with all pretense rode through him hard and fast.

She was right. He hadn't trusted her fifteen years ago. Physically and emotionally beaten, he hadn't wanted to face the brutal possibility that she might dump him, so he had dumped her first. And now, when she needed his trust just as much as she'd needed it then, he couldn't give it to her without endangering her life.

He had to keep her in the dark as long as possible. She didn't have the training necessary to deceive a man like Kiley while they searched for enough evidence to convict him of her brother's murder. In fact, if Kiley had read her as easily as he, the man already knew she had lied about the missing papers. There was also a possibility that she might be tempted to take matters into her own hands if she thought Kiley was responsible for David's death. Lucas's blood ran cold at the thought of her confronting Jonathan Kiley on her own.

Yet he wanted to tell her the truth about himself. He didn't want to represent himself as an employee of an import/export company. He wanted her to know that he worked for the United States government. He wanted her to know that as a result of his experience in Vietnam, he had had only one goal in life—to work for the Drug Enforcement Agency. But if he told her who and what he really was, he would also have to tell her why he was in Houston. He simply couldn't take the risk.

When all was said and done, he had no choice but to continue his charade, despite the fact that it was getting harder and harder to do. He needed her trust on a professional level. If gaining it meant lying to her, he would do it. Unfortunately, the more lies he told her, the more furious and unforgiving she would be when, eventually, inevitably, she began to understand how thoroughly she had been deceived. But by then his job would be done, and he'd be gone. So her anger wouldn't affect him, would it?

Unable, or perhaps unwilling to answer Kate's question, Lucas broke the silence stretching between them with a question of his own. "What have you got in here, anyway?

Rocks?'' He lifted her purse, his long fingers kneading the medium-size, soft leather bag.

She had sat quietly, watching the play of emotions across his face, wondering at the internal war she sensed he was waging. For a moment, regret and longing had lingered in his silvery green eyes, then disappeared with the startling suddenness of a door slamming shut.

"Yeah, I've got rocks in my purse, Lucas. And I've got rocks in my head for putting up with you. Now, give it to me.'' Narrowing her eyes, she reached for the bag, but he slid down the bench away from her before she could get her hands on it. "Don't you dare—''

"You *do* have rocks—in your head," he muttered, unzipping the purse and studying the contents. "Carrying a concealed weapon is against the law in Texas. What are you doing with this thing?" He dangled the .38 on his index finger just high enough for her to see it without putting it on public display.

"It's registered and I know how to use it." Her fists clenched in her lap, Kate glared at Lucas.

"Good for you. But that doesn't explain why you're lugging it around in your purse."

"Why I do what I do is none of your damned business. Now, give me my purse, or I'll... I'll...''

"What? Call the cops? Go ahead. But you'll be the one they cart off in handcuffs, sweetheart." He flashed his wicked, wolfish grin, his eyes glittering.

"I hate you." Kate turned away from him.

"Ah, hate—a good, solid emotion. Often runs hand in hand with love," he taunted in a soft, seductive tone of voice.

"In your dreams, Lucas," she muttered through clenched teeth.

"And in yours... Katie." He paused for a moment, his whispered words hanging between them. Then he continued in a more normal tone of voice. "Are you in trouble, Kate?"

"Of course not." She stared off into the distance, unwilling to meet his probing gaze.

"Then why are you carrying a gun?"

He wasn't going to let it go, and if she didn't answer his questions, he wasn't going to let her go, either. She was already late. She had calls to make. And she was so tired of fighting him. Why not tell him . . . everything? Maybe she'd scare him away.

"My brother was murdered less than two weeks ago. His car was stripped and his apartment was ransacked. A few days later someone broke into my town house and tore the place apart. I don't know if the incidents are related, but against the law or not, until David's murderer is caught, the gun goes wherever I go."

"Sounds like somebody's looking for something. Do the police think the incidents are related?"

"The police are working on it, along with hundreds of other cases." She twisted her fingers together in her lap, considering his comment about somebody looking for something . . . something like David's diary?

"What about you, Kate? Are you working on it?"

"No," she replied, too quickly, too emphatically. She glanced at him to gauge his reaction, but he was pawing around in her purse again. "Honestly, Lucas—"

"What's this?" He held up the small, black book, his eyes holding hers in a steady gaze.

"It's a . . . my . . . diary." Again she responded too quickly, stumbling over her words. "It's private."

"It's full of numbers." He riffled through the pages, frowning slightly.

"I told you it's private. I use a . . . a code."

He held her gaze for a long moment, his eyes searching hers. Then, as if he'd made a monumental decision, he dropped the book into her bag and zipped it shut. "Smart girl," he murmured, tossing her purse at her.

"Yeah, real smart," she retorted, her fingers closing around the soft leather as she stood up. "Smart enough to know when to cut and run." She turned on her heel, but before she could take more than a few steps, Lucas was beside her again, his hand closing around hers.

"I'll walk back with you."

"Suit yourself." She shrugged her shoulders, but she didn't try to pull away from him. There was something so heartachingly familiar about the way he threaded his fingers through hers that she didn't *want* to pull away.

She simply wanted to be with him, which was downright crazy considering the way he'd tormented her for almost two hours. She'd run the gamut of emotions, wanting to slap him senseless one minute, wanting to soothe him with kisses and caresses the next, all the while knowing she had neither the time nor the energy to waste on doing either. Someone had murdered her brother, and until she found out who had done it, and why, she couldn't allow herself to be distracted. And Lucas was definitely a distraction. Though she kept her eyes focused straight ahead, almost unconsciously she eased closer to him, savoring his strength, his warmth, his spicy scent for what must surely be the last time.

He squeezed her hand once, gently, but she didn't return the caress, nor did she meet his eyes when he glanced down at her. The cool breeze ruffled through her sleek, dark hair as she lifted her face to the warmth of the sun. He felt her body relax as she drew near to him. For a moment he thought she might rest her head against his shoulder.

He didn't want to leave her alone at the library, but common sense warned him not to do otherwise. If he stayed with her, or forced her to go with him, she would pitch a fit guaranteed to arouse suspicion. Her tail had been in the lobby when Lucas had entered the library earlier, and he had been waiting for them when they'd left the restaurant. Kiley's timely arrival left little doubt about his employer. He couldn't afford to look like anything but the old boyfriend he'd claimed to be, even if it meant leaving Kate on her own with her literal as well as figurative loaded gun.

If the black book in Kate's purse was her diary, he'd eat it page by page. More likely, it had something to do with her brother, but what? Could it be Kiley's missing papers? Much as he disliked the idea, he had no choice but to wait until later to find out.

In the meantime, he'd visit Kiley's antique gallery and pay his respects to the owner, businessman to businessman. Better to beard the lion in his lair when he least expected it. No telling what he'd find out, and if he kept Kiley busy, he wouldn't be able to hassle Kate.

They crossed the brick plaza in front of the library and stopped just short of the revolving glass doors.

"Well, Lucas...goodbye." Without looking at him, Kate tried to free her hand from his.

"Not so fast, sweetheart," He tightened his hold on her hand as he swung her around to face him. "We're not saying goodbye."

"We should." She met his gaze, sadness and regret lurking in her wide, dark eyes. "It's too late for us, Lucas."

"No, it's not." He gripped her shoulders, his fingers warm and hard through the fabric of her blouse and jacket, his silvery green eyes full of determination. "It's not."

"I wish..." *Wish you had come home to me... Wish you had loved me less and trusted me more...* She reached up, placing her palm against the side of his face, tracing the angle of his cheekbone with her thumb. "I wish..." *Wish I had trusted myself more, wish I had gone to you regardless of what anyone said...*

"And I want," he murmured. *Want to hold you, kiss you, touch you... Want to come to you without lies and deceit... Want your love and trust now and always...* Bending his head, he covered her mouth with his.

He had meant the kiss to be nothing more than a chaste promise of better things to be, a vow to himself that one day, when the shadows receded, he would find a way to make her understand. But then she sighed and swayed against him, resting her hands on his chest.

Ignoring the people milling past them, he deepened the kiss. Unconsciously her lips parted, and he slid his tongue between her teeth, his invasion gentle yet thorough as he stroked her slowly, yet surely.

She responded just as gently, just as thoroughly, moaning softly as she moved her hands from his chest, threading her fingers through the thick, dark hair at the nape of his neck. She couldn't think, she could barely breathe, and she wanted, too....

He slid his hands from her shoulders to the small of her back, pressing her into the cradle of his hips so there would be no doubt in her mind how honestly, how completely he wanted her. Then he lifted his mouth from hers, and folded her into his arms. Rubbing his cheek against the sun-warmed softness of her smooth, dark hair, he murmured her name again and again as he tried to regain control.

Finally, placing his hands on her shoulders, he took a step back. When she gazed up at him, her eyes hazy, her moist, red lips slightly parted, he wanted to scoop her into his arms and carry her away. Instead he gave her a good shake and spoke in his deepest, most authoritative tone of voice. "We are not, repeat *not*, saying goodbye." When she tried to protest, he shook her again, then turned her toward the revolving door. "Go inside. We'll talk later."

Dazed by her response to his kiss, Kate did as she was told, moving, as if on autopilot, into the flow of people entering the library. Without a backward glance, she crossed the lobby, absently exchanging greetings with other staff members as she headed toward her office. As she had the day before, she closed and locked her door, then sagged against her desk.

What in the world had gotten into her? She had no business getting involved with Lucas Hunter, not now. And no matter how she tried to deny it, she *was* getting involved with him. She had welcomed his kiss, relishing the deep, probing intimacy of it with embarrassing enthusiasm, clinging to him with hopeless desire, all but begging him to fill the yawning, aching emptiness inside of her.

"Hopeless is right," she muttered, setting her purse on the desktop. "If you think anything will come of it, you *are* hopeless." But he had said they would talk later. She massaged her temples with her fingertips. "Yeah, later. In another fifteen years, so don't hold your breath. Do something constructive, like your job, or you won't have one. And by all means, stop talking to yourself."

With a wry smile, she stood up and walked around to her desk chair, slipping out of her jacket along the way. She had stacks of paperwork to complete, and she'd really overshot her lunch hour. But if she got busy, she might be caught up enough to justify a couple of personal telephone calls during her late-afternoon break. The tennis instructor should be at the country club, and the shoe salesman should be at the department store, but she'd wait until early evening to contact the owner of Vanderbilt's.

He walked away from the library, his long, loose strides eating up the pavement as he tried to relieve the tension that knotted and twisted inside of him. If he was going to rattle Kiley's cage, he was going to have to be able to concentrate. At the moment, however, he couldn't think of anything except how much he wanted Kathryn Elizabeth Evans.

He must be certifiably insane to have kissed her the way he had. He never started anything he couldn't finish, and there was no doubt in his mind that his kiss had started something. But what he'd started with one kiss could not be finished. Not as long as she was unaware of the real reason for his reappearance.

With that fact in mind, Lucas forced himself to focus on his upcoming meeting with Jonathan Kiley. If he hadn't suspected that Kate might have what he was looking for, Kiley wouldn't have questioned her. And though it was possible he had believed her when she denied having anything, it wasn't probable. The man was too cunning to be deceived by someone as inexperienced as Kate. In fact, it was a good bet her response had increased his suspicions. How long would he wait to act on them?

Not long at all, Lucas thought. If he believed that Kate was a threat to him and his "business," Kiley would attempt to get rid of her in the same way he had gotten rid of her brother. In order to protect her, Lucas knew that he'd have to be in control of the situation.

By approaching Kiley on his territory within hours of their first meeting, he hoped to shake him up, maybe force him into acting without thinking and making a mistake. He was taking a calculated risk, endangering Kate as well as himself, but he could think of no better way to goad Kiley into playing his hand. Once he was done, however, he wouldn't be able to let Kate out of his sight. He would have to stay with her day and night until Kiley and his cohorts were behind bars.

Under any other circumstances the prospect would have pleased him. But knowing Kate, he had a feeling she wouldn't allow it simply on the basis of their past relationship. If she fought him as determinedly as she'd fought him so far, he would have to tell her who and what he was, and why he'd been so determined to renew their acquaintance. It would be then that he would forfeit all hope of regaining her trust and love.

By the time he reached the hotel and retrieved his rented car from the parking garage, he was committed to his chosen course of action regardless of what it might cost him personally. It was his job to gather enough evidence to put Jonathan Kiley behind bars, and he would do whatever was necessary to protect Kate until he had.

Thirty minutes later he strolled into Kiley Gallery, any last lingering doubts about what he was doing, vanishing behind a facade of casual curiosity.

Though the gallery was large it retained all the elegance of a smaller, more intimate setting. Expensive pieces of antique furniture were artfully arranged on the lush, dark gray, high-quality carpeting, and decorated with an assortment of fine porcelain, crystal and silver. The walls were covered with pale gray moiré and hung with delicate paintings, most more than a century old. It was comfortably cool, unusually quiet and, except for Jonathan Kiley, unexpectedly empty.

Or perhaps not so unexpectedly empty, Lucas mused, as he sauntered down a narrow aisle, tracing a mahogany tabletop with one finger. According to the information Matt had gathered on Kiley following David Evans's first telephone call, business had not been good for him since the downturn in the oil business several years ago. Not only were his best customers less inclined to indulge in whimsical shopping sprees, but Kiley himself had lost quite a bit on ill-advised investments in several wildcat drilling ventures.

That he had chosen drug dealing as an alternate means to maintain his life-style was believable. Unfortunately, after all Lucas had seen over the years, he could believe just about anything of anybody. But he found it hard to understand how anyone who spent his days surrounded by such beauty could also associate himself with the incredible filth and degradation that went hand in hand with the illegal drug business.

"Nice place. Kate told me all about it. Since I had the afternoon free, I thought I'd see for myself." Lucas stopped several yards from Kiley, picked up a porcelain vase and weighed it first in one hand, then the other, as he met the older man's gaze.

"You like antiques...Mr. Hunter, is it?" Kiley questioned, his tone polite yet unusually cold and uninviting.

"Sometimes." He replaced the vase on the table and sauntered toward a cluster of Chippendale chairs on his left. "Not too busy, are you? Guess it's just as well since you're here alone. You haven't found a replacement for Kate's brother yet, have you?"

"Are you auditioning for the job?"

"Depends on what's involved..." Lucas glanced over his shoulder, flashed his wicked grin, then moved on to a seventeenth-century Welsh dresser resting against a wall. He opened one drawer after another. When Kiley didn't respond, he changed tack. "She's upset about David's death, you know. She doesn't think it was the result of an attempted robbery. She thinks he might have been involved in something . . . I don't know . . . illegal. What do you think, Mr. Kiley?"

"I think Kate Evans has a vivid imagination. I also think she is overcome with grief for her dead brother, and as a result, she's grasping at straws. The police have assured me, as I know they've assured her, that they are working on the case. It may take some time, but I'm certain that eventually the murderer will be caught."

"You think so, huh?" Lucas turned and faced Kiley, meeting his gaze. "Well, I'll have to tell Kate how you feel. Knowing you have faith in the police department should help to put her mind at ease."

"You'll be seeing Ms. Evans again?"

"As often as possible. I'm relocating to Houston." He picked up a heavy crystal bowl with both hands and turned it from side to side, watching the light scatter and sparkle on its surface. "Miami's gotten kind of...hot for me lately. Say, you bring your stuff in yourself, or do you buy from someone else?" Again Lucas flashed his wicked grin as he set the bowl down.

"It's hot in Houston, too, Mr. Hunter. In fact, you'll find it's getting hotter every day. And I'm satisfied with the way I obtain my...stuff."

"Things change," Lucas murmured. "Keep me in mind." Wheeling around, he started up the aisle leading to the front door, then paused for a moment to glance over his shoulder. "And, say, if Katie comes across those papers you mentioned, I'll let you know, Mr. Kiley...sir."

"You do that, Mr. Hunter," Kiley replied, his pale gray eyes cold, his hands, now at his sides, clenched into fists.

Without looking back, Lucas walked through the door, crossed the sidewalk and climbed into his rented car. Taking a deep breath, he turned the key in the ignition. As he pulled away from the curb, he looked at the clock on the dashboard. It was nearly five o'clock. Kate would be on her way home before he could get to the library. Might as well go back to the hotel. He could check in with Matt, and while he was there, he'd change clothes.

He could catch up with her at her town house. He'd give her a little time to get settled, then pay her a visit. He had the perfect excuse, he thought, smiling slightly. He had returned her purse, but they'd both forgotten about her pair of glasses, which was tucked inside the breast pocket of his suit jacket. She'd be grateful to get them back, maybe grateful enough to invite him in for a drink. And he'd take it from there....

Chapter 5

"I don't give a damn what he does or doesn't do in Miami. He was in the gallery this afternoon, tossing off sly hints and innuendo. He's a smooth character, and he's smart, too damned smart. If Kate has any suspicions about her brother's death and she tells him, he's going to put two and two together. And she must suspect something. She's contacted three of my clients since four o'clock."

"So, what do you want me to do, Mr. Kiley? She's at home, alone. Want me to take care of her for you?"

"Not at her house, and not until you find out how much she knows. If she has any physical evidence, I want it destroyed. At least Sanders had his wits about him when she contacted him. He told her he'd get back to her, then called me. I advised him to invite her to the club for a little chat. I want you there in Sanders's place. When she arrives, I want *you* to talk to her. Then I think it might be best if she had an...accident, a fatal accident. And, Jackson, this time don't bungle it. If I have to clean up another one of your messes..."

"Yes, sir, Mr. Kiley. But what about the boyfriend? What if he's with her?"

"If he's with her, then get out of there. I'll think of something else. If she's alone, get rid of her."

Kate gazed at her reflection in the long mirror hanging on the bathroom door. Turning first one way, then another, she tugged at the pencil-slim skirt of her jade-green knit dress. It seemed shorter than she remembered. Maybe without the wide, black leather belt... But no, she looked more... together, more businesslike with the belt. And she didn't want to trade the added height of her three-inch heels for the comfort of flats. Although she wanted to blend in with the crowd at Vanderbilt's, she also wanted to exude a certain amount of dignity and control when she faced Eddie Sanders.

Moving across the bedroom, she glanced at her watch. It was nearly eight o'clock. Mr. Sanders had told her he'd see her between eight-thirty and nine, before the live band began their first set. So, she should be going, not ogling herself in the mirror. But she had hoped... She stared at the telephone sitting silent on the nightstand and shook her head.

We'll talk again later....

"You are such a sucker," she chided herself as she dumped the contents of her navy blue purse into an almost identical black leather bag. "He probably meant later in the century, not later in the day. Right, Caesar?"

The huge black cat yowled softly, rolling onto his back in the middle of her bed. Kate rubbed his tummy for several seconds, smiling at the way his silvery green eyes narrowed at her gentle touch. "Nice to know somebody cares, even if it's somebody dressed in a cat suit," she murmured.

Of course, considering the way she'd behaved earlier, there was no reason for Lucas to assume she still cared about him. So, how could she expect him to act as if he still cared about her? And since she had no way of contacting him, short of calling every hotel in town, he couldn't know how much she wanted him with her when she walked into Vanderbilt's. She hadn't known it herself until a few minutes ago when she realized she had no desire to enter one of Houston's hottest night spots on her own.

More than that, she had no desire to meet with Eddie Sanders on her own. Just talking to him on the telephone had left her feeling uneasy. After the responses she'd gotten from the others, responses that had ranged from outright denial of ever knowing her brother to stuttering, stammering confusion, his eagerness to meet with her had set off warning bells. But if she wanted to find out why David had been killed, she'd have to start somewhere, and starting with Eddie Sanders was better than spending another night wringing her hands and wondering.

She might find out something. Then again, she might not. In any case, she'd be able to cross off another name on her list. Lots of women went to Vanderbilt's alone. And she *did* have a gun. Clutching her purse in one hand, she flicked off the overhead light and headed for the coat closet at the foot of the staircase.

Lucas tapped the rim of the rented car's steering wheel with his fingers, trying to decide what to do. He'd been parked outside Kate's town house for almost an hour, slouched in the front seat of the car, watching and waiting. Within minutes he'd determined that he was the only one doing so. Still, he hadn't approached her front door. He'd followed her progress through the house via the lights she'd lit, first through the downstairs and then the upstairs, giving her time to get settled. He wanted to be sure she was staying home for the rest of the evening, too. She'd parked her car in front of the house rather than in the garage behind it. If she was going out—

She was. The front door opened, then she stepped into the pale glow of the porch light and turned to pull the door closed. Lucas's eyes narrowed as he watched her set the alarm. They narrowed even more when she walked down the sidewalk to her car, and his first impression of how she was dressed was confirmed. The hem of her skirt was only an inch or two longer than the hem of her oversize, black wool jacket. Only a hooker would consider her shoes sensible, and her hair looked as if it had been raked by a wild wind.

"Well, well, well... What happened to Pure Prudence, the librarian?" he muttered, as she climbed into her car, revealing most of her left thigh in the process.

Sitting up, he reached for the key in the ignition, but waited to start the engine until she had driven almost a block. She had specifically stated that she didn't have a boyfriend. So where was she going dressed the way she was? Unless styles had changed drastically, he didn't think she was spending the evening at the opera.

He thought of the way she'd kissed him that afternoon. She'd been as hot and hungry as he, and despite all her misgivings and murmured protests, she had molded her body to his with an eagerness, an abandon that had surprised him. Now he wondered if she had wanted *him*. Perhaps any man would do...

Lucas twisted the key in the ignition. She had given him no reason to doubt her words or actions. She had been honest about why she couldn't trust him. And she had simply given what he would have taken when he'd kissed her despite her protests. He had kissed her in the deeply, completely sexual way of a man deeply and completely aroused. And she had responded as she had always done, with eagerness and honesty.

So, what the hell was the matter with him? Why was he so intent on thinking the worst of her? Why was he determined to label her a cat in heat because she was going out on a Friday night in a short skirt and high heels?

Because it's easier to justify your deception if you believe she's deceiving you in some way, in any way.

Sick of himself and the direction his thoughts were taking, Lucas forced himself to concentrate on his driving.

Swerving around a slow moving car, he fell in behind her and shortened the distance between them to less than a city block. Although traffic was light, and she was a slow, careful driver, she was winding a weaving path along boulevards and back streets with the ease of long practice, often making turns without signaling until the last moment. Unfamiliar with the area, Lucas realized how easy it would be for her to lose him if she wanted. But then, she probably didn't expect to be followed. He'd be surprised if she'd glanced in her rearview mirror once since he'd pulled in behind her.

"Little innocent," he muttered. Moments later, when she pulled into the parking lot outside Vanderbilt's, he amended his comment slightly, shaking his head in disbelief. "Crazy little innocent. Now what are you going to do?"

He cruised past the entrance to the club's parking lot, stopped at the stop sign at the intersection beyond and watched her progress in his rearview mirror. She parked her car in the first available space, then walked toward the entrance, head down, arms at her sides. She looked more like a woman on her way to an execution, her own execution, than a party girl on the prowl. Frowning slightly, Lucas waited until she stepped through the narrow, hole-in-the-wall front door, then turned the corner.

Even though it was relatively early, Vanderbilt's was packed with people. Small, round tables surrounded by clusters of four or six wooden chairs filled every inch of the wide, semicircle of floor space in front of the stage. All had been claimed, as had the padded banquets lining the side walls and the high stools ringing the long, wide, oak bar. Kate had never heard of Six Dead Men, but judging by the less than patient crowd awaiting the first set, she decided that the band must be quite popular, at least among those favoring leather clothing, tattooed body parts and jewelry she'd always thought better suited to mean dogs and cats.

It had been several years since she had been in the club. Had she known how drastically the clientele had changed, she certainly wouldn't have agreed to meet the owner here on a Friday night. But it was too late now, and since she had come for a good reason, she might as well stay.

That the owner's name was mentioned in David's diary had to mean something. Perhaps her brother had had some sort of secret life. Unappealing as the thought was, Kate was beginning to believe anything was possible. Why, any minute now she might even unglue herself from the back wall and walk up to the bar.

Eddie Sanders had been very specific about his instructions. *Come to Vanderbilt's between eight-thirty and nine o'clock, go to the bar, give the bartender your name.* Unfortunately he had failed to add that she might feel more at ease carrying a club. She did have the .38, but it was tucked deep inside her purse. The way her hands were trembling, she doubted she'd be able to retrieve it without shooting herself in the foot first. Ah, well, in for a penny. . . .

Taking a deep breath, tightening her hold on her purse, squaring her shoulders and keeping her eyes straight ahead, she threaded her way through the crowd, ignoring the snickers, the whistles, the catcalls and comments that followed in her wake. Finding a narrow opening among the people milling around the bar, she edged forward. Her gaze fixed on the emaciated man mixing drinks, she willed him to slow down long enough to look in her direction.

"Yeah, waddaya want?"

He hadn't so much as glanced at her, not even for a second, yet his slurred question seemed to be aimed in her direction.

"I . . . um . . . I—"

"Come on, girlie, I ain't got all night." He did look at her then, his beady, bloodshot eyes sliding over her, leaving her with the sickening sensation that she'd been stripped. "What you need, baby cakes? I got it." He leaned toward her, leering, his breath fetid, his beastly grin revealing stained and broken teeth, his scalp glistening with sweat beneath thin strands of pale, greasy hair.

Gripping the edge of the polished oak bar with one hand, Kate forced herself to meet the man's gaze, her eyes steady. "Mr. Sanders, please. Mr. Eddie Sanders. I'm Kathryn Evans. He's . . . he's expecting me," she replied in a low voice that only quavered a little.

"Oh, yeah?" The bartender raked her with his eyes again as his grin faded. "He told me all about you, girlie." Stepping back, he slapped a palm against a button on the wall behind him, then gathered up a handful of heavy, frosted mugs and moved to the opposite end of the bar to draw beer from a huge keg.

Turning away from him, Kate pressed against the bar. If possible, it seemed that the crowd had grown even more, and onstage the band was setting up, tuning their instruments, and testing the microphones by emitting a variety of incredibly crude noises. The audience, what she could see of it through the thick haze of cigarette smoke, was delighted.

Why on earth had her brother been meeting with the owner of a place like this? She could understand a tennis instructor or a shoe salesman, but Eddie Sanders? She hadn't met him yet, but she couldn't believe he was much better than the crowd he catered to. Of course, Vanderbilt's might be nothing more than a profitable investment for him. He might be a suave, sophisticated man. He might—

"Kathryn Evans?"

He wasn't much taller than she, but he was very broad. He had short, wavy brown hair that was beginning to thin on top and his brown eyes were close-set under thick, bushy brows. Though he wore a dark suit, white shirt and striped tie, his appearance was more menacing than that of anyone else in the club including the bartender. And he had wrapped the fingers of one hand around her upper arm as he said her name.

"Yes, I'm Kathryn Evans." Instinctively, she moved away from the bar as she tried, unsuccessfully, to free herself from his hold. "Are you Mr. Sanders?"

"Ah, Mr. Sanders couldn't make it tonight." He tightened his grip on her, taking a step forward, looming over her, forcing her to back up. "But that's okay. You and I can have a little talk, just the two of us, someplace nice and quiet instead."

"Let go of me." She jerked her arm back, once again trying to loosen his hold. She only succeeded in throwing herself off balance. Unused to high heels, she stumbled backward several steps. Scanning the crowd, she searched for someone, anyone, who might help her, but nobody seemed interested in her plight. The lights had dimmed considerably and onstage the band roared into its opening song with eardrum-shattering intensity.

"I don't want to talk to you," she shouted, clawing frantically at his beefy fingers with fingernails too short to do any real damage. His face twisted in a vile grin, he continued to force her back. They were drawing closer and closer to the exit door at the end of the bar. "Let... me... go."

"You heard the lady. Let her go."

Kate's head snapped up, her gaze focusing on the figure standing just behind and to the right of the man holding her arm. Lucas... It was Lucas. He had the man by the shoulder, and he was pulling him away from her.

"Hey, buddy, mind your own damn—"

Before he could finish, Lucas moved in on him, a feral gleam in his silvery green eyes. "She *is* my business," he snapped. "I thought you'd know that by now. Guess I'll have to jar your... memory, won't I?"

The kick he delivered was swift and vicious, a low and dirty blow guaranteed to do devastating damage. The man doubled over, clutching himself, cursing and sobbing. When Lucas hooked a hand into his shirt collar and tugged his head up, he cried out in a mixture of agony and fear.

"If I see you anywhere near her again, I'll kill you," he promised, his mouth to the man's ear, his voice soft and steady. Then he slammed the man's head against the side of the bar.

As Lucas sent him sprawling, unconscious, onto the floor, a cheer went up among the people around them. Ignoring them, Lucas stepped over the man, wrapped an arm around Kate's waist, and all but carried her through the exit door. Without a word, he hustled her across the parking lot, shielding her with his body. At his car, he unlocked the door, pushed her inside and over onto the passenger seat and slid in beside her. He started the engine and pulled out onto the street.

He drove in silence for several blocks, his headlights out, zigzagging up and down side streets, keeping an eye on the rearview mirror. Finally satisfied that they weren't being followed, he eased the car to the curb in front of an old house and shut off the engine.

"What the hell—"

"I might ask you the same thing, Lucas," Kate snapped.

Hunched into her jacket, clutching her purse in her arms, her knees drawn up and her back against the passenger door, she reminded him of a cornered kitten. She was breathing hard and her hair was a mess, and if he wasn't mistaken, she was shaking so hard her teeth ought to be rattling. She had come close, too damned close, to being badly used by a very nasty man. Yet she was ready to go a few rounds with him because he'd come to her rescue. Lucas wasn't sure whether he wanted to hug her or shout at her.

"What were you doing there, Lucas?"

"I followed you. What were *you* doing there?"

"You followed me? Well, you certainly have a lot of nerve," she huffed, turning her face away.

"Yeah, don't I? And lucky for you, too, isn't it? Because if I hadn't been there, right about now that piece of garbage would be turning you every way but loose. Not a very pretty picture, is it, sweetheart? Unless that's what you were looking for."

"Do you really think . . . ?" She glanced at him, her eyes wide, her face pale in the darkness.

Lord, she'd been so stupid. Though she couldn't prove it, she was sure that Eddie Sanders had set her up. The man in the suit had known she was expected, and he'd been waiting for her. If Lucas hadn't followed her . . . She shivered violently, squeezing her eyes shut as she considered what could have happened.

"I'm sorry," she murmured, her voice barely above a whisper.

"Well, sorry doesn't cut it, baby. What were you doing in there?"

Caught in the crowd at Vanderbilt's, he had experienced several agonizing moments when he'd been afraid that he wouldn't get to her in time. Now all he wanted to do was pull her into his arms and hold her, but he couldn't do it, not yet. She had gone to Vanderbilt's for a reason. He wanted to know what it was. He hated digging at her when her guard was down, but he had to get her to talk to him.

"I went there to meet the owner, Eddie Sanders," she retorted, goaded by his biting sarcasm. "David knew him, and I thought he might . . . he might—"

"Know something about your brother's murder?" Lucas cut in, his voice suddenly soft.

"Yes," she admitted, her voice equally soft. "I called him early this evening just before I left work. He couldn't talk then, but he promised to call me back. When he did, he told me to stop by Vanderbilt's between eight-thirty and nine. He told me to go to the bar, give the bartender my name."

"Was that guy Eddie Sanders?"

"I don't know. He told me Eddie couldn't make it, so I guess not. But then, I wouldn't know Eddie Sanders if he walked up to me and shook my hand."

"Why did you think Sanders might know something about your brother's murder? Were they friends, or what?"

"I don't think they were friends. He was just somebody David knew."

"In what way?"

"I don't know."

"But you knew about him."

"Yes."

"How? Did David talk about him?"

"Aren't you supposed to read me my rights or something before you give me the third degree?" Kate asked, her voice suddenly, unexpectedly cool and more than a little sarcastic.

Her question caught him off guard. He'd been grilling her like a suspect without realizing it, stirring up her suspicions all over again. "I'm sorry, Kate. It's just that when I saw that guy with his hands on you, forcing you... Damn it, you scared the hell out of me." He turned away from her, resting his forearms on the steering wheel, gazing out of the windshield at nothing in particular.

"Why were you following me, Lucas?"

"I was sitting in my car outside your house, wondering how hard you'd slam the door in my face if I had the nerve to ring your doorbell. I wanted to return these." He pulled her glasses out of his shirt pocket and tossed them in her lap. "Anyway, you came out, got in your car and drove off. I was ... curious. So, I followed you."

"I wouldn't have slammed the door in your face," she murmured, reaching across the space separating them to touch the sleeve of his black leather jacket.

He neither glanced at her nor acknowledged her hand on his arm. "All you've been doing since yesterday is slamming doors in my face. I've got feelings, too, Kate."

He was right. One way or another, she had been determined to shut him out. She hadn't wanted to hear what he had to say. She had been evasive and uncooperative each time they'd been together. And when he'd saved her from certain harm, she'd snapped at him as if *he* were her enemy.

If she knew anything, Kate knew that Lucas wasn't her enemy. He had loved her once, loved her enough to give her up rather than risk hurting her. Why would he go out of his way to hurt her now? What could he hope to gain by it? And what did she hope to gain by hurting him? Revenge?

She drew her hand back as she realized what she had been doing. Turning away, she tipped her head against the window and closed her eyes. Every chance she'd had, she'd tried to wound him, and now she had finally succeeded. She ought to feel pleased. Payback time had come at last. Instead she felt like a childish, silly, little fool.

"I'll take you home." Lucas broke the strained silence, his voice rough as he turned the key in the ignition.

"What about my car?" She turned to look at him. His mouth was set in a grim line, his gaze focused on the street straight ahead.

"We can pick it up in the morning. I don't think we ought to risk going back there anymore tonight."

"Whatever you say," she agreed, her voice soft and low as she tucked her glasses in her purse. Given a choice, she'd never go back to Vanderbilt's again, but since she had to retrieve her car sometime, she'd just as soon do it in the daylight.

Lucas glanced at her, surprised by her easy acquiescence. He had been braced for another battle, but she was sitting with her head against the window, her eyes closed. In the darkness, she looked small and fragile, her face pale and drawn. And although it wasn't cold in the car, she was still trembling.

All that had happened over the past couple of weeks was beginning to catch up with her, and his special brand of poking and prodding wasn't helping. He couldn't promise to stop digging for the evidence they needed to put Kiley away, but he could let her know that he'd be there for her. She was frightened, and well she should be, but she wasn't alone anymore. The next time Kiley went for her, either through his henchman or on his own, Lucas vowed that he would be waiting. And in the meantime, he would make sure that Kate was safe.

Reaching out, he smoothed a hand over her hair. "Whatever I say, huh? I never thought I'd hear those words from you."

"You caught me at a weak moment. The one and only weak moment I plan to have in the next twenty years," she muttered, refusing to give in to the urge to crawl across the seat, curl up against him and wait for another of his gentle caresses.

"Twenty years? You wouldn't want to bet on it, would you?" he asked, a hint of laughter under the solemn tone of his voice as he pulled up to the curb in front of her town house.

"No, I wouldn't."

They walked to her front door in silence. Lucas waited patiently while she shut off the alarm system, then took her key from her and opened the door. Putting an arm around her, he held her back while he stepped inside. He scanned the hallway, the staircase and what he could see of the downstairs rooms, thankful that she had left lights burning in the hallway, living room and kitchen. When he was reasonably sure no one was lurking in the shadows, he pulled her inside and closed the door.

"Stay here until I come back," he commanded. "And if I tell you to get out, get out, take the car and go to the nearest police station." He pressed his car keys into her hands, then started down the hallway.

Too tired to protest, Kate sagged against the front door, following Lucas's progress through the living room, dining room, kitchen and breakfast room with her eyes. Without a word, she watched him climb the stairs to the second floor. When he had disappeared down the hallway, she kicked off her shoes, walked to the steps and sat down, listening to him move from the guest bedroom to the study to her—

"Ouch! Son of a . . . what the hell—"

"Lucas, meet Caesar, the flying cat." Kate allowed herself a tiny smile as she rested her chin on her hand. There was a thud, followed by a yowl of displeasure. "Caesar, meet Lucas, my hero. Love at first sight, right, guys?"

She set her purse on the floor, then slipped out of her jacket and tossed it over the stair rail as the cat marched past her, tail high, refusing to acknowledge her presence. Moments later Lucas walked down the steps, cursing under his breath as he rubbed his chest with one hand.

"Why didn't you tell me you had an attack cat?"

"You didn't ask."

"Don't get cute." Lucas frowned down at her. "I thought I told you to stay by the door, not sit on the stairs half-undressed."

"I'm not half-undressed. I took off my jacket and shoes," she protested, but he wasn't paying attention to her. He was striding across the entryway and tinkering with the panel of buttons near the front door.

"How do you set the alarm system?"

"I'll do it after you leave. I guess I ought to call the police, too." Kate pulled herself up off the steps and moved to stand beside him. "Thanks for—"

"What makes you think I'm leaving?" He met her gaze, his eyes steady.

"You should."

"Why? Afraid you'll have another weak moment if I stay?" He traced the line of her jaw with his fingertips. He had meant to speak the words in a teasing tone of voice, but somehow they hadn't come out that way at all. And he hadn't meant to touch her....

"Of course not." She took a step away from him.

"Are you afraid of me?"

"No...."

She wasn't afraid of having another weak moment, nor was she afraid of him. She simply didn't want to depend on him for anything. She didn't want him fighting her battles, or coming to her rescue, or spending the night out of some false sense of chivalry. Because sooner or later, he'd be gone, and she'd be forced to function on her own again.

"I've been alone for a long time, Lucas. I think it would be better if I stayed that way. Sometimes I think I'm just better off...alone...."

"I've been alone for a long time, too, Kate. But I think I've been alone long enough." He took a step toward her, and when she didn't back away, he reached out and pulled her into his arms.

She went willingly, sighing softly as she pressed her palms against his chest and rested her head on his shoulder. Had it been possible, she would have curled up inside of him and stayed there forever.

"Ah, Katie, haven't we been alone long enough?" he murmured, rubbing his cheek against her soft, dark hair.

Her only answer was to cling to him more tightly, twisting her fingers into the fabric of his shirt. She couldn't, *wouldn't* let him go.

She had finally stopped fighting him. She would allow him to stay. He should be relieved. But Lucas found no solace in her acceptance. He was there to protect her, nothing more. He might want to lift her into his arms and carry her to her bedroom, but he couldn't do it. He might need to make love to her until he was too weak to stand, but he wouldn't.

For a few moments longer, though, he'd savor the weight of her body pressing against him. And, he decided, threading his fingers through her hair and tipping her face up, he would kiss her. Closing his eyes, he dipped his head and covered her mouth with his. When she sighed again, and parted her lips, he curled his tongue against hers, hot, wet velvet stroking hot, wet velvet, as he gave in to the hunger deep inside of him.

He slid his hands out of her hair and caressed her back, then her buttocks, drawing her body closer and closer. Finally, unable to stop himself, he trailed one hand up her side, then cupped her breast in his palm, rubbing his thumb over her nipple until it hardened beneath the soft knit of her dress.

She drew in her breath, pressing against him, wrapping her arms around his neck. She was throbbing, aching with desire, the pleasure of his hands and mouth on her too much, yet not enough. She whimpered softly, shifting restlessly in his embrace, her hands slipping down to the buttons on his shirt, to the buckle on his belt. She wanted to touch him, wanted to smooth her hands over his bare chest, then down . . . down through the crisp dark hair, across his flat, hard belly. . . .

She wanted him, needed him. She had been in grave danger at Vanderbilt's, but he had come to her rescue. Now she couldn't get enough of him. He was so warm, so alive. She craved his warmth, and she wanted proof of the most primitive kind that she, too, was alive. Rolling her hips forward, she moved against him, fitting herself to him as intimately as several layers of clothing would allow.

He sensed her sudden desperation in the way she tore at the buttons of his shirt and tugged at his belt buckle as she writhed and twisted in his arms. He had to stop her before she came apart. He had to stop her while he could still stop himself. He braced an arm against the small of her back, holding her still, then closed his hand around hers before she could unfasten his belt. Lifting his head, he dropped soft, gentle kisses on her cheek, her jaw, her forehead.

"Easy, easy. . . . You're going to be all right."

"Lucas, please. . ." she pleaded, pressing her warm, moist lips to the pulse pounding at the base of his throat. "I need you."

"And I'll be here for you. But I'm not making love with you tonight."

"Why not? Don't you want me?" she whispered, burying her face against his chest. Perhaps he had only meant to comfort her, after all. And she had responded like a silly, sex-starved—

"I want you more than I've ever wanted any woman." He tightened his hand on hers as he pulled it down to cover himself. Shifting against her palm, he offered her proof of the full extent of his arousal. It was true, gut-wrenchingly, heartachingly true. He...wanted...her. "But not like this, Kate. Not with you still scared and shaky and not quite sure of you or me. When we make love, I want you to be very sure of you and me." *And I want to be sure, too, sure that I won't hurt you again.*

She sagged against him, blinking back a quick rush of tears. All he wanted was her trust, but how could she trust him when she hardly knew him? He might look like the man she had known and loved, he might sound like the man she had known and loved, but was he?

Yes, a little voice whispered deep in her soul. *Yes.* The man she had known and loved had never taken advantage of her. The man holding her in his arms right now wasn't taking advantage of her, either. Sighing softly, she rubbed her cheek against his chest, letting him know in her own way that she understood all that he had said.

"Show me how to set the alarm and then I'll take you upstairs." Sliding his arm round her shoulders, he guided her to the front door.

She did as he asked, punching in the specially coded series of numbers that activated the security system. She also explained the relatively simple deactivating code.

"In case you have to open the door for some reason."

"To let the cat out?" he asked, unable to disguise the note of hope in his voice as they started up the staircase.

"Oh, no, don't let Caesar out. He always gets into trouble. Comes home all battered and bloody." Kate glanced at Lucas, a smile twitching the corners of her mouth. "He really is a nice cat."

"I'm allergic to cats, especially ones that attack first and ask questions later."

"You're not sneezing, Lucas."

"I will be...." He stopped at her bedroom doorway and turned her to face him. "Do you have any whiskey or brandy?"

"Both in a cabinet in the kitchen. Why?"

"I think we'll both sleep better if we have a drink." He dropped his hands from her shoulders and took a step back. "Speaking of which . . ."

"The bed in the guest room is made up with fresh sheets, and there are towels, toothbrushes, razors, soap and shampoo in the linen cupboard in the hall bathroom. If you leave a glass of brandy on the nightstand, I promise to drink it." She tipped her head to one side and smiled slightly. "Anything else, or should I just say thank you and good-night?"

"Don't thank me yet," Lucas muttered, turning on his heels and heading for the stairs.

"What about good-night?"

"I'll be back in fifteen minutes. You can say it then, all right? Oh, and I'll take care of calling the police while I'm downstairs."

"All right," Kate agreed, more to herself than to Lucas. Unfastening her belt buckle, she crossed the bedroom and entered the bathroom on a wave of weariness. It had been a very long day, a very long week, and suddenly she wanted nothing more than to crawl into bed and sleep.

Chapter 6

At the foot of the staircase, Lucas paused to pick up Kate's purse. With his long fingers kneading the fine leather, he turned down the hallway and walked into the kitchen. Resting a hip against the white tile counter, he parted the zipper and sifted through the contents for several seconds. Wallet, keys, checkbook, a small, clear plastic case containing tissues, tubes of lipstick and mascara, a sewing kit, safety pins, a mirror and comb, and at the bottom of the bag, the .38 and, as he'd hoped, the black book.

She had insisted it was her diary, but Kate wasn't the type to keep a coded diary. Not only did she live a simple, solitary life, she was too open, too honest about her thoughts and feelings. If she chose to write down those thoughts and feelings, she'd do so in the usual manner. On the other hand, her brother had had every reason to use a code to record the dangerous information he'd been collecting.

Dropping the purse on the counter, he thumbed through the book, glancing at page after page of neatly printed numbers. It might be nothing more than a chronicle of

Kate's activities. Or it might be the source of the information that had led her to Vanderbilt's and Eddie Sanders. It could be the evidence he needed to put Jonathan Kiley behind bars. Though he wasn't a betting man, he was willing to lay odds on the latter.

Once she was asleep, he'd find out if he was right or wrong. Unfortunately, cracking codes had never been his forte, so it would probably take him all night. Of course, if he was right, if the diary *was* her brother's, and she'd begun decoding it, then her transcription had to be somewhere. Not in the book, or in her wallet, or in the zipper pocket in the satin lining of the purse. But she'd been carrying a navy blue purse earlier in the day. Maybe she'd forgotten to remove her notes when she'd changed from blue to black.

With a muttered curse, he tossed the diary into the purse. Raking a hand through his hair, he forced himself to slow down. "First things first," he cautioned, turning to the cabinets lining the walls on either side of the window above the kitchen sink. He would have more than enough time to work on the diary if Kate slept soundly until morning. A glass of brandy would guarantee it.

He found the snifters easily but had to go through all the cabinets under the counter before he found the liquor bottles. Sitting on his heels, he reached for the brandy, hesitated a moment as his nose came to life with an uncomfortable prickling sensation, then sneezed.

"Ah, I forgot about you." Lucas glared at the black cat sitting less than a foot away, watching him with silvery green eyes. "Isn't there anywhere else you'd rather be than in here with me?" He wrapped his fingers around the bottle, sneezed again and stood up.

As quickly as possible, he measured brandy into the glasses, trying to ignore the annoying urge to sneeze himself silly. Then, carrying the snifters in one hand and the bottle in the other, he headed out of the kitchen. At the foot of the staircase he stopped. Glancing over his shoulder, he saw the cat sitting in the kitchen doorway, watching him.

"Listen, buddy, you better not follow me upstairs, or else..."

Without batting an eye, the cat yawned, flicked his tail, raised a paw and licked it with his tiny pink tongue.

"Yeah, okay, so you're a tough guy, too. You know it and I know it, but *she* thinks you're nice." His mouth tipped into a rueful smile as he started up the stairs. "Hell, maybe there's hope for me yet. Then again, maybe there isn't. At least not as long as I'm talking to a cat."

"Were you talking to me?"

He turned into the doorway of Kate's bedroom and ground to a halt. Like a man who had ambled precariously close to the edge of a cliff, he took a step back. His hands tightened on the bottle and glasses, and his heart began to pound as if he'd run for miles.

She was standing near the dresser, hairbrush in one hand, wearing an ankle-length, long-sleeved, white cotton gown. Tiny pearl buttons fastened the front and fine lace edged the cuffs and collar. In the pale glow of lamplight, her face devoid of makeup, her dark hair falling smooth and soft against her shoulders, she looked as young and innocent as a virgin bride awaiting her groom.

But he had given up his chance to have her as *his* virgin bride. The realization hit him with the stunning impact of a brutal blow. In his mind he had known she had married another man, but in his heart he had never really accepted it...until now. If only he had trusted her.... She would have waited for him, she would have helped him heal, and she would have been *his* bride. If only he hadn't been so hurt and so afraid.

He was neither hurt nor afraid now. And she could still be his...tonight.... There was wanting in her eyes and on the soft curve of her lips, matching the wanting inside of him that had never died. Though she had been another man's wife, he wanted to believe, *had to believe,* there was a part of her that had remained untouched, that had belonged to him, that would always belong to him. He ached to claim that part of her, ached with a need that went beyond desire. Yet he stood in the doorway, still and silent.

"Were you talking to me?" Kate set her hairbrush on the dresser, repeating her question as she took a step toward him. "I thought I heard your voice a few moments ago." She hesitated, then took another step toward him, wanting to banish the bleak, blank look in his eyes.

He shook his head and forced himself to smile. There was no way he could ease the unwanted burden of his conscience, nor was there any way he could justify making love with her. All he could do was ease the anxiety that had crept into her voice, and see her safely, soundly asleep.

"I was talking to your cat. We had a discussion about territorial rights." He sauntered into the room, stopping less than a yard away from her. Extending his hand, he offered her a choice of the two glasses he held.

Arching an eyebrow, Kate eased one of the snifters from his fingers. "You *were* sneezing, weren't you?" she asked, a teasing note in her voice, a twinkle in her wide, brown eyes. "I thought you were kidding when you said you're allergic to cats."

"Ah, sweetheart, would I kid you?" Lucas's smile widened into a wolfish grin as he moved past her to stand beside the bed. He set his glass and the brandy bottle on the nightstand and tugged back the topsheet, blanket and green-and-rose striped comforter with a flick of his wrist. "Come on, I'll tuck you in." He stood back, hands on his hips, waiting for her.

"How do you know I sleep on this side of the bed?" She stopped in front of him, tipping her head back so she could meet his gaze.

"Because I sleep on the other side," he muttered, unable to stop himself from making the simple admission. Turning away from her, he retrieved his glass and the bottle.

"Oh." She slid her legs beneath the covers, pushed her pillows up against the mahogany headboard and sat back, cradling her glass of brandy in one hand. "Really?"

"Really." He pulled the covers up with a quick jerk, careful not to touch her, then switched off the lamp on the nightstand.

She tasted her brandy as he strode around the end of her bed to the nightstand on the opposite side. The warm, heavy liquor offered some comfort as its heat spread through her body. But it was a poor substitute for the heat and comfort she really wanted.

"Lucas, wait."

He paused, his hand outstretched to switch off the lamp. Reluctantly, he turned to face her.

"Now what?" He was nearing the end of his self-control, and it was beginning to show in the worst possible way. She didn't deserve his anger, but he wasn't sure how much longer he could look at her lying in bed and remain passive.

She hesitated for a moment at the sharp edge in his voice and the cool glint in his eyes. Then, clinging to her dwindling courage, she forced herself to ignore his displeasure. If she didn't speak, in less than a few seconds she would be alone in the dark, and suddenly that was one place she didn't want to be.

"Don't go," she whispered, unable to control the tremor threading through her voice.

"I won't. I'll be—"

"No, don't go now. I don't want to be alone." She despised herself for pleading, but she was desperate.

"Kate, I—"

"Please, Lucas…" She turned away from him, unable to face the final refusal she fully expected. Lifting her glass to her lips, she swallowed another mouthful of brandy.

He wasn't sure what he would end up doing if he stretched out on the bed beside her. But she was frightened, with good reason. And she had no one else but him. If he walked away from her now, it would be nothing less than cruel, and he didn't want to hurt her... again.

He thunked his glass and the brandy bottle on the nightstand, braced his hands on his hips and stared at the lush pile of pale rose carpet beneath his feet. Then he sat on the edge of the bed, his back to her. He shouldn't do it. He shouldn't....

With a heavy sigh of resignation, he pulled off his boots, dropping them on the carpet one after the other. He would just sit with her until she fell asleep. Reaching behind him, he plumped up the pillows and settled back, stretching his long legs in front of him and crossing his arms over his chest.

"Thanks, Lucas."

"What did I tell you about thanking me?" he muttered, focusing his gaze on the silk flower arrangement atop the chest of drawers across the room.

"You told me not to thank you yet."

"So, don't."

She sipped her brandy, watching him out of the corner of her eye. For several minutes she was too relieved that he was staying to say or do anything else. But there was a difference between giving in and giving in gracefully. If he intended to maintain his rigid pose indefinitely, she'd never get to sleep, even though she was very, very tired.

"Did you call the police?" Maybe a little light conversation would help.

"They're working on it." He'd had no intention of calling HPD, but offering to do it, then pretending he had was the simplest way to keep her away from them. They'd do nothing but stir up trouble. Yet he was uncomfortable with the lie hanging in the air between them. *Liar, liar, pants on fire*... He shifted on the bed. *How appropriate*....

"Are you cold, Lucas?"

"No." The single word of denial came out of his mouth on a strangled groan.

"Then why don't you take off your jacket?" She turned to face him, smiling sweetly. "You could turn off the lamp, too."

"Anything else?" he asked, his brow arched, his tone sarcastic.

Take off all your clothes, crawl under the covers and hold me in your arms.

"No." She turned away from his probing gaze, her cheeks tinged with red. He was so close, close enough that she could feel his heat, yet so very far away.

He cursed sharply, succinctly, under his breath. It would be a miracle if she didn't drive him out of his mind. Then without another word, he reached out and switched off the lamp. In the moments before her eyes could adjust to the sudden darkness he shrugged out of his jacket and removed the holstered automatic from the small of his back. After wrapping the gun inside the jacket, he set the bundle on the floor beside the bed, then unbuttoned his shirt, slipped out of it and dropped it on top of his jacket. Almost as an afterthought, he stood up, removed his belt, dropped it on the floor and unsnapped his jeans.

"Are you finished with your brandy?"

"Yes."

Her voice was barely audible, but in the moonlight threading through the shutters on the windows, he could see her face, the angles of her cheekbones, the curve of her mouth, her hair, soft and dark against the pale pillowcase, her wide eyes watching him. Muttering another curse, he jerked back the covers and slid beneath them.

"Well, then, come here."

She didn't hesitate a moment. Before he could blink twice she was in his arms, her body pressed against him, her cheek smooth and cool against his shoulder, her hair drifting soft and fragrant over the curve of his elbow. Her sigh shuddered through him. He closed his eyes and pressed his lips to her forehead.

"Good night, Katie."

"Lucas, I—"

He caught her hand in his, the hand that had begun to stroke his bare chest slowly, steadily, moving down, down through the coarse hair. "Go to sleep, Kate. Just...go to...sleep."

She brushed her lips over the back of his hand, then settled against him when he tightened his hold on her in gentle warning. "Good night, Lucas."

As her breathing deepened, he closed his eyes, allowing himself to relax. Welcoming the weight of her body, he shifted slightly, holding her close. He'd stay a while longer, just a little while longer. And then, when he was sure she was asleep, he'd get busy on the black book. But for now, well, for now what could it hurt to savor the soul-deep satisfaction of holding her in his arms while she slept.... While...he...slept....

She awoke slowly, almost unwillingly. The dream had been so real, so wonderful that she wanted to cling to it as long as possible. Lucas holding her, kissing her, cradling her in his arms in the deep night darkness, the heat of his body warming her, relaxing her, his scent surrounding her. She took a deep breath. Old, well-worn leather, a hint of spice, and the rich, warm muskiness of his masculine body... Blinking her eyes open, Kate smiled softly, moving her hand over the cool, cotton sheet.

"Lucas?"

She was alone in the bed. Had it only been a dream, after all? No.... She moved across the mattress to the place where he had lain, and buried her face in the pillows where his head had rested. No, it hadn't been a dream. She had fallen asleep in his arms. But where was he now? Had he gone while she slept?

After her frightening experience at Vanderbilt's she didn't relish being alone, even in the daylight. And considering the way Lucas had kissed and caressed her, how could he disappear without a word? Closing her eyes, she rubbed her cheek against the pillow, unwilling to accept the painful possibility that he had done it quite easily. Not so early in the morning, and especially not when it was raining.

"Raining?" she murmured, opening her eyes again. Brilliant sunshine poured through the bedroom windows.

Clutching a pillow in her arms, she rolled onto her back, smiling once more. He hadn't gone. He was in the hall bathroom using the shower. If she hurried, she could have coffee brewing and eggs ready to scramble by the time he finished. Cooking breakfast for him was the least she could do. It was also a good way to guarantee his company, at least for a while longer.

Ignoring the little voice that insisted she was a fool, Kate tossed back the covers, slid out of bed and padded barefoot into her bathroom. She washed her face, brushed her teeth and ran a comb through her hair, then returned to her bedroom. Ignoring her ancient, blue terry robe, she rummaged through her closet until she found the almost new embroidered one that matched her nightgown.

As she shrugged into it, she realized how much she wanted Lucas to stay. And, being honest, she admitted that it wasn't only because she'd had a bad scare. It was because she had begun to trust him. He had promised to stay with her, and he had. Yet he hadn't taken advantage of her in any way. She wouldn't have resisted his advances. In fact, she would have welcomed them.

Maybe all he wanted was an honest second chance. And maybe she wanted one, too. Maybe... She walked down the staircase and into the kitchen, her thoughts a jumbled mess. Unfortunately, one thing hadn't changed in the past couple of days. She hadn't found her brother's murderer, and until she did, she didn't have any right worrying about a second chance with Lucas Hunter.

If it had done anything, last night's escapade had confirmed her suspicion that David's murder had been more than the result of a particularly violent robbery. But what had he known or possessed that had put him in danger? She

needed an answer and she needed it fast. Yet she had spent
the night cowering in Lucas's arms when she should have
been decoding the remainder of her brother's diary.

With a sudden surge of panic, she slammed the coffeepot
on the counter and whirled around. "The diary," she whispered, as she scanned the kitchen counters, the chairs and
the tabletop. "What did I do with my purse?"

She hadn't come into the kitchen last night, so it wouldn't
be here. Nor had she brought it upstairs with her. Pushing
away from the counter, she crossed the kitchen and moved
down the hallway. She had left it...there...at the foot of
the staircase. Sighing with relief, she sank onto the steps,
pulled the black leather bag into her lap and unzipped it.
The diary was tucked inside. She pulled it out and flipped
through the pages, making certain none were missing. Upstairs the bathroom door opened. A series of violent sneezes
followed. She dropped the diary into her bag.

"Damn cat, get out of here before I—"

As the door slammed shut, Kate stifled the urge to laugh.
Gathering up her purse and, as he passed her on the steps,
her cat, she returned to the kitchen. Minutes later, she had
coffee brewing, eggs cooking, and Caesar locked in the
laundry room with a huge bowl of his favorite cat food. The
little pig would probably eat himself into a coma, she
thought, as she stirred the eggs with a small wooden spoon.
But at least as long as he was stuffing his face he wouldn't
be ripping at the wooden door with his claws and yowling
his displeasure.

"Ah, the lady cooks. I may forgive her for keeping a cat."

She glanced at him as he entered the kitchen. He was
dressed, but his shirt was only half-buttoned, his feet were
bare and his hair was damp. He was also pressing a wad of
toilet tissue to the left side of his jaw.

"Looks like you found everything all right, including the
shaving cream and razors."

"And the individually wrapped toothbrushes and the
fresh tube of toothpaste. If it weren't for that damned cat,

you'd get top honors in the hostess category." Lucas stopped behind her, wrapped his arm around her waist and pulled her against him. When she gazed up at him in surprise, he dropped a quick kiss on her lips. "Good morning, sweetheart."

"Good morning." She smiled as she reached up to touch his face with her fingertips. "What happened? Cut yourself shaving?"

"Actually, it was attempted homicide. If I get my hands on the vicious perpetrator, I'm going to throttle him."

"He's just a little cat."

"Lady, your *little cat* jumped up on the commode while I was in midstroke with a new razor blade. How he got through a closed door, I'll never know. But if I'd sneezed a moment sooner, I'd have done a hell of a lot more than nick my chin."

"Lucas, he *likes* you." Trying not to laugh at the look of horror on his face, she turned back to the stove. Poor man, his eyes were red, and he was sounding a bit nasal. "Coffee's ready. Cups are in the left cabinet."

"Kate, he hates me. It's his goal to see how long it'll take me to sneeze to death." He found cups and filled them, then set plates and silverware on the breakfast room table while she dropped slices of bread in the toaster.

Unfortunately, he couldn't emphasize his point by telling her how, during the early-morning hours before dawn, the animal had returned to the kitchen over and over regardless of how rudely and consistently he was evicted. Had he mentioned it, he would have had to explain what *he* was doing in the kitchen.

As it was, he hadn't done much at all. With the cat under the table and Kate upstairs in bed, his concentration hadn't been quite what it should have been. He'd managed to get through the notes he'd found in her navy blue purse but he hadn't gotten much further. At least he'd had a list of names to give Matt when he'd checked in with his boss while she was still asleep.

"Well, he's in the laundry room now," Kate assured him as she spooned eggs onto the plates. "So, come and eat while the food is hot."

They sat across from each other at the small, round table, eating in silence for several minutes. Though they were together, they were each very much alone with their own thoughts.

It seemed so natural to be having breakfast with Lucas, she mused, as if it weren't the first time, but one of many times they'd shared the meal. If only it could be. If only he were a permanent part of her life. Then she could tell him about David's diary, and ask him to help her. Glancing up, she saw him studying her.

"More coffee? Toast?" She pushed away from the table and crossed to the counter, afraid that he might read her thoughts if she didn't move away.

What was the matter with her? She must be crazy. She was wasting her time daydreaming about a permanent relationship with him. He was in Houston on business, and when his business was done, he'd be gone. She had no reason to believe he'd be around long enough to help her find her brother's murderer. And even if he was, she had no right to ask it of him.

"Just coffee." He watched her pour, then return the pot to the coffee maker.

When she was seated in her chair again, he reached across the table and took her hand in his. He sensed her sudden withdrawal, and he didn't like it. She had finally begun to accept him. He didn't want to say or do anything to shatter her acceptance. "Do you have to work today?"

"No." He was rubbing the back of her wrist with his thumb, stroking with a soft, circular motion that spiraled through her entire body.

"Any other plans for the day?"

"Nothing special. Grocery shopping, the cleaners. And I've got to get my car."

"Then you can go to Galveston with me." He squeezed her hand and smiled. "We'll pick up your car, stop by the hotel so I can change clothes, then spend the day on the island. I want to take a look at a couple of warehouses, see which one has the best location. We can have lunch and take a walk on the beach, too. All right?"

Kate hesitated a long moment, her thoughts on the black book in her purse. She shouldn't go with him. She should stay at home and finish decoding the diary. She should try to call the rest of the people on the list she'd compiled. But after last night, she wasn't quite ready to confront any of them alone, even by telephone. And Lucas was looking at her with a teasing, pleading smile, while his thumb and fingers made magic with her hand and wrist. Foolish as it was, she didn't want their time together to end ... yet. He would be gone soon enough.

"All right," she agreed, squeezing his hand and returning his smile. "I'll go to Galveston with you. Do I have time for a quick shower?"

"We could make time for a long, slow shower...." Though still teasing, his smile made her think of a big, bad wolf.

"Maybe later," she replied, her voice soft and seductive, her eyes wide and innocent, offering a bit of her own brand of teasing.

At the sudden, surprised look on his face, she laughed out loud. Then, slipping her hand free, she stood up. "But right now, you've got twenty minutes to clean up the kitchen ... sweetheart." Afraid to wait for his reply, she turned and fled.

She was ready, as promised, in twenty minutes. She found him in the kitchen, finishing a last cup of coffee. He was completely dressed, including his black leather jacket. And, Kate noted with a hint of amusement, he had stacked their breakfast dishes in the dishwasher.

"Are you always so obedient?" she asked, as she stopped beside him.

"I had a weak moment." He rinsed his cup, set it on the top rack of the dishwasher and closed the door. "The only weak moment I plan to have in the—"

"Next twenty years?"

"Yeah, something like that," he agreed, as he followed her down the hallway.

Actually he was having another weak moment even as he spoke. Only rigid self-control kept him from reaching out and pulling her into his arms. He shouldn't have made the crack about a long, slow shower. The sound of water running in her bathroom coupled with several extraordinarily erotic mental images had left him with jeans just a tad too tight.

He'd slung dishes into the dishwasher with such force it was a miracle he hadn't broken every one of them. And just when he'd finally gotten himself settled down, she'd bounced into the kitchen looking more like a college coed than a thirty-four-year-old woman.

She was wearing faded jeans that hugged her bottom like a second skin, an oversize, hot pink pullover sweater, slouchy, hot pink socks and white leather running shoes. She'd tied her hair into a ponytail with a hot pink scarf and fastened small gold hoops in her ears. He wanted to start with the scarf and work his way down her body, removing everything except her earrings. And then, he wanted to...

She was standing just inside the open door of the hall closet, gazing at him with a questioning look in her eyes. "Earth to Lucas, earth to Lucas...come in, please." She held up the black wool jacket she'd worn the night before. "Have you been outside yet? Do you think I ought to take a jacket?"

"The sun's warm, but the air is cool. It'll be even cooler near the water. Guess you'd better take it." He fiddled with the alarm system, swung open the front door and stepped outside.

Thank God he'd mentioned the warehouses at Harry's, he thought, as he waited for Kate to follow him. Not only did they provide an excellent excuse for an excursion to Galveston Island, but he'd also have a chance to poke around the warehouse Jonathan Kiley rented without arousing her suspicion. And as long as they were out in public, he'd have to keep his hands off her. But tonight . . .

He stood and watched her lock her door and set the alarm, forcing himself not to think about the night. He was staying with her to protect her and to search for evidence against Kiley—nothing more, nothing less. He couldn't allow himself to forget it, not even for a moment, especially now that they were leaving the relative safety of her house. Clicking into years of training, he surveyed the street and surrounding houses with practiced skill and tried to concentrate on the day ahead.

They retrieved Kate's car and returned it to her garage without any problems. When he had talked to Matt earlier, Lucas had asked him to send someone to Vanderbilt's parking lot to make sure no one had tampered with it. The man was waiting for them, sitting in a doorway, looking more like a wino after an all-night binge than the highly trained agent he was. His salute with a half-empty bottle was the signal that everything was all right, yet Lucas insisted on checking out the car himself and, despite her protests, driving it while Kate followed in his rental car.

At the hotel, she prowled around the room while he gathered an armful of clothing, then disappeared into the bathroom to change. When he reappeared, wearing fresh jeans, a white shirt and a bulky black pullover sweater, she was sitting in a chair flipping channels on the television set with the remote control.

"You're worse than a kid," he muttered as he tossed his dirty clothes and shaving kit on the bed. "Hey, wait, *Pee Wee's Playhouse*. Switch it back."

"Who's worse than a kid?" Kate queried, arching an eyebrow at him.

He flashed a quick grin, then crossed to the closet and removed a medium-size black leather suitcase, which he set on the bed and opened. After stuffing his dirty clothes behind the panel in the upper half, he returned to the closet and pulled out his suit and a couple of fresh shirts. He folded them into the bottom half, along with the clean underwear, jeans and socks he retrieved from the dresser drawers.

"What are you doing?"

Lucas glanced at Kate as he snapped the locks on the case. "Checking out." He turned to the telephone on the nightstand and dialed the front desk. After notifying the clerk that he was vacating his room, and requesting that his bill be mailed to the address he'd given at check-in, he picked up his bag and walked over to Kate. "Ready?"

She stared at the television set for several seconds, seemingly absorbed in the antics of Pee Wee Herman and a talking chair. Finally she shut it off. When she met his gaze, her eyes were shadowed. Any trace of animation had drained from her face.

"Are you leaving after you look at the warehouses in Galveston?" she asked softly, putting her painful thoughts into words.

Of course she had known he wasn't going to stay forever. However, she had hoped that he would stay a few more days. But he was a businessman on a business trip. He had commitments in other places, commitments to other people. He might even have someone waiting for him somewhere, someone special.

Though he didn't seem like a stranger anymore, Kate realized that in many way he was. There was so much she didn't know about him, and he hadn't offered to enlighten her. He had spoken of the past almost unwillingly, as a last resort, and except for his answers to Jonathan Kiley's questions, he hadn't spoken of the present at all. Perhaps he hadn't done so because he hadn't planned to be around long enough for it to matter.

Surprised by the sudden sadness in her eyes, Lucas dropped his suitcase, wrapped his hands around her shoulders and hauled her to her feet. "I'm not going anywhere, sweetheart, at least not for a while."

She glanced down at the suitcase, then up into his eyes. "But you're not staying at the hotel?"

"Do you want me to stay at the hotel?"

Kate tipped her head to one side, a smile edging up the corners of her mouth, her eyes sparkling once again. Suddenly, what she didn't know didn't matter, at least not for the moment. "No," she admitted. "I want you to stay with me."

He pulled her into his arms, giving her a quick, fierce hug. He could hardly bear the simple honesty of her answer. "And I want to stay with you, Katie." He held her a moment longer, his eyes closed, his heart aching as he realized it was all he really wanted. To stay with her not because it was his job, or a duty to be done, but because she was all he'd ever needed to make his life complete.

"We'd better go." Releasing her, he took a step back and picked up his suitcase.

Accepting the arm he slipped around her shoulders, Kate went with him gladly.

They drove to Galveston Island without exchanging more than a few sentences. Neither wanted to say anything that might break the tentative bond that had begun to form between them as they'd held each other in the hotel room.

Kate guided Lucas through the maze of downtown streets to the freeway entrance, then tipped her head back and closed her eyes. She sat quietly, but her mind whirled a mile a minute. She was pleased that he was going to stay with her, yet it seemed more important than ever that they talk.

She needed answers to her questions. And she was going to have to make a decision. But not until she had sorted through her thoughts and feelings, her needs and desires one more time. She wanted to be very sure of where she was headed before she confronted Lucas, because she knew that once she did, there would be no retreat.

She was quiet, too quiet, he thought, as he guided the rental car down the Gulf Freeway, skillfully weaving in and out of the Saturday-morning traffic that thinned gradually as they left the city behind. She was quiet in the kind of way that warned him she would be asking questions, serious questions sometime soon. And truth or fiction, he was going to have to have some answers for her.

Once again he debated the wisdom of telling her the truth. Once again, he decided to wait. He wanted to finish with her brother's diary first, to find out exactly how much information it contained, and how useful it would be. A list of names alone wasn't enough to convict Kiley of murder. At best, it would give them a basis to start investigating him. But when he'd talked to Matt, David Evans had mentioned photographs as well as a list of names. Perhaps there was a reference or a clue in the diary as to where the negatives had been hidden. He had every intention of finding out to-night.

In the meantime, he would answer Kate's questions as best he could, staying as close to the truth as possible without giving himself away. And he would ask her some questions, too, questions that a file full of information had failed to answer, questions that had been eating at his insides since last night.

She had been another man's wife, but only for a short time. Then, by choice, she had been alone. Had she given up the hopes and dreams she'd had so many years ago, her hopes and dreams of a home and a family? Had she given up on love? Or was there a chance for her...a chance for him...a chance for them to find happiness?

Somewhere over the rainbow, pal... The thought was as bitter and sarcastic as the half smile twisting his lips.

Turning slightly, he glanced at Kate, then away. He was crazy to think about the future, especially a future that included her. But maybe, just maybe, anything was possible. *Maybe somewhere on the other side of tomorrow...*

Chapter 7

"Wake up, Sleeping Beauty. I need your help," Lucas growled as he drove off the bridge connecting Galveston Island to the Texas mainland. "There's a map of the island and a piece of paper with some addresses on it in the glove box. I've traced the streets with a yellow marker, but you'll have to guide me to them. I thought we'd take care of business first, then have lunch."

Kate blinked in the bright sunshine as they stopped at the first of the many stoplights that lined the main artery into downtown Galveston. Somewhere along the Gulf Freeway past Nasa Road 1, her mind had stopped spinning, and she'd fallen asleep. What a mistake. She should have been psyching herself for her confrontation with Lucas, not drifting in dreamland, she thought, as she sat forward to retrieve the map and the list. But, oh, the dream she'd been dreaming....

"Do you want to look at them in the order they're listed?" Shifting in her seat, she hoped he wouldn't notice the hint of red that had crept into her cheeks.

"Yes, let's start with Logan Brothers."

She opened the map across her lap and studied it for several seconds. "Left at the next light, then." She glanced at the list again. "The others are within a block or two, so we can park near Logan Brothers and walk to them if you want." She checked a street sign as they crossed an intersection. "Right at the next street, two blocks, and left again. We should run right into it."

Lucas grunted something unintelligible as he followed her directions. She glanced at him, but his eyes were focused on the rows of huge metal buildings looming just ahead of them at the end of a narrow street. Suddenly, the hustle and bustle of a sunny Saturday morning in Galveston seemed a million miles away. She frowned slightly, scanning the empty sidewalks and the littered alleyways, her eyes darting nervously from one side to the other as he pulled to the curb and switched off the engine. It certainly wasn't an area of the island she'd choose to visit on her own. Even with Lucas.

"Come on, let's take a look around."

He was out of the car before she could voice her uncertainty. A moment later she stood beside him on the cracked pavement. Though the day was bright, the buildings shaded the sidewalk. A cool, crisp breeze ruffled her hair, sending a shiver down her spine. "It looks like everything is closed." She hesitated, holding back when he started toward the warehouses. "Are you supposed to be meeting someone?"

"No, I just want to check access and get an idea of what the neighborhood is like. If I'm satisfied with what I see, I'll contact the owners on Monday." He turned to face her, his eyes searching hers as he tucked a wisp of hair behind her ear. "Are you scared?" The corners of his mouth twitched into a smile. "I won't let the bogeyman get you, sweetheart."

"After your performance last night, I believe you," she replied, acknowledging the teasing tone in his voice with a tiny smile. Then, remembering his behavior at Vanderbilt's, not to mention the way he'd gone through her town house and inspected her car, she frowned again. "Lucas, where did you learn to fight so, so..."

"Dirty?" At her nod, he shrugged. Taking her hand in his, he moved down the sidewalk toward the Logan Brothers warehouse, his eyes roving over the area.

While Kate was uneasy about the deserted atmosphere of the neighborhood, he appreciated it. Anyone following them would stick out like a sore thumb. Although it was a good bet Kiley's henchman was still seeing double, Lucas was wise enough not to let down his guard for a moment.

"We live in a dirty little world, Kate. Thank God most of us don't have to face it on a daily basis. I faced it for the first time fighting the dirty little war in Vietnam, and I've never forgotten it. I've never forgotten how the army taught me to fight, either. It comes in handy in my line of work."

The time had come to walk the fine line between truth and fiction. She had begun to ask questions just as he'd expected. He had to give her some information about himself to quell her suspicions, but he'd have to keep tabs on the lies. The more lies he told her now, the more furious and unforgiving she would be later. He'd have to divert her attention as quickly as possible. The longer they discussed the life and times of Lucas Hunter, the harder it would be to skirt potentially dangerous territory.

"In the import/export business?" she asked, glancing up at him in surprise. "You have to bash heads against bars as part of your job in the import/export business? What exactly do you import and/or export?"

"Look around you. Are these warehouses located in a *nice* neighborhood? When I pick up a shipment at a dock in Miami, do you think I deal with elderly gentlemen in three-piece suits? No matter what kind of goods we handle, and we've handled just about everything at one time or another, the warehouses we use for storage are almost always in an unsavory area. And on the docks I deal with long-shoremen who'd just as soon kick me as look at me. Believe me, there have been times when they've done just that.''

"Is that where you live? Miami?''

"Yeah, I've been there for a while.''

"Do you own your own business?''

"No, but I've been with the company long enough to be able to choose what I do and where I go, and I have a voice in the decision-making process.''

"Are you thinking of relocating to Houston?''

"It's a possibility.''

"How will your girlfriend feel about that?'' She tossed out the question too softly, too casually. She knew that she had no right poking into his private life. It was none of her business. But now that he was talking to her, she wanted to know everything, good and bad. She had to know.

"I don't have a girlfriend, but my wife won't be too pleased. She loves Cuban food,'' he replied in a solemn tone of voice. Glancing down at her he saw the utterly shocked and appalled look on her face. Unable to stop himself, he burst out laughing. "Katie, sweetheart, I'm teasing.''

"You...you rat.'' She punched his arm with all her might. Then, wrenching her other hand free of his, she turned on her heel and started back to the car.

He caught her within a couple of strides, gripping her arm and spinning her around to face him. The pain and confusion in her eyes grabbed at his gut. Damn it, he *was* a rat. She had only been trying to assure herself that she was emotionally as well as physically safe with him. And if he owed her anything, he owed her the assurance that he wasn't a philanderer.

"Wait, I'm sorry.'' He wrapped his hands around her shoulders, holding her still when she tried to pull away. "It wasn't funny. I guess I just assumed you'd know I was free. I wouldn't have approached you otherwise.''

"You don't have to apologize to me, Lucas. Your love life is your business, not mine. I had no right asking about it in

the first place.'' She felt small and stupid, and she wanted
nothing more than to curl up under a rock.

"Well, so you know, I've never been married. In fact, although I've had a couple of serious relationships, I've never
considered marriage. In a sense I guess I've been married to
my job for the past several years. But,'' he murmured, his
voice lowering as he tipped her chin up and kissed her cheek,
"things change.'' Sliding an arm around her shoulders, he
hugged her close for a moment. Then, taking her hand in
his, he started down the street again. "Come on, Saloman
and Sons is just two blocks away.''

She trailed along beside him, her fingers woven through
his, repeating the words he'd spoken over and over in her
mind. *Things change*... She had no reason to doubt him,
none at all. And more than anything, she wanted to believe
him. So, she did.

"I like this location better than Logan Brothers', and the
buildings are newer. What do you think?''

"It does look a little cleaner here,'' she offered. Otherwise, she couldn't tell the difference, but she didn't want to
admit it. "What about Meacham Limited? I think it's on
this street, too.''

"Yeah, there it is.'' He pointed to the building at the end
of the block. "It's even better because it's on the corner.''
They stopped across the street from it. "If the price is rea-
sonable, and the inside looks as good as the outside, it
would be my choice.'' He paused for a moment, scanning
the surrounding buildings. "I guess you wouldn't know how
much Jonathan Kiley paid for his warehouse.''

"No, I don't.'' She glanced at him, a puzzled expression
on her face. "Why?''

"That's his building next to Meacham.''

Kate followed the direction of his gaze and noticed, for
the first time, the small Kiley Gallery sign above a set of
huge overhead doors. Though she had never seen the warehouse, she had known one existed. According to what David had told her, it was used for storage of new items until a

place was found for them in the showroom. It was also used for refinishing and restoration work. Come to think of it, according to the notes in his diary, all of the people he'd listed had had restoration work done there on every item they had purchased.

"Have you ever been in the warehouse?"

"No."

"Does he use it for storage?"

"Yes, and if a customer wants something restored or refinished the work is done there, too."

As she stared at the large metal building, she realized, for the first time, how odd it was that all of the people named on the list had had all of the items they had purchased sent to the warehouse for refinishing. Odd because ninety percent of the pieces offered for sale in the showroom, including the less expensive items, often were in excellent condition.

Had something else been done to the pieces at the warehouse? And if so, what? More important, how and why had David been involved? He had gone to the warehouse very rarely. In fact, in the past year, she couldn't recall a time when he'd mentioned making the trip. Jonathan had preferred to supervise the activity there, leaving David in charge of the gallery whenever he went to Galveston.

"Something wrong?"

Though she shivered slightly, Kate shook her head. "Just . . . thinking."

"About what?"

She hesitated a moment, then turned to face Lucas, her eyes shadowed. "Do you think David might have been involved in something illegal?"

"Do you?"

"I don't know. I don't think so. But after everything that's happened I'm beginning to believe that anything is possible."

"Do you know any reason why he'd do something illegal? Did he need money to pay off debts? Was he into...drugs?"

"If he had needed money, I would have given it to him. But as far as I know, he didn't. He lived on his salary. Except for an occasional game of penny-ante poker, he didn't gamble. As for drugs, he wouldn't touch them. When he was in high school, a good friend of his overdosed and died. It really scared him."

"Then I doubt that he was involved in any illegal activities."

"So why was he killed?" she demanded, anger and urgency edging into her voice. "Damn it, why?" She couldn't help feeling as if something was eluding her, some vital piece of information that was within reach. Maybe she would find it in the part of the diary she had yet to decode.

"Whatever the reason, his murderer will be caught and punished. Believe it."

"I want to believe it. More than anything, I want to believe it." *But I'm not going to sit by idly and wait for it to happen,* she vowed, as they turned away from the row of buildings.

They retraced their steps along the sidewalk until they came to Lucas's car. Anxious to get away from the oppressive atmosphere of the deserted warehouses, Kate suggested they go to The Strand, a part of Galveston's once-thriving business district where several blocks of old buildings had been restored and refurbished.

He agreed easily, willing to do whatever was necessary to change the direction of her thoughts. He wasn't ready for her to put two and two together and come up with Jonathan Kiley, at least not yet.

After driving the short distance and parking the car, they joined the crowd of people milling along the sidewalks. The two strolled hand in hand past shops, stores and restaurants, weighing the pros and cons of where to stop for lunch. They finally agreed on a small, corner café decorated in the art deco mode, and were rewarded with a secluded table for two tucked in the tiny bay window overlooking the street.

Her spirits gradually lifting, Kate sipped iced tea while she watched the men, women and children wandering past. The warm March sunshine coupled with cool breezes had lured scores of people who, at a distance, appeared to be completely carefree.

She knew it was just an illusion. Everyone had problems, everyone experienced their own private pain and sorrow. She wasn't alone. But at the moment there was little she could do to find her brother's murderer. And while she had no intention of forgetting about what she had to do, on a day like today who wanted to brood about the past or worry about the future? *Not I. I want to hope a little, dream a little, love a little. . . .*

"You're awfully quiet. If you're thinking again, I hope it's good thoughts."

"It's good thoughts," she admitted, as the waitress set bowls of steaming seafood gumbo and a loaf of crusty French bread on the table.

"Like what?"

"Like how good this looks." Kate tore off a piece of bread, then offered the loaf to Lucas. "I am so hungry."

"I'm hungry, too." His fingers brushed hers as he took the bread, his eyes holding hers in a steady gaze for a moment before his lips curved into a smile.

Only a fool would have missed the double meaning behind his words, and she was no fool. Neither was she the type to lie to herself. In two days her life had been turned upside down by the man sitting across from her. When she had thought of little hopes and dreams, when she'd thought of love, she had been thinking of him.

She knew exactly where they were headed, where they had been headed from the moment she looked up and saw him standing in front of her desk at the library. There was unfinished business between them. Regardless of the ultimate outcome, until it was resolved, neither of them would be at peace. And until they were at peace with themselves and with each other, there would be no foundation for her little hopes and dreams, nor any basis for her love.

"I know," she murmured, returning his smile as she ducked her head and picked up her spoon.

For several minutes they focused their attention on their meal, murmuring occasional comments about the excellent quality of the food as well as the generous portions. His leg brushed against hers beneath the table. She glanced at him, then away, her fingers trembling slightly as she reached for her glass of tea. He reached across the table, tucking a wisp of hair behind her ear, trailing the back of his hand down the side of her face in a gentle caress. She sighed, smiled, shifted in her seat. It was so good just to be—

"Why did you marry him, Kate?"

His words, so totally and completely unexpected, caught her by surprise. Her spoon clattered to the table. Her head snapped up. For several seconds she stared at him, willing him to withdraw his question. She didn't want to talk about her ex-husband, not now, not ever.

Of all the mistakes she had made in her life, marrying Alan Stevens was the worst. And though they had parted as they'd started, as friends, when she thought of him it was with regret for the years of unhappiness she had caused him. He had married her hoping that one day she would love him. She had married him knowing she never would. Though it had seemed like the right choice at the time, looking back she wasn't very proud of having made it.

Lucas watched the play of emotions on her face. He was almost sorry he'd broached the subject. As she had insisted so many times, nothing could change the past. Yet he needed to know the answer. If he had driven her into the arms of another man by betraying her trust and love, he would live with it. And if she had given Alan Stevens the love and trust he'd betrayed, he would live with that knowledge, too. In any case, he had to know.

"We started out as friends." Turning her face away, Kate propped an elbow on the edge of the table and rested her chin on her fist. "We were assigned to be lab partners in a biology class neither one of us wanted to take. We both needed a science credit in order to graduate, and we both thought biology would be the simplest choice."

Smiling slightly, she shook her head. "Boy, were we wrong. Anyway, we made it through the class...together. When the semester was over, I didn't think I'd see him again, but he called one evening and asked if we could meet for coffee the following afternoon. Since I knew he wasn't interested in a serious relationship and he knew all about you, I couldn't see any harm in it. He was more like a big brother than a boyfriend."

"I'll bet," Lucas muttered, his face grim.

At the tone of his voice, she turned to face him. "Believe what you want, but Alan Stevens was my friend, nothing more, for a long, long time. He was very popular and he dated several women. But he was there for me when I needed a friend. He was the only one who advised me to go to you when you didn't contact me, but I was too proud. When I didn't, well, our relationship began to change." She shifted her eyes away from his, refocusing her attention on the activity outside the café window. "A month before graduation, he asked me to marry him. He had gotten a good job with a company in Houston, and he wanted me to go with him."

"Did you love him?"

"I liked him. I liked him a lot. I thought it would be enough, especially since I didn't think I'd ever feel for another man what I'd felt for you. And I was so grateful, so damned grateful that *somebody* loved me.... I accepted his proposal out of gratitude. But he deserved so much more." She felt her mouth twisting in a bitter little smile as she paused for a moment. Then she turned to face Lucas again. "Do you want to hear something really amusing?"

"Kate, don't—"

"Don't what? You're the one who started it." She held his gaze, her eyes steady. "The night you called was the night of our engagement party. And do you know I almost, *almost* agreed to meet you? Talk about not having my head screwed on straight. I should have known then that marrying Alan was a mistake. But I'd made one mistake trusting you. I wasn't ready to admit that I'd made another.

"We were married for five years. I tried to be the lover he wanted and needed, but I...couldn't.... I wasn't very good at...having sex." She dropped her gaze, embarrassed by her admission. "He was kind and gentle and understanding, but after a while, he just...gave up on me. I can't say I blamed him. In fact, I was relieved.

"Toward the end, we were living more like roommates than husband and wife. When he was offered a promotion and a transfer to Dallas, we agreed to a legal separation. A year later he met someone who really loved him, so we were divorced. I hear from him occasionally. They have two children and a lovely home in Arlington. I'm so happy for him."

Though her voice was soft and low, her words were spoken with complete and utter honesty. She *was* happy for Alan. He was a good man and he deserved the good life he was living. She had never begrudged him his home and family. If not exactly what she'd dreamed of so many years ago, she'd had a home and a family of her own. And if not inordinately happy, her life had been relatively satisfying.

Lucas wanted to grab her and shake her until the cool, distant look in her eyes disappeared. Then he wanted to sling her over his shoulder, carry her away to some dark, secret place, and claim her as he should have done fifteen years ago. He wanted to take her beyond the mistakes they'd made in the past. And he wanted to show her the difference between having sex and making love.

Making love? Yes, with Kate it would be making love. Long, slow, deep love to last a lifetime.

Shaking his head at his foolishness, he pulled his wallet out of his back pocket. "Come on, let's go." He counted out bills to cover the check the waitress had left on the table, and he reminded himself for the umpteenth time that they probably weren't going to have a lifetime together. It was something he really ought to remember.

"I'll split the bill with you. How much do I owe?" she asked, her voice as cool and distant as her eyes, as if they were nothing more than mere acquaintances.

In reply, he glared at her, then prefaced his curt refusal with a swearword.

"Well, pardon the hell out of me," she snapped, the fire back in her eyes. She grabbed her purse and slid out of her chair. "I was only trying to be nice." Sweeping past him, she headed for the door.

He caught her just outside, wrapping his fingers around her wrist, and jerking her to a stop. "I don't want *nice* from you, Kate." His voice was low and rough, like the growl of an angry animal, but his eyes were shadowed with uncertainty.

"What *do* you want from me?" she demanded, tipping her chin up.

"I'm not...sure." He eased his hand down her arm, weaving his fingers through hers. "Maybe I want the impossible."

Smiling slightly at the sudden gentling of his voice and the possessive warmth of his hand on hers, Kate shook her head. "Changing the past is impossible, Lucas. If that's what you want, you're out of luck. But anything's possible today, tomorrow or the next day."

"So we can take a walk on the beach?"

"If that's what you want."

"That's what I want...for now..."

They returned to the car, then drove up Seawall Boulevard past hotels and motels, souvenir stands and restaurants, avoiding the more crowded and commercial Stewart Beach area for the relative peace and quiet of the state park to the west. On foot and wearing their jackets, they followed a narrow trail through the dunes, crossing the flat expanse of sand to the water's edge. In silent agreement, they stopped for a few moments, slipping off their shoes and socks, and rolling up their pant legs. As they headed up the beach, the icy water curled and foamed around their bare feet at regular, rhythmic intervals, wiping out the footprints they left in the damp sand.

Thick clouds had begun to build to the north, the wind had picked up and the temperature had dropped, driving most of the beachcombers away. But the storm would take a while arriving on the island, and neither of them minded the wind and cold. Hand in hand, they walked in silence as the sun arced overhead and dipped toward the horizon.

For the first time in weeks Kate felt the knot of tension inside her begin to ease. Despite her original hesitation to talk about Alan, suddenly she was glad that she had. It was as if another barrier between them had been torn down.

The gentle lapping of the waves, the gritty sand beneath her feet and the salt air stinging her cheeks reassured her in a way that was hard to describe. So much had changed in a short space of time. She had suffered a terrible loss, she had been alone and frightened, her life threatened. Yet today, with Lucas by her side, she could almost believe that better days were ahead.

"I love the beach," she confessed, breaking the silence stretching between them.

"Is that why you stayed in Houston after your divorce? So you could be close to the beach?"

"It's one reason," she admitted with a smile. "Of course the summer months can be awfully hot and humid. The mild winters do make up for it, though. I don't miss driving in ice and snow at all. But I really stayed because of David.

"He'd won a full scholarship to Rice University before Alan and I separated. It seemed foolish to move back to St. Louis when he was going to be moving here. And it seemed foolish for him to live in a dormitory when I had the town house all to myself. Then, our parents died within months of each other, and there wasn't really any reason to go back. My job and my home and my friends were here. After he graduated, David decided to stay, too. He got a job with a small oil company and moved into his own apartment.''

''How did he end up working for Jonathan Kiley?''

''He loved antique furniture. He used to haunt the local flea markets, buying odd pieces and refinishing them. As he began earning money, he graduated to antique stores. Kiley Gallery is one of the best in the city, and David was a regular customer. When Jonathan's assistant left to open a small store of her own in Austin, he offered her job to David. With his business background, his C.P.A. and his love of antiques, it was the perfect job for him. He was so...happy.''

''You were really close, weren't you? Remember how he used to tag along with us when we went to the swimming pool or the park? And I'll never forget that night we caught him hiding in the bushes by the front porch.''

Kate nodded her head, smiling at the distant memory. Her little brother had been lurking in the shadows while she and Lucas had been saying good-night with a lot more than words. ''If he'd told my mother what we were doing... But he didn't. He was a good kid.'' Her smile faded as she blinked back a sudden rush of tears. ''I'm going to find out who killed him and why, if it's the last thing I do,'' she swore, her voice barely above a whisper.

Lucas's hand tightened on hers. ''Hey, I told you, his murderer will be caught. There are trained professionals looking for whoever did it.''

''Yeah, sure.'' She shrugged, wishing she could believe him, yet knowing that her brother's murder was just one of many, many crimes waiting to be solved by an overworked, understaffed police department.

''Hey, I don't know about you, sweetheart, but my toes are starting to turn blue,'' he grumbled, trying to lighten her mood again as he pulled her to a halt. ''Why don't we ease up the beach and head back to the car? We might make it before it starts to rain."

"Sounds like a good idea." She scanned the sky as they turned. "I didn't realize the clouds were building so fast."

They scuffed through warmer, drier sand in silence for several minutes. Then, wanting to change the subject as much as Lucas, Kate decided to pick up where she'd been sidetracked earlier.

"How did you end up in Miami?"

"Company transfer." She was asking questions again, questions he didn't want her to ask because some of his answers would be lies. But once again there was no way to avoid it without arousing her suspicions. She had grown more and more comfortable with him as the day progressed. He didn't want to say or do anything to make her uneasy again.

"Do you like it there?"

"It's all right."

"Are your parents . . . do your parents still live in Ohio?"

"They decided to stay in Columbus when my dad retired. Their house was paid off, they had a lot of friends there, and my sister and her family live in a neighboring suburb. Bev has three kids, two boys and a girl. My folks have them spoiled rotten."

"Do you see your family often?" She couldn't mask the wistful note in her voice. He was so lucky to have his parents and his older sister's family to help fill the empty places in her life. She had a feeling his mother and father weren't the only ones who spoiled his niece and nephews rotten.

"Not often enough. I try to go to Columbus for a week in the summer. And we meet on Sanibel Island for two weeks at Christmas. We have standing reservations at a small resort there. You'd like it. The cottages are secluded, and it's just a short walk to the beach. I wish..." He paused, staring off in the distance. *Wish we were there now, just you and I, alone together, forever and ever....*

Kate gazed up at him, at the hard line of his jaw, the grim twist of his lips, the bleak look in his eyes, and wondered what he wished. She could ask, but she didn't. She simply squeezed his hand. "I wish, too, Lucas," she murmured as they angled toward the trail that led to the parking area and his car.

Ignoring the rising wind and the bone-chilling dampness in the air, he paused, turning to meet her gaze. Her dark eyes were warm and reassuring. Her smile was soft and seductive. She reached up to touch his face, tracing the curve of his cheekbone with her fingertips.

He caught her hand in his and pressed his open mouth against her palm, stroking her tender flesh with the tip of his tongue as his eyes held hers. Her breath caught in her throat, and she swayed toward him. Folding her fingers around the moist heat in her hand, he dropped a chaste kiss on her cheek.

"Be careful what you wish, little girl. You might get it."

"I could be so lucky."

"Are you sure, Katie? Are you very, very sure?"

Her gaze unwavering, she nodded her head. "Very sure, Lucas."

In that instant he knew that she would give him anything he wanted, everything he needed, whether he deserved it or not. And what he wanted, needed, was to bury himself deep inside of her, to claim her in the most intimate way possible. They wouldn't have any future together. Not after she realized how he'd deceived her. But they had today. They had tonight....

"Hang on to that thought," he muttered, as much to himself as to Kate, as he led her up the trail.

They beat the rain, but just barely. By the time they'd dusted the sand from their feet and put on their socks and shoes, a thin drizzle had begun to fall. Several minutes later, as Lucas pulled onto the freeway, joining the long line of stop-and-go traffic heading toward Houston, larger drops began to splatter against the windshield.

"I don't suppose there's a shortcut back to your house," he asked as he flicked on the heater and turned the windshield wipers up a notch. At the rate they were going, it would take two hours to get to Houston.

"Nope." Kate snuggled into her black wool jacket, blinked sleepy eyes, and yawned as the warm air in the closed car seeped into her bones.

"Don't you dare fall asleep on me. If I have to drive in this mess, the least you can do is keep me company."

"But I'm tired," she muttered. "Must have been all that fresh air."

He risked a quick glance at her. Her face was turned toward him, her cheek resting on the back of the seat. Her eyes were closed. She looked small and fragile and utterly exhausted. He reached over and brushed back her tumbled hair.

She smiled slightly. Her hand snaked across the car seat, and settled on his thigh. "I'm awake." She smoothed her hand along the inside of his leg, slowly, surely....

"Maybe you better sleep, after all," he growled, covering her hand with his and holding it still. "Otherwise, I may end up running off the road. Or pulling off the road... sweetheart."

"I've never gone all the way in a parked car. Have you, Lucas?" Her voice was whisper-light and dreamy. "I remember we came close a couple of times in the back seat of your dad's car. But you always stopped. And then there was the night we were driving home, and it was really late, and I was really tired, sort of like now, and I put my head in your lap, and I unzipped—"

"Kate!"

"It would be so nice if I could stretch out and—"

"For your well-being and the well-being of everybody else on the freeway, stay under that seat belt."

"But, Lucas—"

"Kate!"

"Yes?"

"Shut . . . up."

Chapter 8

It took them just over an hour to reach her neighborhood. She dozed most of the way, lulled by the rhythm of the rain and the soft music playing on the radio. But as Lucas exited the freeway and braked at a stoplight, she shifted in her seat, sighed and stretched her arms over her head. Outside the sky had darkened into early evening, and if anything, the weather had gotten worse instead of better.

"Where are we?" she asked, blinking her eyes and trying to get her bearings.

"About ten blocks from your house. Feeling better?"

"Mmm, yes. But I'm hungry." Brushing her hair out of her face, she slanted a glance at him out of the corner of her eye, trying to gauge his mood. She had pushed him to the edge with unmerciful teasing, and she had no idea why she'd done it. *Oh, sure, little Miss Innocence, no idea at all....*

He turned his head and gazed at her, his silvery green eyes glinting in the glow of a streetlight. Not even a hint of a smile softened his rugged features. "Somehow, I'm not surprised. What do you want to do about it?"

"Depends on what you want." Ignoring the subtle suggestion underlying his words, she smiled as she ticked off the choices she was willing to give him. "Mexican, Italian, Oriental, something southern-fried?"

"You're going to cook? Great. I like a woman who knows the way to a man's heart is through his stomach." Lucas grinned as he pulled away from the stoplight. If she wanted to play a while longer, it was fine with him. But later...
Little girl, we're going to finish what we've started....

"Who said anything about cooking? There's a Taco Hut, a pizza parlor, a Chinese restaurant, and Mr. Archie's Fried Chicken between here and my house. I'll eat anything. Pizza or Chinese we can have delivered. Tacos or fried chicken we'll have to pick up. So, make a decision quick. And, Lucas?"

"Yes?"

"If you ever make another male-chauvinist-pig remark like that again, I'll lock you in the laundry room with the cat."

"You're a coldhearted woman, Kathryn Elizabeth Evans."

"Don't you forget it, Lucas Daniel Hunter. Now, hurry up and decide. We're almost at Mr. Archie's."

"Is that a hint?"

"Well, their chicken is the best, and their biscuits are better than my mother used to make, and the dirty rice is seasoned to perfection."

"Okay, okay. You talked me into it."

"Turn right at the next light. It's two blocks ahead on the left."

They pulled into the line for the drive-thru window and proceeded to argue about what to get. They ended up with far more food than they could ever eat at one sitting since Lucas wanted to try the red beans as well as the dirty rice, and Kate begged for a small order of onion rings.

"Hey, give me another onion ring," he said as he turned onto her street.

"Sorry, all gone."

"What do you mean—"

He stopped speaking in midsentence. Switching off the headlights, he allowed the car to roll slowly to the edge of the curb half a block from the town house.

"Did you leave any lights on when we left this morning?"

At the sudden, serious tone of his voice, Kate's grin faded. "I...I don't remember. But I don't think so. I thought we'd be back before dark." Even at a distance she could see that lights were lit in the first floor of her house. Beside her, Lucas was digging in her purse. "What are you doing?"

He pulled out her keys and the .38 and tucked them in his jacket pocket as he reached for the door handle. "Wait here."

"Oh, no. You go, I go. Either that, or we drive to a service station and call the police." She released her seat belt and pushed her door open.

Lucas caught her wrist, yanking her back. "Don't be silly."

"Calling the police is silly?"

"Does anyone have a key to your house?" he demanded, ignoring her question. "Were you expecting anyone to stop by for a visit today?"

"Of course n—" Clapping a hand over her mouth, she gazed at him, her eyes wide. "Oh, no..."

She grabbed her purse and was out of the car, trotting up the sidewalk before he could stop her. Muttering a savage string of curses, he ran after her, catching her around the waist and holding her still just yards from her front door. "You little fool. Get behind me," he snapped, his voice low, his mouth pressed close to her ear.

"But, Lucas—"

"Shut up and get behind me. The car keys are in the ignition. If I tell you to go, you go, damn it."

He moved toward her front door, swiftly, silently, her keys in his left hand, his right hand wrapped around the butt of the revolver in his jacket pocket. He punched in the code to release the alarm system, then slid the appropriate key in the lock and turned it slowly, soundlessly. Reaching behind him, he pushed Kate to the side so she stood along the brick wall next to the door. Then shoving the keys in his pocket, he eased the door open.

"Stay here," he commanded, his voice barely above a whisper, glaring at her when she opened her mouth to speak. "Just do it, Kate. No arguments."

He hesitated a moment longer, tightening his grip on the revolver as he released the safety. It wasn't likely that Kiley or his cohort would wait for them with lights blazing. However, it was possible that one or the other or both had been and gone, leaving behind a booby trap of some sort. In any case, he wasn't going to take any chances. He stepped over the threshold and moved into the hallway, searching for any sign of disturbance, any sign that he wasn't alone in the town house.

He heard her an instant before he saw her. Drawing in a sharp breath, he pulled the .38 from his pocket, brought his left hand up to meet his right, and aimed the weapon straight ahead, pointing the muzzle at the tall, thin red-haired woman lounging in the kitchen doorway.

"Don't get excited, buster. No harm done. Just back out the way you came in, and we can forget we ever met," she advised in a gruff voice, slowly raising her hands palms up.

"Who the hell—"

"Grace! I'm sorry. I forgot all about our plans for lunch," Kate called out, pushing past Lucas. "I tried to tell him, but he wouldn't give me a chance. Put that thing away, will you, Lucas?"

As she moved in front of him, he tipped the .38 up so the muzzle pointed at the ceiling. "Who else is in here?" he asked, his voice low and rough, his gaze riveted to a point past the redhead's right shoulder.

"Just me."

The man walking out of the kitchen clutching a black cat in his arms and smiling beneficently at the embracing women was none other than Matthew Owen. Grinding his teeth around a string of swearwords, Lucas flicked the safety on the revolver, shoved it in his jacket pocket and raked a hand through his hair.

Walking past the chattering women and the grinning man, he entered the kitchen, found a glass and the brandy bottle and poured himself a double shot. As the first mouthful of liquor burned its way into his belly, he leaned against the counter for a moment and willed his heart to stop pounding.

One day he was sure he'd find the entire episode highly amusing, but that day was far off in the future. Right now he couldn't decide which one of the three standing in the hallway he wanted to throttle first. He finished the brandy in a couple of gulps, then slammed the glass on the counter and crossed the kitchen.

"... and I kept calling and calling. After David ... I was really worried about you. It was getting later and later, and it's not like you to forget. Since I have a key, Matt suggested we stop by. We parked in back by the garage so you'd see the car. Kate, this is my old friend, Matthew Owen. Matt, this is Kate Evans."

"And I'm Lucas Hunter, an old friend of Kate." He sauntered into the hallway, offering his hand to Grace, then to Matt, a charming smile pasted on his face.

"I'm Grace Stone. And," she continued, surveying Lucas from head to toe, a sly grin curving her lips, "I can see why Kate forgot all about our lunch. You're enough to muddle any woman's mind. And I'd say you're just what the doctor ordered. She needs someone like you, in more ways than—"

"Grace!" Kate glared at her irrepressible friend, her cheeks tinged with red. "Please ..."

"Please, hell. Young woman like you living like an old maid, it's a damned shame. You do something about it, you hear?" Grace poked a bony finger at Lucas's chest and winked at him. "Then maybe I'll forgive you for pointing a gun at me. Knew what you were doing with that thing, didn't you? Sure you boys don't know each other?"

"Say good-night, Gracie," Matt admonished. He was almost a head shorter, but as she turned to smile at him, there was no doubt who was in charge.

"Right, Matt. I'm rattling again, but so, what else is new? Anyway, I guess we'll be seeing you."

"Yeah, we gotta be going, kids." With a wicked grin, Matt shoved the cat at Lucas. "Take good care of my buddy," he advised as Caesar sank his claws into the front of Lucas's shirt.

"Well, I'll be damned," Grace paused for a moment as Matt took her arm, her blue eyes sparkling as her gaze swung from Lucas to Kate to Lucas. "Now I know why you're so attached to that cat. They could be brothers, couldn't they?"

"Grace!" Kate protested, feeling her cheeks burning brighter and brighter. But as she took a good look at Lucas and the cat, she couldn't help but smile, especially when she realized that her friend was probably right. "Actually, there is a resemblance, isn't there? In the eyes."

"And the attitude," Matt added as he urged Grace into the kitchen.

"I'll give you attitude," Lucas growled, then sneezed as Caesar's tail tickled his nose.

"Nice meeting you, Lucas," Grace offered, trying not to laugh.

"Grace, Matt, wait," Kate cut in as they started toward the French door. "We have bags of fried chicken and dirty rice and red beans and biscuits in the car, more than enough for four. Why don't you stay and have dinner with us?"

"No!" All three turned to face her as they voted unanimously against her idea.

"Okay, okay. It was just a thought. I guess you two have plans." She traded a secret smile with Grace and Matt, trying not to laugh as Lucas struggled to keep the cat from crawling onto his shoulder.

"I have a feeling you two have plans, too. In fact, if I were you, girlie, I'd forget about fried chicken and concentrate on that hunk—"

"Grace."

"Coming, Matt." She trotted behind him as he double-timed to the French door. "I'll call you in the morning, no, afternoon . . . late after—" The door slammed shut on her last word.

Beside her, Lucas snorted with laughter. "I'm glad you think she's funny," Kate muttered, dropping her purse on the hall table. She started toward the front door.

"Hey, wait. If you leave me here alone with your damned cat, I may resort to vio—" He stopped, drew in a deep breath, and sneezed. *"Kate. . . ."*

She retraced her steps, pausing in front of Lucas long enough to free him from Caesar's hold. Murmuring reassuring nonsense, she set the cat on the floor as Lucas sneezed again . . . and again. "I think you're faking, Lucas," she muttered, heading for the front door again.

"Faking, hell," he grumbled, catching up with her in a couple of strides. "Where do you think you're going now?"

"To retrieve our dinner."

"Not going to listen to your friend's excellent advice, huh?"

"Unfortunately, I can't concentrate on anything on an empty stomach."

"But once you've eaten?"

"Mmm, I'm sure I'll be able to . . . concentrate then." She glanced at him over her shoulder, smiling sweetly as she reached for the door handle.

He caught her hand and pulled her around to face him. "Is that a promise?"

"That's a promise." Tipping her head back, she kissed his chin. "Now, can I get the food?"

"You stay in here. And put this away, will you?" He pulled the .38 out of his pocket and pressed it into her hands. "Preferably somewhere other than your purse. One of these days you're going to shoot your foot off."

"You know, Grace was right. You are pretty good with a gun. Is it like fighting dirty, something you've never forgotten, something you have to use in your line of work?" She frowned as she considered how dangerous his job might be.

"Don't worry, sweetheart. I use a gun a lot less than dirty fighting." He touched her face with his fingertips for a moment, then turned to open the door. "Better lock it behind me. I'll let myself in with your keys, okay?"

Kate murmured her agreement and did as he asked. However, she ignored his suggestion to put the .38 somewhere besides her purse. She tucked it in the bottom of her bag, shrugged out of her wool jacket and hung it in the closet, then headed for the kitchen.

By the time Lucas returned, she'd set the table and poured tall glasses of iced tea. While he retreated to the second floor to stow his suitcase, she transferred the food to several dishes and, as she ran them through the microwave, tried not to think about which room he'd chosen to occupy. He had been sending mixed signals all day, but then so had she, teasing him mercilessly one minute, backing away the next. The time was coming when they'd have to make a decision about where their relationship was going, and do something about it. Kate knew where she wanted to go, but she couldn't go there alone....

"Smells good." He strolled into the kitchen, a lazy smile tipping up the corners of his mouth. "I guess food first wasn't a bad idea, after all."

He'd taken off his jacket, sweater and the holstered automatic, draping one over the chair in Kate's bedroom, tucking the other under his side of her bed. Standing beside the counter, he rolled his shirtsleeves up to his elbows, then washed his hands at the sink while she transferred dishes from the microwave to the table.

"I knew you'd feel that way once the food was on the table."

"Think you're smart, huh?"

"I know I'm smart, Lucas. Now, shut up and eat."

As if it had been a few days instead of a few hours since their last meal, they gave their undivided attention to the food, eating in silence for a few minutes. As their initial hunger was satisfied, however, they began to talk. At Lucas's prompting, Kate told him how she had met Grace Stone, adding several anecdotes about interesting experiences they'd shared over the years.

Lucas realized that Kate had no idea who Matthew Owen was. Although Grace had mentioned an old boyfriend on several occasions over the past few days, she hadn't given his name. Apparently Kate had met him for the first time that night.

"I wonder if he works for an import company, too," she mused, pulling apart her second biscuit and popping a piece in her mouth.

"Grace never mentioned what he does for a living?"

"She just said he was someone from her lurid past. But then, she commented on how you handled a gun and wondered if you were in the same business."

Growing more and more uncomfortable with the direction of her thinking, yet curious about Grace's relationship with Matt, Lucas guided the conversation back to her friend. "Lurid past, huh? What was she, a mobster's moll?"

"Of course not. She worked for the government for several years. Since she's never discussed any details, I've always assumed her job was classified or top secret. Anyway, she was in love with a co-worker and wanted to marry him. But he was married to his job."

Kate wiped her hands and mouth on her napkin, then reached for her glass of tea. She took several swallows, set her glass down and met Lucas's gaze, a smile tipping up the corners of her mouth. "Sounds like you. Maybe you are in the same business. In any case, she quit her job, moved back to Houston and married her high school sweetheart."

"And lived happily ever after?"

"Until her husband died two years ago, yes, I think she did." Kate stood up and reached for his plate. "Do you think Matt Owen is the man who chose his job over Grace?"

Lucas shrugged as he pushed away from the table. He carried a couple of half-full covered dishes to the counter while she scraped chicken bones into the garbage can. "Could be," he admitted, wondering if his boss had put duty first and, as a result, lost the woman he loved.

The man had led a very solitary life, one Lucas had never envied. Yet it was a life he might end up leading, too. Unable to accept the possibility, he blocked it out by changing the subject. "What do you want to do with the leftovers?"

"I'll put them in plastic containers and store them in the refrigerator if you take out the garbage. Otherwise Caesar will find a way to get into it and make a mess."

"Take out the garbage? Wow, my favorite job. How did you guess?"

"Told you, I'm just smart." She tossed a grin in his direction as she tied the ends of the bag together and pulled it out of the plastic pail. "The cans are in the back by the garage. If you want, you can put your car in the garage, too. It's a double. Have you got my keys? Here, it's this one."

Grumbling about bossy women in general and Kate in particular, Lucas ran upstairs to retrieve his jacket and the automatic, then picked up the plastic bag and headed for the back door. He disposed of the garbage bag, and, doing as she suggested, moved his car from the street in front of her house to the empty half of her garage. Taking advantage of a break in the rain, he also made a quick survey of the area, walking to the end of the block in both directions, first along the sidewalk in front, then along the alley in back, to assure himself that no one was watching the house. Either he had done more damage to Kiley's associate than he thought, or Kiley had taken the hint and called off his dog. In any case, he didn't find anyone or anything out of the ordinary.

He returned to the garage and checked the locks one more time, then crossed the patio and reentered the house. As he paused to set the alarm system just inside the French door, he heard a radio playing in the kitchen. He dumped his jacket and weapon in her bedroom. Then, following the music, he walked down the hallway to the kitchen doorway where he stood in silence, hands tucked in his pockets, watching her.

Her back to him, she moved from the counter to the refrigerator, storing leftovers. She swayed to the toe-tapping beat of an oldie by the Lovin' Spoonful, a song about magic, the magic in a young girl's eyes, the magic in the music. *The music in me.* The years seemed to fade away, and with them all the pain and loneliness he'd endured. All that remained was a woman in faded jeans, a baggy sweater and a jaunty ponytail, and the man who had never stopped loving her.

"Do you?"

She spun around, startled by the sound of his deep, rough voice filling the void between the end of the song and the disc jockey's patter. She wanted to scold him for scaring her, but the grave look in his eyes stopped her.

"Do you?" He repeated his question as he crossed the kitchen.

"Do I what?" She tipped her head back to meet his gaze.

"Believe in magic." He traced the line of her jaw with a fingertip, his touch as light as the brush of a butterfly's wing.

"Sometimes...." Her voice was whisper-soft, yet sure. "What about you?"

"I don't know. It's been such a long time. I don't know what I believe in anymore." He dropped his hand to his side and turned his face away.

She reached up and pressed her palm against the curve of his cheek, forcing him to look at her. "Then start with me. Believe in me, Lucas. Believe in . . . us. If anyone deserves a second chance, we do."

His eyes holding hers, he covered her hand with his and brought it down to rest against his chest. Beneath the cotton fabric of his shirt, she could feel his heartbeat quicken. "They're playing our song," he murmured, curving his arm around her waist. "Will you dance with me?"

In answer, she lifted her arm, threading her fingers through the thick, dark hair at the nape of his neck, resting her head on his shoulder. On the radio, the Righteous Brothers sang about time going by so slowly, about time doing so much. As they moved to the unhurried rhythm of the music, the words washing over them, their bodies drew closer and closer.

"Lucas?" As she settled into the cradle of his hips, she felt his arousal, thick and heavy against her. And she felt her body's response, the deep, moist heat of desire spreading between her legs, the aching emptiness begging to be filled.

"I know, sweetheart, I know. . . ." His arm tightened around her, holding her near as he bent his head. Tracing the curve of her ear and the narrow column of her neck with his lips, he savored the salty tang of the ocean air on her skin. Then he nipped at her earlobe, toying with her gold earring, tugging at it gently with his teeth and tongue.

She closed her eyes and tilted her head, giving him easier access, murmuring her pleasure as his lips followed the line of her jaw. When his mouth finally opened over hers and his tongue delved deeply, possessively, she matched him stroke for stroke, her hunger as insatiable as his. And when he pulled away, she cried out, unwilling to let him go.

"I want you, Katie." His lips were close to her ear, his breath hot and damp against her skin, his voice ragged. His hand still covering hers, he moved it down between their bodies, until her palm curved over the evidence his arousal. "I want to be inside of you, so . . . deep . . . inside of you."

She pressed her hand against him, caressing him as she tipped her face up to meet his gaze. "And I want you, Lucas. I've always . . . wanted . . . you." *I have always loved you.*

She wanted to say the words aloud, but she didn't, not wanting to bind him with an emotion he might not be able to feel. She smiled, a small, sad smile, as she moved her hand back to his chest. "But . . ." She hesitated, not quite sure how to warn him. She had disappointed one man, and despite her growing desire, she was afraid of disappointing Lucas, as well. "I'm not . . ."

"Don't worry, sweetheart, I'll protect you." He dropped a gentle kiss on her cheek.

"Oh, I didn't think of that," she murmured, a blush creeping up her cheeks. "I'm not using any . . . I don't have any kind of . . . birth control."

"But I have." He paused a moment, studying her face, seeing the uncertainty in her wide, dark eyes, feeling the sudden stiffness in her body, as if she were drawing away from him. "I would never do anything to hurt you, sweetheart."

"I know. It's just that . . . that I'm not . . . very good at . . . this. I don't want to disappoint you."

"At what?"

"Having . . . sex."

"We're not going to have sex, Kate."

"We're not?" She gazed at him in confusion, unable to keep the mortification out of her voice. "But what—"

He stopped her question with a kiss, his mouth on hers very gentle, very soothing, yet very insistent. When he finally raised his head, she had relaxed in his arms again. "We're not having sex. We're going to make love upstairs in your bedroom . . . slow, sweet, love . . . all night." He dropped a light kiss on her lips, then stepped back. "But, first, why don't you lock up your cat while I check the doors."

"My cat?" She stared at him, a puzzled frown on her face.

"That *is* your cat sitting on the kitchen counter, isn't it?"

She followed the direction of his pointing finger, making a valiant effort to get a grip on herself. Seeing Caesar sitting on the counter polishing off the piece of fried chicken he'd filched from the foil package that hadn't made it to the refrigerator did the trick.

"Caesar, *no*," she scolded, as she spun away from Lucas. "You're going to end up sick as a dog."

Ignoring Lucas's laughter, she scooped up her pet, deposited him in the laundry room and closed the door firmly. She returned to the kitchen where she finished cleaning up, then turned off the radio and the overhead light.

In the semidarkness she stood by the sink and watched the rain beat against the window with renewed vigor. She tried not to think, but thinking was all she seemed capable of doing. Thinking about the past, thinking about the mistakes she'd made, thinking about—

"I did tell you it was too late, didn't I?" He came up behind her, put his hand on her shoulder and turned her so that she was facing him.

"Too late for what?" she asked, her voice barely above a whisper.

"Second thoughts." He slid an arm down her back, caught her behind the knees and lifted her into his arms, a wicked glint in his silvery green eyes. "But you weren't having any of those, were you, sweetheart?"

She hesitated for an instant, then smiled shyly as she wrapped her arms around his neck. "Not anymore," she assured him, tipping her head up so she could kiss the hard line of his jaw.

"Good." His grin was as wicked as the glint in his eyes. He bent his head and took her mouth, his kiss hard and possessive and over all too soon. Then, without another word, he started toward the staircase.

Only the small, lacy-shaded lamp on the dresser was lit, its gentle glow transforming her old, familiar bedroom into a warm, intimate haven meant to be shared. Her heart beat a little faster when she saw his jacket draped over the chair, saw his suitcase on the floor beside it, saw the bed turned down. Any lingering uncertainty vanished in an instant. Despite the past, and no matter what the future might bring, this night belonged to them.

She expected him to stop beside the bed, but he surprised her by moving across the bedroom to the bathroom doorway where he set her on her feet.

"What—?"

"Remember that *maybe later* you tossed at me this morning?" He reached up and began to untie the knot in the hot pink scarf securing what was left of her ponytail. As her soft, dark hair drifted to her shoulders, he dropped the scarf on her dresser. "Well, sweetheart, I've thought about it all day." He bent and kissed her cheek, then switched on the light, walked to the shower stall and started the water.

"I said *maybe* later, Lucas," Kate pointed out, hanging back in the doorway, suddenly feeling very shy, yet very, very excited.

"Sounded like a definite *maybe yes* to me. And I can't think of a better way to get rid of the salt spray and sand we picked up on the beach this afternoon." He grinned as he leaned against the door frame and pulled off his boots and socks. Then he knelt in front of Kate and disposed of her shoes and socks. "Okay, now we're even," he declared, as he stood up and faced her. His grin faded. He buried his fingers in her hair and opened his mouth over hers.

As if with a will of their own, her fingers found the buttons on the front of his shirt. Her tongue playing with his, she released one, and another, and another, until they were all undone. Then she hesitated a moment, her hands on his chest, once again feeling shy and unsure.

When he raised his head, she opened her eyes and met his gaze. He smiled and with the tip of his tongue, traced the line of her lips which were already moist and swollen. "Take it off, sweetheart," he murmured, his eyes holding hers.

His encouragement was all she need. Tugging at his shirt, she freed it from the waistband of his jeans, smoothed it off his shoulders and down his arms, letting it drop to the floor as Lucas used his lips, his teeth, and his tongue on the nape of her neck. When she reached for the hem of his T-shirt, however, he moved back a step, covering her hands with his.

"Uh-uh. It's my turn." He reached for the hem of her hot pink sweater, drawing it up and over her head in one smooth movement. His eyes still holding hers, he tossed it aside. Then he lowered his gaze and touched her.

As if she might break, he traced the line of her neck and shoulders, then trailed his fingertips down to the gentle swell of her breasts rising above the pale silk and lace of her bra, to her nipples pressing dark and hard against the fabric. Cupping her breasts in his hands, he brushed his thumbs over the tight peaks again and again as he dropped swift, soft kisses on her neck and shoulders.

Her hands braced on his chest, she shivered under his touch. And then she cried out, her voice low with surprise and delight as he slid his hands to her hips and took first one nipple, then the other into his mouth, laving her through the fine fabric of her bra with his hot, moist tongue. Deep inside of her the ache intensified. And when he used his teeth on her... It was too much, yet not enough.

"Take it ... off," she whispered. "Please...."

She reached for the hook at the front of her bra, wanting nothing more than to be rid of the thing, but once again, he caught her hands in his, guiding them to his soft, white cotton T-shirt. She didn't hesitate a moment, pulling it up and, with his help, over his head.

As it fell to the floor, he released the hook on her bra and pushed the straps down her arms. Then he pulled her into his arms, holding her tight, her head resting against his shoulder, her cheek smooth and cool against his bare skin, her breasts nestled in the coarse, curly hair that veed down his chest and into his jeans. He smoothed a hand down her bare back to her bottom, pressed her into the cradle of his hips and moved against her.

Whimpering softly, she turned her face into his chest, kissing him, licking him, nipping at him with her teeth as she fumbled with his belt buckle. She was burning up, she was achingly empty, she was going to explode....

"Easy, little girl, easy," he murmured, stepping away from her and stilling her trembling fingers. "Not yet."

"But, Lucas, I want—"

"So do I, but we have all night, sweetheart...all night." His smile was as gentle as his kiss on her lips. He wanted her so much, but not hard and fast against a door frame. They had waited so long, they could wait just a little longer. "Take your jeans off and get in the shower before the water runs cold."

She hesitated, wanting to argue, her eyes on him as he shucked his jeans and briefs in one quick movement. But words died in her throat as she gazed at him, at his masculine strength and beauty, at his awesome arousal, at the breadth of his shoulders, his narrow hips, his firm bottom, his powerful thighs. As he disappeared into the shower stall, Kate unsnapped her jeans.

He moved back as she opened the stall door, allowing her to stand under the warm pulsing spray for several seconds. Then, changing places with her, he shielded her with his body as he rubbed fragrant soap into a fresh washcloth. When a thick lather had formed, he began to wash her, his hand stroking her in slow, circular motions as he worked his way down from her shoulders to her breasts to her belly....

He stopped, turned her around and started again, following the elegant line of her back to her buttocks. He paused for a long moment. Then, one arm around her waist, he pulled her against him, rubbing his soapy fingers between her legs, caressing her with steady, rhythmic strokes.

She sighed deeply, arching into him, opening herself to him. Her eyes closed, her lips parted, she rested her head on his shoulder. Bending his head, he took her mouth, claiming it in undeniable imitation of the ultimate claiming to come as the warm water pounded down upon them.

She twisted in his arms, one hand locked on the forearm he'd wrapped around her waist, the other covering his hand on her, urging him to deepen his caress as she moved against him with increasing urgency. She couldn't get enough of him, yet all too soon, he lifted his head and shifted his hand, pressing the washcloth into her palm.

"My turn?" she asked, her voice soft and unsteady as she turned toward him.

"Yes, please." He handed her the soap, then reached up to smooth her wet hair away from her face. "Back first," he advised, shifting positions.

"Oh, Lucas...." She saw the scars then. Though most had faded after so many years, she had no trouble imagining the pain he'd suffered as she traced the marks on his back, his buttocks, the tops of his thighs.

"Shrapnel makes a hell of a mess, doesn't it? But, it's all right now, Katie. It was a long time ago. You won't hurt me when you touch me."

His gentle voice reassured her as she rubbed thick mounds of lather over his skin from his shoulders to his buttocks, waiting a moment for the water to wash it away before turning him around. Starting at his shoulders again, she slid the soapy washcloth over him, watching as the bubbles clung to the coarse, dark hair on his chest, then gathered in the coarser, darker hair curling between his legs.

Smiling slightly, all shyness gone, she dropped the washcloth, rolling the bar of soap in her hands. Then she cupped him in her palms, her touch incredibly gentle as she explored the very essence of his masculinity.

"*Enough,*" he groaned, taking her hands in his and moving them away.

"But, Lucas," she protested, gazing up at him through her damp, dark lashes. "Aren't you going to give me... equal time?"

"I'll give you equal time," he muttered, shutting off the shower and opening the stall door. Stepping out, he grabbed a thick, fresh towel, tossed it to Kate, then claimed one for himself.

He rubbed the towel over himself quickly. She did the same, her dark eyes gleaming as she gazed up at him. He finished first. Then, taking a fresh towel, he soaked up the moisture clinging to her hair. Setting the towels aside, he walked out of the bathroom, waiting for her just outside the doorway. When she stopped beside him, a questioning look on her face, he grinned his wolfish grin, grabbed her and tossed her over his shoulder.

"*Lucas!* What are you doing?" She giggled like a schoolgirl, smoothing her palms down his bare back, savoring the warm, damp press of her bare body against his.

"Why, sweetheart," he drawled, his voice rich with barely suppressed laughter as he started across the bedroom. "I thought we'd satisfy your curiosity about *doing it* in the car."

Chapter 9

"Lucas, you're crazy," Kate declared, flattening her palms against his smooth skin, trying to get her laughter under control. "I was teasing you. Anyway, it's cold outside. Why don't we save the car for another time?"

"Teasing, huh?" He halted halfway across the room, easing her down the length of his body, until she stood facing him. "Bad habit, teasing. It can get you in a lot of trouble, little girl." He feathered light kisses along her cheek. "But it *is* cold outside, and it's so warm...inside...." He cupped her breast in one hand, stroking her nipple with his thumb.

"Mmm, yes, so warm," she murmured, threading her fingers through his thick, dark hair, tilting her face up to trace the curve of his mouth with the tip of her tongue. "Come to bed, Lucas." She closed her teeth over his full, bottom lip, tugging gently yet insistently. "Come to bed *now*." She stepped away from him, taking his hand in hers. "And stop teasing *me*."

"Yes, ma'am. Anything you say, ma'am."

He stretched out beside her on the cool, crisp sheets and gathered her into his arms, marveling once again at how small and fragile she was despite the womanly curve of her breasts and hips. "I won't hurt you," he whispered, his light mood darkening. Resting his cheek on her damp hair, he ran his hand down the length of her body, hesitating... hesitating.... He wanted her more than he had ever wanted anything or anyone in his life, and he wanted her always and forever. But he knew, deep in his heart, that tonight might be all he'd ever have of what he wanted.

Sensing his uncertainty, she shifted in his arms, sliding her hands between their bodies to caress him. "I know, Lucas. I ... trust you."

He groaned as she cupped him in her palms and stroked him. What had he told her earlier? *Too late, too late for second thoughts....* She trusted him. He groaned again as her fingers closed around him possessively. If only she would trust in his love, as well, maybe they would have a chance. It was a risk he was willing to take.

Shackling her wrists with one hand, he dragged her arms over her head as he rolled her onto her back. "Slowly, sweetheart...slowly...." He nuzzled her neck, his lips moist and warm, then dipped his head lower, lower, nipping her, kissing her until at last his lips closed around her nipple.

"Lucas..." she cried out, her voice high and surprised, her body arching up as he drew her into his mouth and suckled her. Deep inside of her the aching intensified, then intensified even more as his fingers trailed down her belly to tease the dark curls between her legs, to delve gently, ever so gently into her velvety softness. She shifted her hips, opening to his touch. "Lucas, please ... please ..."

He lifted his head, his eyes meeting hers. He released her wrists and smoothed her damp hair away from her face. "You're special, sweetheart, very, very special, and I want you so very, very much. I want to make love with you. I want to bury myself deep inside of you." *Tonight and every night from now until the day I die....*

Her dark eyes glowing in the pale lamplight, she stroked his cheek with her fingertips. They were good together, so right and good together. It had been true long ago, and it was still true. He warmed her heart and settled her soul. He was a strong man, a kind man, a man who had suffered, a man who had made mistakes and paid the price. He deserved to be loved, to be cherished. And finally... finally he had come home to her.

"I want you, too. I want you inside of me." She smiled slightly as she trailed her fingers down his chest, over his belly and along the hot, hard length of him. "Now, Lucas, *now...*"

He rolled away from her for one long moment, reaching for the foil packet on the nightstand, fulfilling his promise to protect her. Then, resting his weight on his forearms, he moved over her, positioning himself between her legs. His eyes holding hers, his self-control slipping, he sheathed himself inside of her with one sure, certain stroke, filling her with his heat. He was so close to coming apart, but he wanted her with him all the way. Trembling with the urge to claim her completely, he forced himself to remain still.

She wrapped her arms around him, clinging to him with her legs and the deep, velvet folds of her body, relishing the weight and warmth of his body over her, inside of her for several moments. Then, her need building, she arched her back and rolled her hips, drawing him in deeper and deeper. She was hot, so hot, and on the very edge of a place she'd never been before.

He bent his head to take her mouth, meeting her sudden demand with his own. Sliding his forearm under her hips, he lifted her, thrusting into her with a slow, steady rhythm that built and built again until he was driving into her, hard and fast, eating her cries as she pulsed around him, coming apart with a force that claimed him as completely as he claimed her. Then, with a hoarse groan, he arched into her one last time, holding her still as he filled her with his love.

Their bodies hot and slick, their breathing quick and harsh, they clung together, silently savoring the heavy, throbbing, aching aftermath of their mating. When, at last, he tried to ease away from her, she tightened her grip on him, unwilling to let him go.

"Not yet," she protested, her voice barely above a whisper as she rubbed her cheek against his chest.

"Ah, Katie, I'd better...get rid of..." He brushed his lips against her hair as he slid out of her, then rolled to his side. "Be right back," he murmured, tugging the sheet up over her body.

"Promise?" she asked, as she watched him swing his legs over the side of the bed, stand up and stride across the bedroom. The sight of his long, bare back, his hard, tight bottom and his heavy, powerful thighs stirred her with an intensity that belied her earlier satisfaction.

"Promise," he agreed, glancing over his shoulder to flash his wicked grin as he stepped into the bathroom and closed the door.

A few moments later, he switched off the lamp on the dresser. Then he was beside her again, turning toward her, pulling her into his arms. She settled against him with a soul-deep sigh, curling into his warmth without hesitation. She closed her eyes and tried to lie still. Despite the words left unsaid, she didn't want to talk. Yet despite the long, tiring day, she didn't feel like sleeping. To be honest, what she felt like doing was...impossible.... Wasn't it?

Smiling against his shoulder, she trailed her hand down his chest, her palm smoothing over bare skin and coarse hair.

"Kate?" He caught her hand, holding it still for an instant as he gazed down at her.

"Don't you want to make love again?"

"What do you think?" he asked, moving her hand down his body. "But, sweetheart, if we make love again the way we just did, you're going to be sore in the morning."

"Mmm, I've heard of . . . other ways."

"So have I, Katie," he muttered, pressing his lips to her throat, her breast, her belly as he slid down her body. "Gentle ways. . . ." He nuzzled the dark curls between her legs, glorying in her seductive woman scent, and her hands in his hair. "Very gentle . . . ways. . . ." He caressed her with his lips, then his tongue, stroking her with intimate care, delving into her, his claiming soft and subtle, his pleasure her pleasure as she twisted and shuddered and called his name into the night.

She couldn't sleep. Easing away from Lucas, she turned on her side and stared at the dull glow of the digital clock on her nightstand. It was four-thirty in the morning. She rolled onto her back, unable to contain a soft sigh as she gazed into the predawn darkness.

She should have been sound asleep. The events of the past few weeks had left her bone-weary, and under normal circumstances she'd be worn out by Lucas's lovemaking. A smile tipping up the corners of her mouth, she shifted slightly, testing the tenderness between her legs. He had been right. She *was* sore, but just a little, and it really was her fault. He had been so gentle, but then she had demanded equal time. One thing had led to another, he had ended up inside of her again, and again they had spiraled out of control, clinging to each other with quiet desperation.

Tonight was their first night together, but Kate knew she wasn't alone in her fear that it might also be their *only* night. It was as if something, some shadow, hung over them, marring the bright possibility of all their tomorrows. Turning her head, she gazed at Lucas. He was lying on his side, facing her, sleeping soundly, snoring softly. She raised her hand, wanting to touch him, wanting to smooth the thick, dark hair from his forehead. If she touched him, he would awaken and take her in his arms again. Turning away, she closed her fingers into a fist and pressed it against her chest.

There *was* a shadow hanging over them, she thought, staring into the darkness once more. The shadow of her brother's death, a shadow she had ignored for a while but could no longer avoid. Never one to shirk responsibility, she knew that it was up to her to find out who had murdered David and why. Until she did, there would be no peace, no happiness for her. If she wanted anything, it was peace and happiness. And she wanted it with the man lying beside her.

Moving slowly, quietly, she eased out from under the bed covers, sliding her feet to the floor and standing up. Barefoot, she padded across the bedroom and into the bathroom where she retrieved her old, terry-cloth robe. Tightening the belt around her waist, she paused for a moment, trying to remember what she'd done with her purse. If she wasn't mistaken, she'd left it on the small table in the entryway. But her notes were still in the outside zipper pocket of the navy blue purse propped on her dresser.

Casting a last glance at Lucas, she assured herself that he was sleeping soundly. Then she picked up her navy bag and after pulling the bedroom door closed behind her, headed for the staircase. With luck she'd be through with the diary in a couple of hours. And once she was, she would give Lucas the trust he seemed to want. Whatever she had discovered, good or bad, she would tell him. Then she would ask his advice about what to do next.

Still half-asleep, Lucas rolled onto his back and stretched beneath the blanket. He couldn't remember the last time he'd slept so deeply, nor could he remember the last time he'd awakened so completely aroused. He wanted the warmth and weight of Kate's body next to his, wanted to bury himself inside her slick, hot depths, wanted to watch her come apart in his arms again . . . and again. Turning on his side, he reached for her, but she was gone.

His eyes flew open as panic gripped his gut. *What the hell?* Propping himself up on an elbow, he rubbed a hand over his eyes, trying to clear away the cobwebs. Her side of the bed was empty, and judging from the coolness of the sheets and pillow, it had been empty for quite a while. Sitting up, he glanced around the room, aware of the utter silence surrounding him. Pale sunlight slanted through the shutters on the windows, and according to the clock on her nightstand it was just past seven. The clothes she'd worn yesterday were piled on the floor near his, but the bedroom door was closed.

"Kate!" he shouted as he threw back the covers and swung his legs over the side of the bed. It took him only seconds to pull on his jeans and stride across the room.

"Kate!" Throwing open the bedroom door, all but running down the hallway, he shouted her name again. Cursing himself for sleeping like a dead man, he pounded down the staircase. Oh, God, if she had left the house alone and Kiley's henchman had been watching and waiting...

She had left her purse on the table in the hallway, but it wasn't there. And though there was a fresh pot of coffee brewing in the kitchen, she wasn't there, either. Heart pounding, breathing hard, as if he'd run for miles, he turned into the living room and skidded to a halt.

"Damn it, Kate, why didn't you answer me?" he snapped, raking his fingers through his hair as he glared at her, his fear and anger not quite overcome by his relief at finding her safe inside the house.

She was huddled on the pale green-and-beige striped love seat, staring into space, her hair a tumbled mess, her bare feet peeking out from under the hem of an old blue robe. The black cat was curled up in her lap, his throaty purr the only sound in the room as she ruffled his fur with one hand. For one long moment, she remained still. Then, very slowly, she turned her head and met his gaze.

The expression on her face, the look in her eyes, hit him like a body slam, her pain and uncertainty so deep, so com-

plete that he felt it inside himself, along with the fear that he
was responsible. For several seconds, he couldn't speak and
he couldn't move. He could only hope that he wasn't the
reason why she was hurting.

"What's wrong, sweetheart?" He moved toward her, his
footsteps muffled by the thick carpeting, his eyes holding
hers in a calm, questioning gaze.

When she didn't respond, he glanced at the coffee table,
then drew in a quick, sharp breath. Her brother's diary lay
open on the polished wood surface, and beside it were several sheets of yellow legal paper filled with Kate's distinc-
tive handwriting, a pencil and her reading glasses. She had
been working on the diary, and from what he could see, she
had gotten to the last page. What had she discovered? The
shadows in her eyes and the faint quivering of her lips
warned that it was nothing good.

"Want to tell me about it?" he asked, his voice soft as he
settled a hip on one arm of the love seat. He wanted to sit
beside her and wrap his arms around her, but he forced
himself to maintain the distance she seemed to need.

She tipped her head down, turning her face away. She had
to tell him what she'd found in David's diary. Then she had
to ask for his help. But first she had to admit that she'd lied
to him. After last night, it wasn't an easy thing to do. He
had taught her the true meaning of making love, of giving
without taking, and getting for giving. And he had done it
with a gentle honesty that had warmed her heart and soul.

He had done it, too, despite her earlier efforts to drive him
away. He had accused her of slamming doors in his face,
and she had. But he had simply reopened them, then waited
patiently for her to realize how much he still cared for her.
He did care for her, didn't he? Otherwise, why would he
have put up with her bad attitude and her sarcastic smart
mouth?

And she still loved him, more than she had ever loved him
or any man. She trusted him, too, trusted that he would see
her through the painful hours ahead and help her decide

what to do with whatever she found at Grace's cabin. She glanced at the open diary and the pages of notes, remembering the last words her brother had written.

If you've gotten this far, sis, then I'm not around anymore. So, do me a favor. Go to our favorite place, the one by the river, and remember the first time.

The message had been written in code, but the numbers had been scrawled across the page quickly, carelessly, as if they had been added as an afterthought. *If you've gotten this far, sis...* David had been afraid of someone, and hard as it was to believe, Kate had a good idea of whom he'd been afraid.

Beneath her hand, Caesar's purring turned to a yowl of disapproval. Glancing at him, she realized she had curled her fingers into his fur, tightening her hold on him to an uncomfortable degree. Murmuring an apology, she released him and watched as he scampered off her lap and across the room. Then, she turned to meet Lucas's gaze, taking comfort and courage in the warmth and concern radiating from the depths of his silvery green eyes.

"I lied to you on Friday," she confessed, willing her voice to hold steady. "When you asked me about the black book in my purse, I told you it was my diary. It's not. It was my brother's. He mailed it to me that day he was killed." She paused for a moment, uncertain how to continue.

"And you've been decoding it?" Lucas asked, his voice warm and reassuring. It was all he could do to mask his inner turmoil, to remain calm and in control. She had decided to trust him, yet in trusting him she was forcing him toward the moment when he, too, would have to admit to lies and deception. It was a moment he wasn't ready to face.

"It's mostly a record of meetings with people I don't know, people like Eddie Sanders, the owner of Vanderbilt's. But toward the end..." She hesitated, dropping her gaze for a moment. She didn't want to mention David's discovery of the desk with its drawers full of cocaine. Not yet...not yet until she found out what was hidden at Grace's cabin. Not until she was sure her suspicions were correct....

"You can tell me, Kate. You know I'll help you any way I can."

"I know." Her dark eyes met his once again. "There's somewhere I have to go, something I have to do, but I don't want to go alone."

"You're not alone anymore, Katie." He pushed away from the arm of the love seat and sat down next to her, taking her hand in his. "So, where are we going and what do we have to do?" he asked, weaving his fingers through hers, trying to ease her uncertainty.

"My friend, Grace... She has a cabin on the Trinity River. It's a two-hour drive from here." Tightening her grip on his hand, she rested her head on his shoulder. "David and I borrowed it for an occasional long weekend. It was our... favorite place." They had gone there often when he was in school, but since he'd begun working for Jonathan, their trips had been much fewer.

"And once we get there?" Lucas prodded as gently as possible. He didn't want to push her, but he had to have some idea of what she had in mind. He had to be prepared to deal with any unwelcome company, and, equally important, prepared to tell Kate the truth about himself.

"I think David hid something at the cabin. I'm not sure what, but I know where." Though she still held onto his hand, she lifted her head from his shoulder and eased away from him. "Can you be ready to leave in thirty minutes?"

"I think so." Turning to meet her eyes, he smiled as he rubbed a palm across his beard-roughened jaw. "Of course, if your cat wanders into the bathroom while I'm shaving, it may take me longer."

"Why is that?" Kate asked, returning his smile.

"I'll be forced to make good on my threat to get rid of him myself, and I have a feeling it might take awhile." He stood up, pulling her with him. "He might have you buffaloed into believing he's a nice cat, but I have my doubts."

"Are you trying to tell me that I'm too easy, Lucas? Because, you know, I believe you're a nice cat, too, especially after the way you growled and purred last night."

Her voice was light and teasing, but her dark eyes radiated warmth and honesty. The meaning behind her words hit him low and hard. Caesar wasn't the only one who had her believing he was something more than he was.

"Only for you, little girl, only for you. Last night, and every night you'll have me until the day I die. No matter what happens, don't forget it." He traced the line of her cheek and jaw with his fingertips. Then he released her hand, turned and walked out of the living room.

Surprised by the solemnity of his vow, yet oddly shaken by the sudden hint of desperation in his voice and eyes, Kate stood beside the coffee table for several seconds, staring after him. At the sound of running water in the guest bathroom, however, she sat on the sofa again. She tucked the diary and her notes in her purse, slung the strap over her shoulder and headed for the staircase. She'd worry about the underlying meaning of Lucas's words later. Right now, she had less than thirty minutes to shower and dress. Then, during the drive to the cabin, she was going to sort out the information she'd discovered in David's diary. And she was going to try to figure out exactly what had been going on at Kiley Gallery and why her brother had been involved in it.

The storm that had caught them in Galveston had blown through during the night, leaving behind a first taste of spring in the sunny skies and a last taste of winter in the crisp, cold air. Kate and Lucas dressed in fresh jeans, shirts, bulky sweaters and heavy jackets, but fifteen minutes into the drive, as the car heater kicked in, they both shed their jackets. When they reached the outskirts of the city, Lucas pulled into a McDonald's drive-thru, but neither of them wanted more than coffee.

Aside from offering directions, Kate remained silent. She turned away from him slightly and stared out the window as if entranced by the passing scenery. Lucas wasn't deceived. From the corner of his eye he saw the way her fingers flexed around her coffee cup while it was full, then how they shredded the paper cup once it was empty. Finally, unable to stand the distance she demanded, yet unwilling to talk himself into a place he wasn't ready to go, he plucked what remained of the torn cup from her grasp and tossed it on the floor. Then, without a word, he caught her hand in his and brought it to rest on his thigh.

"I'm sorry. I'm just kind of nervous," she murmured, glancing at him.

His eyes caught hers and held them for a long moment before he focused on the road ahead of them once again. "I know, sweetheart. But no matter what's waiting for us in Grace's cabin, we'll get past it...together. Just...trust me."

"You know I do."

"Yes, I know." He tightened his hold on her hand. She had meant the words to be reassuring. Unfortunately, he was only reassured of how much he might lose once she knew the truth about him.

But what was the truth? Lord help him, he didn't know anymore. Why had he agreed to approach her in the first place? To protect her while he gathered enough evidence to convict her brother's killer? Yes. But within moments of seeing her sitting at her desk in the library, he had known that his reasons were as much personal as professional.

At first he had wanted to be free of her once and for all. Yet last night he had bound himself to her in the most intimate way. And the bond was one he had no desire to break. Nor would he allow her to break it. She would be angry and disillusioned, but ultimately he would find a way to make her understand that despite his deception, their love had been right and true.

"Lucas, slow down. We have to get off the freeway at the next exit."

"Sorry, sweetheart. I was a million miles away." He squeezed her hand again, then released it to switch on the right turn signal. Checking the rearview mirror as he pulled up to the stop sign at the crossroad, he assured himself that they weren't being followed, at least not closely. "Which way to the cabin?"

"Left," she advised, then admonished as he turned right, "Lucas, I said *left*."

"I heard you. Just thought we'd take a ride in the wrong direction for a few minutes, see if we've got company. If our friend from Vanderbilt's or anyone else is following us, I want to know before we go to the cabin."

"I've . . . I've got my gun."

"I thought I told you to put that thing away." He glared at her, narrowing his eyes. "You're going to end up shooting your foot off, or worse, shooting *my* foot off. When I told you to put it away, I meant it."

"I did put it away. I put it away in my purse," she huffed, crossing her arms over her chest and glaring back at him.

"One of these days, Kate . . ." He veered left off the two-lane asphalt road onto a narrow dirt and gravel track that ran between two barbed-wire fences, drove about five hundred yards, executed a neat one-hundred-eighty degree turn and stopped under a small stand of pine trees.

"One day what, Lucas?"

"One day," he ground out, his voice soft and dark in the sudden silence, "I'm going to turn you over my knee and whack the living daylights out of you for all the torment you've caused me the past couple of days."

"Oh, yeah? Think so, huh? What about all the torment *you've* caused *me*?"

"I've caused you torment, Katie?" He stared at her with wide, innocent eyes, his eyebrows arched in exaggerated inquiry, wanting nothing more than to make her smile one more time.

"What do you think, *sweetheart*?" She grinned at him as she used his nickname for her.

"I think it's damn good to be home again," he murmured, raising her hand to his lips for a quick kiss. "I also think we ought to go to the cabin before I'm tempted to drive off with you into the sunset."

"You know, I kind of like that idea," she admitted as he guided the car onto the two-lane road. "If I had a choice, a *real* choice, I'd definitely opt for a drive into the sunset. But I don't have a real choice, do I?"

"Neither do I, Kate, neither do I."

Puzzled by the desperation that had edged into his voice, she turned to face him, started to speak, then stopped. She knew why she had no choice about going to the cabin. She was determined to find out why her brother had been murdered and, if possible, by whom. But what about Lucas? Though he had promised to help her, something in the set of his shoulders and the grim twist of his lips as he watched the road warned her that his talk of choices had been on another level altogether. Kate wasn't sure it was a level she was ready to explore.

"How much farther?"

He knew that she was watching him and weighing the meaning of his words. He knew, too, that she had questions he would have to answer. But not yet, please, not yet.... He wasn't ready to reveal his true identity. Though he had no doubt that he would have to do it very, very soon, he hoped that when he did, she would remember and understand that he had had no choice, either.

"Turn right at the second crossroad, then left onto the third dirt road. The cabin is tucked in the woods at the end of the dirt road, about three miles from the main road." Kate paused for a moment. Then, uncomfortable with Lucas's cold, quiet withdrawal, she forced herself to speak again. "Is something wrong? Are you... are you mad at me?"

Without looking at her, he let go of the steering wheel with one hand, reached across the seat and squeezed her shoulder. "I'm not mad, sweetheart. I'm just...thinking." He moved his hand to the back of her neck, stroking her gently. "How are we going to get into Grace's cabin? Have you got a key?"

"She leaves one under a rock near the back door."

"So David could have come up here anytime and gotten into the cabin?"

"Yes . . . anytime."

"Did the two of you come up here often enough that he might have talked about it to someone else?"

"In the past couple of years David might have come up here two, maybe three times. He was busy with his job and his friends. And I doubt if a weekend at a cabin with Grace and me was something he'd discuss with anyone in any great detail."

"Third dirt road to the left, huh? This should be it."

Lucas moved his hand back to the steering wheel so he could make the turn and minimize the car's slipping and sliding in the gravel strewn mud. After about a mile, just past a curve, he stopped, rolled down his window and waited. The wind sighed and whispered through the tall pine trees while birds twittered in the underbrush. Inside, they sat in silence for several minutes, until he was sure they were alone on the road.

"Do you still think someone might be following us?" Kate asked as Lucas pressed down on the accelerator.

"Let's just say I don't like surprises."

Five minutes later, at Kate's direction, he turned onto a narrow, overgrown track that curved around a stand of pines, then opened into a clearing. At the end of the clearing was a rustic log cabin and a small wooden shed. Behind the cabin the cleared area sloped down to a narrow dock that angled out into the river. As he guided the car to a stop near the front porch of the cabin, they could hear the rush and tumble of rain-swollen water flowing past.

"Stay here, all right? I want to take a quick look around."

Knowing better than to argue with him, Kate waited until he was halfway across the clearing. Then, putting her purse strap over her shoulder, she slipped out of the car and stood beside it as she watched him survey the area. When he turned back to the car, she moved forward to meet him.

"I didn't notice anything out of the ordinary, but before we go inside I want you to walk around the cabin with me. If you see anything that seems out of place, tell me."

Acknowledging his request with a nod, she fell into step beside him. They circled the cabin, the soft, wet ground squishing beneath her sneakers and the crisp, cold air ruffling her hair. Shivering slightly as they passed through a patch of shade, she wished she'd grabbed her jacket out of the back seat. But then, Lucas put an arm around her shoulders and drew her close to his side, and she was glad she'd left it.

"Nothing unusual?" he asked as they completed their circuit.

"Nothing. Why don't we get the key and go inside?"

She led him to the back again, counted the stones in the odd arrangement to one side of the door, stooped down and lifted one. It was medium-sized and should have been heavy, but Kate handled it as if it weighed ounces instead of pounds. When she turned it over, Lucas realized why. It wasn't a real rock, but rather a good imitation. And inside the small sliding panel on the flat bottom was a key to the cabin.

"Neat, huh?" she asked as she replaced the stone. "Grace loves gadgets."

"Very neat," he agreed, taking the key from her hand before she could insert it in the back-door lock. "You—"

"Wait here," she finished for him, unable to contain a sigh of exasperation. "You know, there's such a thing as being too careful."

"Not where you're concerned. Now that I've found you, I'm not going to lose you." He reached out, threading his fingers through her hair, tilting her face up for one quick, hard, possessive kiss. "And don't you forget it."

Releasing her, he turned back to the door and inserted the key in the lock. A moment later he stepped into the cabin's combination kitchen, living room and dining room. Scanning the wide, open area, he assured himself that no one was waiting for them. Then he reached behind him to grab Kate's hand, pulling her across the threshold before he closed and locked the door.

"What's upstairs?"

"Two bedrooms and a bathroom."

"I'll be right back."

As Lucas disappeared up the narrow staircase, she reached for the light switch. With one quick flick, she turned on the light above the kitchen sink as well as several lamps scattered around the living room. It was easier than opening the window shades, especially since they'd only be there a short time.

It had been awhile since the cabin had been used. The air was stale and musty, and there was a fine layer of dust on the tabletops. As far as she could tell, there was nothing out of the ordinary anywhere in the room. If David had been here before he was killed, he'd left no outward sign. But then, she hadn't expected he would.

Crossing her arms over her chest, she tipped her head down and closed her eyes, remembering the last words he'd written in the diary. *Go to our favorite place, the one by the river, and remember the first time.*

They'd come for the day. They had fished from the dock without any luck. They'd barbecued steaks and eaten at the picnic table overlooking the river. And after they'd done the dishes, Grace had given them a tour of the old cabin, showing off all the cunning little nooks and crannies she used for storage. One in particular had fascinated David. It was the one behind the hidden door in the fireplace.

"Nothing upstairs." Lucas turned from the staircase and started toward her, only to stop as he met his gaze.

"It's down here," she murmured, more to herself than to him as she dropped her purse on the kitchen counter and moved across the living room. "In the fireplace."

He glanced at the large stone fireplace in one corner of the living room, wondering if she had lost her mind. Except for a couple of ancient andirons, the hearth was empty. But she seemed to know what she was doing, and what she was doing was awfully odd. She was running her hand along the bricks on the right side and muttering to herself.

"Can I help?"

"No, I think . . . I think I've got . . . it."

With a loud grinding noise, a large gray stone at the base of the right side shifted away from the wall. Only vaguely aware of Lucas hovering over her, Kate dropped to her knees, shoved the stone out of the way and reached inside the gaping black hole. Her fingers came in contact with cold metal, and a moment later she had the long, narrow box in her lap. She hesitated, barely breathing. If she was wrong, if the box was empty . . . But the box wasn't empty.

Chapter 10

She pulled the thick manila envelope out of the metal box. Her name was scrawled across the front in her brother's familiar handwriting and it was sealed. She tore the flap with trembling fingers, afraid of what she might find. Someone had been using the gallery and the warehouse as a front for illegal drug distribution. She had determined that much from the final entries in the diary. She couldn't believe it had been her brother. But if it hadn't been David, then who—

With surprising suddenness, the envelope opened, spilling its contents into her lap. She picked up one thing, then another—a sheaf of photographs, strips of negatives tucked into protective plastic sleeves, and a slim, white, legal-size envelope, again with her name scrawled across the front. Inside she found a list of names and addresses, the same names and addresses her brother had included in his diary. And there was a letter.

Good girl, Kate. You've gotten this far, you can go all the way. Sorry to dump this mess on you, but I wanted to be sure that if I couldn't stop Jonathan, somebody would.

She raised her eyes for a moment, blinking back the hot threat of tears that blurred her vision. Jonathan? As she recalled the entries in the diary, all the pieces began to fit together. It had been Jonathan Kiley who had met with the people David had named. It had been socially prominent, wealthy, well-respected Jonathan Kiley who had been dealing drugs. And as surely as she knew her name, Kate knew that it had been Jonathan Kiley who had killed her brother.

Her fingers tightened on the paper in her hand as pain and anger coursed through her, weaving into bitter rage and single-minded determination. No, there was no doubt in her mind that Jonathan had killed her brother. And there was no doubt in her mind that she'd do whatever was necessary to prove it.

"What is it, Kate?" Lucas crouched beside her and touched her shoulder. He had seen the pain and anger in her eyes and he wanted nothing more than to hold her in his arms and comfort her. But he couldn't do it, not yet, not until he had her brother's evidence in his hands. Not until he ended his deception.

"I'm not sure," she replied, her voice soft and full of uncertainty. She glanced at him, shook her head, then turned back to her brother's letter.

The pictures are of the people on the list, the ones Jonathan supplies with cocaine. There's also a picture of the man who supplies Jonathan with cocaine, and a couple of pictures of the setup inside the warehouse. From what I could determine the dealing is done between the tenth and twentieth of the month.

Kate riffled through the photographs. In each one Jonathan was standing with a different person at a party he'd hosted at the gallery. David had noted the names on the backs of the pictures, and the names were the same as those on the list. There was also a photograph of Jonathan and a Hispanic man. The name on the back was Diego Garcia. And there were photos of what looked like a small lab set up inside what she assumed was the warehouse.

How had David stumbled onto Jonathan's sideline? And why had he chosen to investigate on his own rather than go to the police? Perhaps, like her, he had found it impossible to believe that a man like Jonathan would be involved in drug dealing. Perhaps he had known that without some sort of proof no one would believe him. But without her brother, how effective was the meager evidence he'd collected? And what was she supposed to do with it?

"Can I see those?"

She had been so deep in thought, she had forgotten about Lucas. He had withdrawn his hand from her shoulder, but he had stayed beside her, waiting patiently, allowing her to deal with what she'd discovered in her own time and in her own way. She couldn't begin to tell him how much his kindness and understanding meant to her.

"He . . . he found out that Jonathan was using the gallery to distribute illegal drugs." She met his gaze as she handed him the photographs. "He took pictures of the people he named in the diary. There's one of Eddie Sanders. And there's one of the man he assumed was Jonathan's supplier, and . . . one of the inside of the warehouse. Lucas, I think . . . I think Jonathan Kiley killed my brother."

Not saying a word, he shuffled through the photographs, checking them against the list of names. It wasn't enough. Without David Evans to testify, names and photographs alone wouldn't bring Jonathan Kiley down. They could try to get someone into the gallery undercover. But Kiley was a smart man. He wouldn't be in any hurry to hire a replacement, and he'd kept his operation small enough to shut down or to relocate with little or no trouble.

And in any case, they didn't want Kiley for drug dealing alone. They wanted him for murder. In order to get him, they'd have to force him to show his hand. They'd have to use Kate as bait, just as they'd planned in case her brother's evidence wasn't enough. Unfortunately, as far as he was concerned, using Kate was no longer an option.

While he studied the photographs, she retrieved her brother's letter, turned to the second page and continued reading. He must have had a plan in mind.

Whatever you do, Katie, stay away from Jonathan. He's dangerous. Very, very dangerous. Contact Matthew Owen through the local DEA office. Tell him who you are and what you've got. He will help you. Take care. I love you, sis.

Kate folded the letter and tucked it into the envelope, her mind spinning as she tried to remember. *Matthew Owen...Matt Owen...* Grace's friend... Was it possible that Grace's friend was the DEA agent David had mentioned in his letter? Surely the name was common enough, but Grace's friend *did* work for the government, didn't he? And the DEA was a government agency.

"Matthew Owen." She spoke the name aloud, her voice soft and tentative as she glanced at Lucas.

His eyes met hers for a moment as he handed her the photographs. Standing up, he stuffed his hands in the side pockets of his jeans and turned away from her. He took several steps, stopped, then faced her once again, waiting...waiting....

"Lucas, remember the man who was with Grace last night? His name was Matthew Owen, wasn't it?"

He nodded. Knowing what was coming, he didn't trust his voice.

"In David's letter, he mentioned a man, a DEA agent named Matthew Owen. Do you think they're the same person?"

She sat on the stone hearth, looking so small, so fragile, her wide, dark eyes questioning. And he had all the answers. The time had come to tell her who and what he was. The time had come to reveal his deception. She would be furious, he was sure of it. But he would get her past it, he would make her understand. Then everything would be all right. Everything had to be all right because he had no intention of losing her again.

"I don't think, Kate, I know."

"You *know*? But, Lucas, how..." Her words drifted away as she tried to make sense of what he was saying. He couldn't possibly know... Could he? The two men had hardly acknowledged each other.

"I know because he's my boss."

"Your...boss?" Somewhere in the back of her mind, she chided herself for repeating his statements as if she were hard of hearing.

And finally she realized why he had barged into her life so suddenly and stayed with such determination. Finally she realized why he had put up with her smart mouth and her slamming doors. Finally she realized why he'd been so patient, so kind, so damned understanding. Not because he wanted or needed her love, but because he wanted, needed her as a means to an end. And even though she wanted the same end, to see Jonathan Kiley in prison, she was having an awfully time hard justifying his means.

At the moment she was finding it hard to do anything except stare at him. How could she have been so stupid?

"I'm a DEA agent, Kate. Matt Owen is my supervisor. Normally I work undercover in Miami, but when your brother was killed, Matt asked for my help. He needed someone to get close to you, to find out if you had David's diary and the negatives, and to protect you without arousing any suspicion. It's not unusual for old friends to meet and get together again."

He paused, wanting her to say something, *anything*, but she sat as still as a statue, clutching her brother's letter and the photographs, her eyes glued to his, her face drained of color. If only she would fly at him with fists and angry words. If only she would cut him to ribbons with her biting sarcasm. But it was as if she'd drawn into herself, locking down her emotions and locking him out.

"We decided it would be wiser not to tell you about the real reason for my reappearance. Kiley had someone watching you—the man who tried to grab you at Vanderbilt's. We didn't want you saying or doing anything that wouldn't jibe with the return of an old boyfriend."

"And I didn't, did I?" she asked, her voice whisper-soft. "I played your game like a good *little girl*, didn't I? Do you think you fooled Jonathan? I know you fooled me. Especially last night...."

She turned away from him and picked up the manila envelope. She tucked the letter, photographs and negatives inside, silently cursing her trembling hands for betraying the fragile hold she had on her self-control.

He was across the room in three long strides. Holding her shoulders, he yanked her to her feet, forcing her to face him. When she refused to meet his gaze, he grabbed her chin with one hand and tilted her head up.

"Listen to me," he growled, barely able to resist the urge to shake her senseless. "*Listen...to...me*. This isn't a game, Kate. This is life and death. Kiley killed your brother. He'd just as soon kill you, too. I did what I had to do to protect you."

Beneath his hands she was as cold and rigid as a steel rod, and her eyes were focused somewhere near his left cheekbone. She was blocking him out again, along with everything he had to say. He tightened his hold on her, vaguely aware that he must be bruising her tender skin. And he shook her once. Then, he released her and walked away. A the kitchen counter, he stopped. Bending forward, he placed his fists on the either side of the sink. "About last night . . . well, sweetheart, you were there. Believe whatever you want."

She wanted to cry. She felt great, gulping sobs dragging at the back of her throat and the hot, wet sting of tears in her eyes. But she wouldn't do it. She wouldn't give in to the pain he'd caused her. Not yet, and certainly not in front of him. When she did, she would do it alone. *And I'll be alone till the day I die,* she swore silently, swallowing hard and blinking her eyes. Her trust had been broken not once, but twice. There wouldn't be a third time.

For now, though, she wanted nothing more than to cope with her humiliation, her mind-boggling mortification at being so stupid. She was so smart about so many things. How could she have been so utterly and completely naive where Lucas Hunter was concerned? He had been too vague about his business in Houston, he had been too glib about fighting dirty, and he had been much too good with a gun. But she had blithely ignored the facts in favor of her fantasy, a foolish fantasy of mutual love and longing.

Over the past few days he had deceived her so many times in so many ways, and she had been too gullible to realize. Why, it was even possible that he had lied to her about why he'd never come home to her. Very possible. . . . It had seemed so hard for him to talk about it, and the pain that had edged into his voice, that had lingered in his eyes, had seemed so real. But he lived and worked undercover, didn't he? And in order to do that he would have to be an expert at deception. Wouldn't he?

And if he'd lied about what had happened fifteen years ago, then he'd lie about anything, including last night, if it suited him. It had been his job to stay close to her, and last night he'd certainly done that. And why not? She had been so willing, so eager, so . . . available. Perhaps he had simply decided to take advantage of the situation and enjoy himself.

No, she couldn't, *wouldn't* believe that last night had been nothing more to him than a pleasant interlude, one more means to his end—another job well done. But for her it had been a very foolish mistake, the last she intended to make where he was concerned.

She closed the metal box and returned it to its special place, then repositioned the movable stone, locking it down with a flip of the hidden switch. Pushing away from the narrow hearth, she stood up, the manila envelope in her hands.

He had wanted David's evidence against Jonathan Kiley, wanted it enough to deceive her in order to get it. Well, she would give it to him, gladly, and then she'd be done with him. She would have to suffer the two-hour drive back to her house, but she would do it in silence. She had nothing to say to him except goodbye and good riddance, which she would do the moment his car stopped outside her front door. With Jonathan out of commission, her purpose would be served, and his job would be done.

She crossed the living room, stopping at the corner of the kitchen counter closest to the back door. When Lucas turned his head to look at her, she avoided his gaze as she set the envelope between them on the tiled surface. With one finger she shoved it in his direction, then drew her hand away.

"I hope you can put Jonathan Kiley away for a very long time." Turning on her heel, she started toward the door "I'll wait for you in the car."

Before she had taken two steps, he caught her arm, pulling her to a stop. Her head snapped up, her eyes met his dark, fierce and forbidding as she strained against him.

"I'm not letting you go this time." He picked up the envelope and moved toward the door without releasing her.

Having no choice, she walked with him, but the words she tossed at him seared into his soul. "You're too late, Lucas. I'm already gone. Long gone."

She was as good as her word, he thought, as he followed the freeway back to Houston, her *long gone* echoing in the rhythmic slap, slap of car tires against pavement. She had closed in on herself completely, sitting as near to the passenger door as humanly possible, her arms crossed over her chest, her face turned away from him. When he stopped at a gas station to use the telephone she neither moved nor spoke. It was as if he no longer existed in her world. She had shut him out with a single-minded determination he found frightening.

He had to talk to her. He had to tell her that her brother's evidence wasn't enough. He had to make her understand that she would be in danger as long as Kiley was on the loose, and that he had no intention of leaving her until he was certain that she was safe. Even then he wasn't going to let her go.

But he knew that she wouldn't listen to him, not in her present frame of mind. So he called Matt and arranged to meet him at one of the agency's safe houses. If anyone could talk sense into her, it was his boss.

There was a flicker of movement from her when he flipped his turn signal on and headed down an exit ramp several miles northwest of the city. He waited for her to say something, anything, but she kept her thoughts to herself as he guided the car down a four-lane road past shopping centers and subdivision entrances. When he turned down a tree-lined street and headed toward a small, secluded apartment complex, however, she could no longer remain silent.

"I want to go home. *Now*," she snapped, barely able to control the high note of anxiety in her voice.

The strain of sharing the front seat of a car that seemed to grow smaller and smaller by the minute, with a man she'd known intimately yet not at all, was starting to make her a little crazy. Screaming was beginning to look like a viable alternative to sitting in silence, but indulging in that pleasure would let him know how badly she was hurting.

So she'd clung to the knowledge that she was almost home, and she'd forced herself to hang on until she could scream and cry all she wanted...without an audience. But suddenly, she had a feeling that she wasn't going home, at least not yet, and that her audience wasn't going to disappear as quickly or as quietly as she'd hoped.

"We're meeting Matt at a safe house. Since you refuse to listen to anything I have to say, I've asked him to talk to you."

"What makes you think I'll listen to him?"

"For one thing, he hasn't hurt you the way I have." He glanced at her as he slowed the car to turn right into the parking lot behind a row of two-story apartments, but she averted her eyes rather than meet his gaze. He tightened his hold on the steering wheel until his knuckles turned white, forcing himself to keep his voice calm and steady. "And I don't think you want to see Jonathan Kiley go free, do you?"

Since answering him would have been a waste of breath, she stayed silent as the car glided to a stop in a parking space near the end of the building. Of course she didn't want Jonathan to go free. But she'd done her part, hadn't she? She'd decoded her brother's diary and she'd led Lucas to the other evidence David had gathered, just as they'd expected her to do. Wasn't putting Jonathan Kiley in prison someone else's job?

Surely DEA agents Lucas Hunter and Matthew Owen, along with the Houston Police Department, could handle it without her assistance. Surely she'd earned the right to go home, alone, to lick her wounds. For just a moment, she was tempted to jump out of the car and run. But then Lucas was opening the door, looming over her. As if reading her mind, he took hold of her arm, and she realized how foolish, and how futile, running would be.

She wasn't as cool and composed as she wanted him to believe. He could feel the tension thrumming through her as he led her up the wooden staircase and along the railed, porchlike walkway to the apartment where his boss would be waiting. Damn it, he'd better be waiting. And he'd better be able to talk some sense into Kate. He'd also better be ready to listen. Because they weren't going to use Kate, not the way they'd planned, not in any way at all.

He rapped on the door of number twenty-five, the banging of his knuckles sounding unusually loud in the Sunday late-morning silence. Most of the apartment dwellers were probably still asleep or out of town. According to Matt at least two-thirds of the residents were airline employees who came and went at odd hours, often staying in one place less than a year, making the complex an ideal spot for a safe house. New neighbors really weren't anything new here.

The door swung open on well-oiled hinges. As Lucas escorted Kate across the threshold, Lucas shut the door, then surveyed the room. It was well furnished, neat and clean. And its sterile, unlived-in look was suddenly all too familiar. Just like the apartment in Miami, it was nobody's home.

"Ouch. Lucas, I'm not going anywhere."

He gazed down at her, seeing the quick flash of another kind of pain in her dark eyes. Without realizing it, he had tightened his hold on her arm. "Katie, sweetheart, I'm sorry. So sorry," he muttered, as he released her, willing her to understand and accept his apology.

"Not nearly as sorry as I am," she declared, rubbing her arm as she turned away from him. She crossed the living room, dropped her purse on the narrow, oak coffee table and flopped down on the navy-and-beige flowered sofa. Folding her hands in her lap, she focused on a point between Lucas and Matt.

"I'm here and I'm listening. Say whatever it is you want to say to me. Then, please, *please*, take me home and let me alone."

When there was no verbal response to her request, she hazarded a glance at Matt, then Lucas. It took her only a moment to realize that neither one of them was paying any attention to her. In fact, they were exchanging a long look, as if they hadn't heard her. And then they were moving out of the living room and into the kitchen.

Straining to see, she watched Lucas open the manila envelope he'd been carrying and empty the contents onto the table. Head to head, their backs to her, they poured over the list, the letter and the photographs. The muted rumble of their deep, low voices offered her not a clue as to what they were saying, much less thinking.

"Damn it," she cursed under her breath, as she scanned the living room. They didn't need her here, and she certainly had no desire to stay. Not only was she confused and tired, she was about as unhappy as she'd ever been in her life, or at least as unhappy as she'd been in the past fifteen years. And she wanted out.

She slipped off the sofa and walked to an end table where there was a telephone book under a telephone. She looked up the number of a cab company and began to dial. She'd pushed all of three buttons when Lucas pulled the receiver out of her hand, yanked the phone cord out of the wall and, without a word, carried the instrument into the kitchen.

Biting back a string of swearwords, she walked back to the couch, picked up her purse and turned toward the door. She was willing to walk halfway into next year if it meant getting away from Lucas. Unfortunately, he had her by the arm within a few steps. Hauling her around none too gently, he ushered her back to the sofa.

"Sit down." His voice was low and dangerous, and there was an angry glitter in his eyes.

When she hesitated, he loomed over her, narrowing the distance between their bodies until his chest brushed against her breasts. She stepped away from him as if she'd been burned. The backs of her knees hit the edge of the couch and, her balance gone, she sat.

"I thought there was a law against police brutality." She glared at him with the first real show of emotion she'd allowed herself since he'd admitted his deception.

"I'll show you police brutality, little girl, if you don't—"

"Now, now, children. We're going to be here a long time if you two don't call time-out. Considering what we're up against, I think your personal problems can wait."

Kate and Lucas turned to look at the short, pudgy, balding man who had joined them in the living room. The expression on his face was as bland as oatmeal mush, but the gleam in his eyes caught and held their attention, reminding them of the real reason they were together.

"Mr. Owen, please, I just want to go home. I did what you wanted, didn't I? I found the evidence against Jonathan Kiley that David gathered. Now that you have it, you're going to pick him up and put him in jail, aren't you? And you don't need me for that. Do you?" Her final question faded on a low note of uncertainty.

The two men were looking at each other again as if they were trying to decide what to say and how to say it. Lucas shook his head in warning, then raked a hand through his dark, shaggy hair. Matt shrugged, stuffed his fists into his pants pockets and rocked back and forth on his heels. And suddenly she realized that something was wrong, very wrong indeed.

"I'm sorry, Kate. Without your brother to testify, we don't have enough evidence to arrest Kiley on drug dealing, much less murder," Matt advised, the kindness in his voice at odds with the speculative look in his eyes. "You know what he's been up to and so do I, but a list of names and some photographs won't prove it to a judge and jury. As it is, several of his people have already left town. We can try to get a search warrant, but it's a good bet he's cleared out the warehouse and warned his supplier, too. We can watch him for a while. But unless we can flush him out somehow, unless we can bait a trap and catch the bastard, he's a free man. And unfortunately, he's demonstrated a certain amount of determination to get rid of you, something he can try to do again at any time."

She stared at Matthew Owen as if he were an alien from another planet. *Don't have enough evidence...bait a trap...determination to get rid of you...* His words whirled and spun through her head with mind-boggling clarity. And though she didn't want to go where her thoughts were leading, she didn't seem to have any choice.

"We can put you in a safe house in another city," Lucas insisted as he took a step toward her.

"For a while," she murmured.

"For as long as it takes to get him," he promised, placing his hands on his hips as he gazed down at her.

"But it could take...forever. I don't want to live like...like this...." She waved a hand, indicating the stylish, sterile room to emphasize her point. "I don't want to give up my job and my home and hide indefinitely unless it's the only choice I have." She put her elbows on her knees and massaged her temples with her fingertips. But it wasn't her only choice, and she knew it. Clasping her hands in her lap, she raised her head, her eyes meeting Matt's. "Why don't you bait a trap, Mr. Owen? And since Kiley's so determined to get rid of me, use *me*."

"No!" Lucas roared, his fingers folding into fists as his gaze swung from Kate to Matt, then back to Kate. *"No!"*

"It's what we planned originally, in case there wasn't enough evidence. You knew going in we might have to use her to get Kiley. You knew what we might have to ask her to do in order to get the job done," Matt pointed out, his eyes bright and determined.

"And you were willing to do anything to get the job done, weren't you, Lucas?" Kate added, her dark eyes full of pain, the pain of his betrayal. "So, get the job done, damn it. Use me, or I'll go after Kiley myself."

Lucas raked a hand through his hair, feeling anger and fear clutching at his gut. She might be willing to risk her life, but he wasn't going to let her do it.

Her jaw clenched, her lips narrowed in a thin line, her dark eyes cold and distant, she turned her face away, shutting him out. He wanted to grab her and shake her until her teeth rattled. Then he wanted to drag her as far away from

Matthew Owen as possible. Instead, he hunkered down beside her, covering her clasped hands with his, holding her still when she tried to pull away.

"Katie, sweetheart, listen to me," he implored, his voice as soft as velvet, as intimate as a lover's touch. "Not everything I did was to get my job done. I didn't sleep with you to gain your cooperation. You and I made love, together. Together, Kate, the way we were meant to be. I know I deceived you, but not in that. Never in that. You're angry, and you have a right to be, but don't let your anger get in the way of your common sense."

For just an instant, her eyes flicked to his, so full of sadness and longing that he wanted to gather her into his arms. But then her gaze shifted away, and when she spoke, her words were for Matt, not for him. "Just tell me what you want me to do, Mr. Owen."

Lucas stood up and strode across the room, stopping less than a foot from his boss. "Damn you, I told you she was out of it."

"She volunteered."

"You led her into it like a lamb to slaughter, and you know it."

"And *you* know it's the only way we've got a chance of getting Kiley. Or you would if you'd start thinking with your head instead of another part of your anatomy. I warned you—"

"And I *told* you, she's out of it."

"I'm not out of anything," Kate interrupted as she stood up. Hands on her hips, she glared at Lucas. "You're the one who claimed to be married to your job. What's the matter? Can't you hack it now that the honeymoon's over?"

"A hell of a lot more than the honeymoon is over." Lucas took several steps away from her. She was defeating him. But although he knew it, he wasn't quite ready to admit it yet.

"How true," she countered, then turned her attention to Matt. "I meant what I said. I'll help you any way I can, or

I'll go after Kiley myself. I'm not hiding like a scared rabbit and I'm not going to watch him go free."

"Are you sure?" he asked, his sharp eyes holding hers. "Because no matter how careful we are, you're going to be in a very dangerous position. We can set a trap. We can check and double-check that we've covered all the angles. But I can't guarantee your safety. You could get hurt, or you could—"

"End up dead." His back to them, Lucas completed his boss's statement, his voice as cold and hard as the icy hand wrapped around his heart. He had one last card to play, one last chance to change her mind. He walked into the kitchen and picked up the newspaper Matt had left on the table.

"I'm sure," she replied, knotting her frozen fingers together to still their trembling. She was so close to coming apart, yet she had to find the strength to hold herself together just a little while longer.

"Sure enough to risk ending up like him?" Lucas shoved the paper under her nose, ignoring her startled cry as she focused on the photograph in the bottom right-hand corner of the front page. "Your friend from Vanderbilt's, right? Ralph Jackson, found dead Saturday afternoon. And he didn't die as a result of having his head slammed into the side of a bar. Somebody shot him. Want to guess who it was?"

She backed away from him, averting her eyes from the all-too familiar face in the mug-shot photograph and the captioned details of his death. Acid burned at the back of her throat as her stomach heaved and rolled. He was trying to scare the spit out of her, and he was doing a damn good job of it. But she wasn't going to let him know it. He knew too much about her already, and he'd used the knowledge against her long enough. He wasn't going to manipulate her into doing what he wanted, not anymore.

"I'm sure," she repeated, ignoring the pounding of her heart and the sick sensation that had settled in the pit of her stomach.

"What about you, Lucas?" Matt questioned, focusing his attention on his associate.

"What about me?" he snarled, tossing the newspaper on the coffee table before he turned to face Matt.

"Are you in or out? If you want out, I'll have to brief another agent. Of course, if you're out, it will increase the risk for Kate. Another man on the scene will definitely rattle Kiley's cage and if you're right about Mr. Newsmaker there, Kiley's already out of control. However, if your behavior the past few minutes is any indication, you're out of—"

"And you're a cold-blooded son of a bitch."

"Whatever it takes, son, whatever it takes. You've never had a problem with it in the past. You got a problem now?" Matt jerked his thumb toward the apartment door. "Take a hike."

One of these days he was going to get hold of his boss by his thick neck and... Shaking his head, Lucas tried to rid himself of the gut-wrenching fear that continued to cloud his judgment. Not fear for himself, but for Kate. She had no idea how dangerous a man like Kiley could be. He was power-tripping out of control. He would just as soon put a bullet in her as look at her. She wouldn't stand a chance against him on her own and, in her present frame of mind, Lucas had no doubt she'd go for him alone if she felt she had no other choice.

She wouldn't have much more of a chance if Matt brought in another agent. No matter how well he or she was briefed, another agent would be less attuned to the situation and to Kiley's particular brand of insanity. There was no doubt that he had an edge, Lucas thought, as he held Matthew Owen's gaze.

Kate wasn't going to back off no matter what he said, and neither would Matt. Talk about being trapped. He could either go along with a plan that would risk her life, or walk away, knowing that he was increasing the odds against her a hundredfold. No one on earth could protect her as well as he could. And when all was said and done, he had no intention of walking away, not now, not ever.

Yet if he didn't rein in his emotions, he might not have any choice. Matt was losing patience, and losing it fast. In fact, if any other agent had indulged in a fit of temper as Lucas had been doing, he or she would have been looking for another job come Monday morning. That he had gotten away with such unprofessional behavior spoke volumes about Matt's faith in him and his understanding of what Lucas had to face.

"No need to get huffy, boss," Lucas advised in a mild tone of voice. "I just wanted to make sure Kate understood what she was doing." He almost smiled at the flash of approval in Matt's bright, beady eyes. "But I want you to understand something, too. She can change her mind anytime, and she's out of here."

At Matt's nod, Lucas turned to face Kate. She was sitting on the sofa, her legs drawn up under her, her arms crossed over her chest. Her face was pale, there were dark circles under her wide eyes and she was trembling slightly. Yet she met his gaze with a spark of defiance. Though she didn't speak, he got her message loud and clear. She wouldn't change her mind.

"And I'm with her all the way. She doesn't go anywhere near Kiley alone." Lucas focused his attention on his boss again.

"You can manage it without tipping our hand?"

"I can manage it."

At his words, Kate felt the knot in her stomach easing just a bit. Her threat to go after Jonathan Kiley alone had been false bravado. If she had to face him, and it seemed she did, then she wanted to do it with Lucas by her side. No matter how badly he'd hurt her, and despite her very real anger at his deception, she knew she would be safe with him. Whatever he had done, he had done it to catch her brother's killer. If anyone could understand his motivation, she should be the one.

As if from a great distance, she heard him say her name. She raised her head, meeting his gaze with a questioning expression in her eyes.

"Are you all right, Kate?" he asked for a second time as he sat down next to her. Exhaustion had deepened the fine lines around her eyes and at the corners of her mouth. Had she slept at all last night?

"I'm fine," she replied, forcing a note of assurance into her voice.

"Well, then, pay attention. This is what we're going to do."

Chapter 11

It took them less than thirty minutes to drive the distance between the apartment and her town house. For most of the way she huddled against the passenger door, hands clasped in her lap, her shoulders rigid, her face turned away. She stared out the window as if fascinated by the passing scenery, her eyes hot and gritty, the weight of too many unshed tears pressing at the back of her throat. She didn't want to think about Lucas Hunter, didn't want to think about Jonathan Kiley. But she could think of nothing else.

Fear flowed inside her with the steadily increasing intensity of waves rolling toward high tide. The desire to run and hide that she'd experienced several days ago was nothing compared to what she was feeling now. Yet she wouldn't do it. She owed it to her brother and to herself to honor her commitment, to do what was necessary to put Jonathan behind bars. Maybe then she could also justify her ludicrous behavior with Lucas. Maybe then she wouldn't feel like such a fool.

Though there was an outside chance that she wouldn't have to face Jonathan, Kate was wise enough not to count on it. From the first he had suspected that she might know about his drug dealing. She had no doubt that his determination to get rid of her would double after Lucas called him. Then he would know that she had David's evidence against him.

Confronting him wasn't going to be a pleasant experience. And as Matthew Owen had warned, no matter how controlled the situation, there was no guarantee that she and Lucas would be safe. But there wasn't any other way to draw Jonathan out, to force him to show his hand, and she wasn't going to let him get away with murder.

At least they had decided to move as quickly as possible against him. She wasn't sure how much longer she could still the shivers that threatened to skip up her spine. She was afraid once she started to shake, she might never stop. And she wasn't sure how much longer she could stand Lucas's company.

"You don't have to do it, Kate. We can have you in another city, another state in a few hours," he advised, his voice soft and gentle.

He placed one large, warm hand over her twisted, frozen fingers. Much as he wanted her to change her decision, he didn't push it. Somewhere in the back of his mind, he knew it was futile. She was determined to see her brother's killer behind bars, and she was willing to sacrifice herself to do so. It was a sacrifice he had no intention of allowing her to make.

"We've been over and over it already. I'm not running away."

With a perversity that was beyond her understanding, she wanted to weave her fingers through his, wanted to cling to his hand, wanted to absorb as much of his warmth as she could. Yet she kept her fingers knotted together in her lap, her face turned away, pretending to do nothing more than tolerate his touch.

Though most of her initial anger at his deception had faded, she was still hurt and confused. How much of what had happened between them over the past few days had been real, and how much had been a lie? She didn't want to know...didn't...want to know....

"You could have trusted me. You could have told me why you were in Houston." She hadn't intended to say the words, especially not in such an unsteady tone of voice. *"I trusted you."* She turned to look at him for the first time since they'd entered the car.

He met her gaze for a moment, cursing himself for the pain he was causing her, yet determined to get her past it. If he didn't, he would end up spending the rest of his life without her, and he'd been without her for too long already. Taking a deep breath, he focused on the road ahead.

"It's not that simple, Kate."

"Then explain it to me. I'm *not* stupid. At least I don't think I am."

"You're not." He squeezed her hands, then released her to guide the car off the freeway and turn onto the street that led to her house. "But for your own good, you were better off not knowing why I was here. You've heard the old saying 'what you don't know can't hurt you.' We didn't want you doing or saying anything to arouse Kiley's suspicions, especially since we weren't sure if you had any evidence against him. And we didn't want to arouse his suspicions. We wanted it to look like you were being pursued by someone from your past, nothing more, nothing less."

"Well, I don't know if you fooled Jonathan, but you sure fooled me," she muttered, her voice tinged with bitterness.

"Would you believe me if I told you I wasn't trying to fool you? Because I wasn't, not in that way. I couldn't trust you with my real reason for being in Houston, but you've got my trust now. Believe me, I'm trusting you with my life.

f I didn't, I wouldn't be planning to go up against Kiley
vith you.''

"I don't know what I believe anymore." She was so tired
and more confused than ever. Rubbing a hand over her eyes,
she tried to sort out her thoughts and feelings. There were
so many questions she wanted to ask. "Did you lie to me
about why you stayed away after Vietnam?''

"I told you the truth, or most of it. What I didn't add was
that because of what happened in Nam, I've spent more
than ten years of my life doing whatever was necessary to get
rid of scum like Kiley. It's my job. I'm good at it and I'm
proud of it. But if you think I enjoyed deceiving you, you're
wrong. It was one of the hardest things I've ever done. And
I didn't do it simply because it was my job. I did it to keep
you safe."

She wanted to believe him. Lord, how she wanted to believe him, but there was another question burning at the
back of her mind, a question she had to ask before they went
any further, although she knew that his answer could de-
stroy the last shreds of her self-respect. "Are you married,
Lucas? Do you have a wife and family waiting for you in
Miami?''

He eased the car to a stop in front of her town house, set
the parking brake and switched off the ignition. She turned
to face him, but he didn't meet her gaze. He stared out the
windshield, his eyes cold and distant, his mouth drawn
down in a narrow line. In the silence that surrounded them,
one second beat into two, then three, then four, an eternity
of time measured in her shallow breathing and the steady
beating of her heart. *Look at me. Look at me and tell me.*

As if her wish were his command, he turned his head, his
silvery green eyes roving over her in a manner she could only
describe as impersonal, as if she were a particularly uninviting stranger. Even before he spoke she realized how
thoughtless her question had been, and how much she'd
hurt him, how much she'd angered him by asking it. He

might have avoided telling her the truth, but suddenly she knew that there were some lies Lucas would never tell, even if his life depended on it.

"I told you the truth when you first asked that question. But if you believe I could make love with you the way I did last night with a wife and family waiting for me in Miami, then believe it, little girl." Turning away from her, he opened his car door, climbed out and started toward her front door.

Grabbing her purse, she hopped out of the car and followed him up the narrow sidewalk. At the door she dug out her keys and handed them to him, not saying a word, not meeting his eyes. Without being told, she stood back, allowing him to enter first. Then, gathering Caesar into her arms when the cat wove around her ankles, she waited patiently while he checked downstairs and upstairs for signs of an intruder.

By the time he'd gone through the house and returned to the hallway, some of his anger had obviously abated. Still, as his eyes met hers, she realized that his attitude toward her was anything but friendly. She wanted to believe his displeasure was aimed at her pet, but she had a feeling it most definitely extended to her. Her teasing friend, her warm and gentle lover had disappeared, almost without warning, behind the facade of a cool, calculating professional, ready, willing and able to get the job done regardless of how distasteful it might be.

He shrugged out of his black leather jacket and tossed it over the stair rail. His bulky black pullover sweater followed. He rolled up the sleeves of his pale blue cotton shirt, then glanced at his watch.

"It's after one. Do you have any idea what Kiley does on Sunday afternoons?" he asked.

She shook her head, wincing inwardly at his rough tone of voice. The chill that had settled in his silvery green eyes wrapped around her heart and squeezed. Without thinking, she dug her fingers into Caesar's thick, soft fur. Not to be outdone, the cat dug his claws into her arm. Ignoring the sharp sting of his discontent, she forced herself to hold Lucas's gaze.

"Well, then, let's hope he's at home. The sooner we finish with him, the sooner I can get out of here. You have his telephone number?" Not waiting for her answer, he turned on his heel and headed for the kitchen.

Her eyes widened when she saw the holstered automatic at the small of his back. She wasn't really surprised that he was armed. She was surprised that she hadn't realized it until now. But then he'd always worn a jacket or a bulky sweater when they'd left the house. This was the first time he'd removed both in her presence. And when he'd held her and kissed her, her hands had rested on his chest or his shoulders or tunneled into his thick, dark hair.

"Come on, Kate, get with the program. You do have Kiley's telephone number, don't you?" He paused in the kitchen doorway and glanced over his shoulder.

At the taunting tone of his voice, she tipped up her chin. "I have it. It's in the address book on the counter by the wall phone," she snapped. "Do you want me to dial it for you, or can you do it yourself?" If he wanted hard and cold, she'd give him hard and cold no matter what it cost her. And maybe if she concentrated on toughing it out with him, she'd be less apt to turn to quivering jelly when they finally faced Jonathan Kiley.

His eyes flashed a warning, but she pretended not to see it as she brushed past him, barely controlling the childish urge to shove Caesar into his arms the way Matt had done last night. The fleeting desire to see him sneeze himself silly was just that—fleeting. Their showdown with Jonathan was coming closer and closer with every passing minute, and she had no intention of saying or doing anything to distract Lucas until it was over. Afterward, she wasn't sure. Maybe by the time they got to the afterward, she would be.

In the meantime, she ignored his ignoring her as she moved across the kitchen to open a cabinet and retrieve a couple of pouches of Caesar's favorite food. While Lucas looked up Kiley's number, she deposited her pet in the laundry room, filled his food and water bowls, then slipped out, pulling the door closed behind her. As she slid into a chair at the kitchen table, she caught Lucas staring at her.

"Thanks. I was about sixty seconds away from a major sneezing session." His voice was faintly begrudging, but his eyes had warmed at least a couple of degrees.

She shrugged and offered a very small smile. "No problem. I'll let him out again when we leave."

"*If* we leave. As we discussed, I'd like to tempt Kiley into coming here. That's the safest way for us to confront him. If he won't come here, I'll try to get him to agree to see me alone. Right?"

"Right . . . boss."

His lips twitched as if he might smile, but in the end he didn't. He lifted the receiver and punched in the first three numbers. "Ready, then?"

She nodded her head, suddenly unable to speak around the thick lump of fear that lodged in her throat as he finished dialing. She wasn't ready to face Jonathan Kiley. She'd never be ready. But better now than later, before she had time to really think about it, before she had time to give in to the temptation to run. *Be there, damn you, be there....*

"Hello? Mr. Kiley? This is Lucas Hunter. We met the other day at Harry's and again at your gallery."

He leaned against the tile counter, crossing his ankles, tucking his free hand in the back pocket of his jeans. He looked so calm, so casual, but Kate saw the lines of tension etching his forehead and the corners of his eyes and mouth. For one odd moment, she wanted to go to him, put her arms around him and offer him . . . what? Twisting her hands together in her lap, she met his gaze. Whatever he wanted, whatever he needed . . .

"Yes, that's right. Kate's *friend*." He paused for several seconds, listening, then continued. "I've got those missing papers you mentioned as well as some interesting photographs. I didn't know you were a friend of Diego. Of course, if you're not interested—"

He paused again, then his lips twisted in a bitter smile. "I thought you would be. And it doesn't matter how I got them. What matters is how much you're willing to pay for them. You wouldn't want the police to find out about your little sideline, would you? And Diego wouldn't be at all pleased with your carelessness, either. From what I've seen, a cut in the business would be . . . nice."

She sat very still, barely breathing. Her fingers curled around the edge of the table until her knuckles turned white as she tried to concentrate on Lucas's end of the conversation, tried to shut out the dull, rapid thud of her pounding heartbeats.

"Fifty thou? Sure, if you've got that kind of money lying around on a Sunday afternoon, I'll take it. I'll be waiting for you at Kate's— All right, tonight, seven-thirty, at the gallery. I'll be there."

He ran a hand through his hair, frowning as he listened to whatever Kiley was saying. Nothing good, she thought, holding her breath. He hadn't gone for a meeting at her house, but the gallery was almost as good. He wouldn't risk another murder there, would he? And it sounded as if she might not have to—

"I'll take care of her. She doesn't have the faintest idea."

She let out her breath in a shuddering sigh as Lucas pushed away from the counter, turning his back to her. His shoulders rigid, his free hand braced on his hip, he listened to what Kiley was saying. Watching him, Kate realized that it had been too much to hope Kiley would forget about her. Contacting the people mentioned in David's diary had been tantamount to signing her own death warrant. And although Lucas had tried to deflect Kiley's attention, the man clung to his determination to be rid of her.

"All right, if you insist. It's not a problem for me. She'll do what she's told. As long as I get my money, you can do what you want with her. I don't need the risk, either."

He hung up the phone, slamming the receiver with a bang that echoed like a gunshot in the quiet room. Resting his palms flat against the cool surface of the tile counter, he closed his eyes, took several deep breaths, tried to bring the anger building up inside of him under control. The bastard was dead set on getting his hands on her. *I'll pay your price, but you bring the woman with you.* He turned to face her.

She stared at him as she had earlier in the day when he'd told her who and what he was, stared at him as if he were some sort of unsavory stranger. And as he had earlier, he tried to find something to say that would wipe the bleak, bruised look from her eyes.

"It was an act, Kate, just an act, a way of baiting our trap. I told him what he wanted to hear, one businessman to another."

"You're a very good actor. No denying that. And you're very good at telling people what they want to hear." She put an elbow on the table and rested her chin in her palm while she drew invisible circles on the tabletop with one fingertip.

He crossed the room in three long strides, stopping beside her, towering over her. He was of half a mind to shake the living daylights out of her. Unfortunately, he was also of half a mind to throw her over his shoulder and carry her up to the bedroom. Common sense warned that if he pursued either course of action now he would only alienate her more. But tomorrow, when they were finally done with Jonathan Kiley, he was going to teach Ms. Kathryn Elizabeth Evans the difference between truth and fiction.

He dragged a chair away from the table and sat down beside her. Cocking an ankle over a knee, he folded his arms across his chest and stared at her, willing her to meet his gaze. Though she was determined not to do it, eventually she did.

"What, Lucas? Damn it, *what?*" she demanded in a less than pleasant tone of voice.

"You would try the patience of a saint, little girl," he mused, his voice unexpectedly gentle. When she responded with nothing more than a shrug, he continued, "For your information, being a good actor has kept me alive for a lot of years. And being a good actor is going to keep us alive tonight when we confront Kiley. But what's been happening between us, between you and me, is no act. And I have every intention of proving that fact once he's behind bars."

"Lucas—" she began, prepared to protest, but he cut her off.

"I'm not going to argue with you about our personal problems now. *Now*, we're going to talk business. You do want to see Kiley in jail, don't you?" He leaned forward, his hands clasped between his knees.

"Of course." She shifted back in her chair, folding her arms at her waist, ducking her head to avoid his penetrating gaze.

"Well, then, we're supposed to meet him at seven-thirty tonight at the gallery. It's not as good as getting him to come here, especially since the building is freestanding. We won't be able to get anyone inside, but Matt will have more than enough time to set up our people outside. And with you wearing a wire, they'll be able to hear everything loud and clear. Given a bit of encouragement, I think Kiley is just cocky enough to want to brag about his exploits. I'll get him talking. Then once we get it on tape, and he hands over the cash, Matt's people will move in, just the way we planned this morning. All right?"

"All right," she agreed, glancing at him, then away. It sounded so simple, but she knew that anything could happen during the actual confrontation. Jonathan was on the edge. If he went over, he could take them down in a matter of seconds. He had already killed two men. Of that she was sure. How hard would it be for him to kill again if he thought he could get away with it? Not very hard at all, she conceded.

"Are you afraid?" Lucas reached across the space separating them, touching her face, tipping up her chin.

Raising her head, she met his silvery green eyes. They were full of warmth and understanding and the barest hint of teasing. "I'm scared to death," she admitted.

"Just do what I tell you to do, and let me do the talking. We'll be all right, sweetheart, I promise." He brushed his thumb over her lips, his touch soft and gentle, then dropped his hand. He stood up and glanced at his watch. "It's after two. Why don't you go upstairs and lie down while I call Matt? You look worn out. A few hours of sleep should help a lot."

She frowned, rubbing her hands over her face. Worn out didn't quite do justice to the overwhelming exhaustion that was settling over her mind and body like a thick, wet blanket. But how could she sleep with the specter of Jonathan Kiley, homicidal maniac, hanging over her? "I don't think—"

"Believe me, you will," he promised, as if he'd read her mind.

Grabbing her hand, he pulled her to her feet and, unable to stop himself, into his arms. The top of her head barely reached his shoulders, and beneath her heavy sweater her body felt fine and fragile. Yet despite her admission of being scared to death, she was so damned fearless. If anything happened to her . . . He tightened his hold on her for just an instant, brushing his lips against her soft, dark hair. Then he released her, pointing her toward the kitchen doorway. "Upstairs, now. You'll be asleep before your head hits the pillow. Trust me." His voice was soft and steady.

For one long moment, she simply stared at him. Then, without a word, she crossed the kitchen and started down the hallway. Halfway along, she stopped, turned. "I do," she confessed, her voice barely above a whisper. "I do trust you, Lucas."

She might not want to trust him, and she might not understand exactly why she did. But she did. And for some strange reason, it suddenly seemed important to let him know. In the space of a few hours she had come full circle, ending at the realization that he needed her trust as much as she needed his if they were to survive the confrontation with Jonathan Kiley. It was all she had left to give him, but then, it was all he'd asked of her from the start. He hadn't said anything about love.

"You won't regret it, Kate. You'll never regret trusting me again. I promise...."

She acknowledged his words with a nod. Then, she retreated down the hallway and up the staircase. In her bedroom, she paused for a moment, staring at the tumbled mess of blankets and pillows covering her bed, recalling bits and pieces of her hours of lovemaking with Lucas. Running her fingers through her hair, she shook her head. *Should have made the damned bed.*

Now she was too tired to do anything but kick out of her sneakers and strip off her jeans and sweater. In bra and panties, she crossed to the windows, slanting the wooden shutters against the midafternoon sunlight. Then she collapsed on the mattress, ignoring the rumpled sheets, nestling against the pillows, pulling a blanket up. Savoring the scent of man and woman, of loving and being loved that clung to the bedding, she closed her burning, aching eyes and, against her every expectation, as Lucas had predicted, she slept.

He called Matt, outlined the details of his conversation with Kiley and finalized their plans for the seven-thirty meeting. Matt would brief the agents he planned to post around the gallery and, well in advance, he would position the small van full of electronics that would record every sound picked up by the wire Kate would be wearing. They agreed on the signal to be given when Lucas was ready for the other agents to move into the gallery. Matt would also be in the van, monitoring their exchange for any dangerous deterioration in the situation that would require immediate backup.

After hanging up the telephone, he paced from one end of the kitchen to the other. Everything was under control, or as under control as possible considering they would be dealing with an out-of-control killer. He'd faced much worse odds on more than one occasion, and he'd come out on top. But then he'd never faced danger shoulder to shoulder with the woman he loved. He'd never risked anyone's life but his own.

Tonight would be different, and yet he couldn't let it be, and expect to survive. He had to block out his personal feelings for Kate, had to stop thinking of her as his friend and lover. Better to think of her as a stranger, better to think of her as expendable. It was the only way he'd be able to stay cool and calm, the only way he'd be able to play his part.

With a vicious curse, he slammed his fist onto the tile counter, welcoming the bruising pain that shot up his arm. *You're a very good actor, Lucas.* She had no idea at all what the past few days had cost him. And that was nothing at all compared to the price he might pay tonight. If Kiley touched one hair on her head, he would tear the bastard in half.

Rubbing his aching hand against his thigh, he walked across the kitchen and sent the refrigerator door swinging back on its hinges. Though he hadn't eaten all day, he wasn't hungry. But with several long, lonely hours ahead of him, a beer would be more than all right. He found a couple tucked at the back of the bottom shelf, and helped himself. Popping the top, he moved into the living room and stretched out on the love seat. He slipped out of his boots, propped his feet on the coffee table and swallowed several mouth-

fuls of the cold brew. Then, although he didn't expect to
sleep, he set the alarm on his watch for six o'clock, and
drank again. Several minutes later, the can empty, he slid
lower on the love seat and closed his eyes.

The steady, piercing beep of his watch awakened him
three hours later. Rubbing a hand across his eyes and over
the back of his neck, he stood up and headed toward the
staircase. With the March sun already dipping into the
western horizon the house was dark as well as quiet. After
switching on the upstairs hall light, he tapped on Kate's
bedroom door. When she didn't respond, he opened it and
padded silently across the carpet.

She was curled on her side, head resting on one arm, and
she was deeply asleep. In the dim light that filtered through
the doorway, her face was drawn and pale, her breathing
light and shallow. When he eased onto the edge of the bed,
she sighed softly but didn't move. The past couple of weeks,
especially the past couple of days, had taken their toll. If he
left her alone, she'd probably sleep until late the next
morning. If only he could....

"Katie, sweetheart, wake up," he murmured, his voice
soft and low as he smoothed tumbled hair from her face and
stroked the angle of her cheekbone with his thumb.

She sighed again, shifting beneath the blanket so that it
fell from her shoulders. Her eyes fluttered opened, then
closed, his name a whisper on her lips as she covered his
hand with hers. She turned her face, pressed her lips into his
palm.

The dream had been achingly erotic. She hadn't wanted
it to end. But Lucas was here beside her, his hand warm and
gentle on her face, her mouth. And last night he had shown
her how pale dreams could be compared to the real thing.
Without a word, she moved his hand to her breast, arching
into his touch. Opening her eyes, she gazed up at him, unable to read his expression in the semidarkness, yet sensing

his hesitation. She threaded her fingers through his shaggy, dark hair, pulling his head down until she could take his mouth with hers.

He rubbed his palm against her breast, his body tightening in response to the budding hardness of her nipple as he kissed her with a fierceness born of desperation. She was still half-asleep, still living out last night. He had no right to take advantage of her now. But he was a man, not a machine, and he might never again be able to hold her in his arms or taste the dark, wet warmth of her desire.

"Make love with me, Lucas," she implored, her breath hot against his lips, her fingers fumbling with the buttons of his shirt. "Come inside me. I want you . . . inside of . . . me. . . ."

With a ragged groan, he caught her hands in his. Holding her still, he kissed her one more time, one last time, his mouth eating hers with a bruising, reckless abandon that begged for forever when they might have no tomorrow. Then, lifting his head, he gazed into her dark, drowsy eyes. "Katie, no, we can't. We have to—"

There was a subtle shift in the tension thrumming through her as fear and uncertainty sank into her soul. She edged away from him, withdrawing physically and emotionally, her body no longer loose, her soft, drowsy expression hardening. When she tried to free her hands, he tightened his fingers around hers for an instant, refusing to let her go. And then, with a muttered curse, he released her and stood up.

She was so cold, and she had no reason to believe she would ever be warm again. She reached for the blanket that had slipped to her waist, and covered herself with it, clinging to it with trembling fingers as she pushed herself to a sitting position. Beside her Lucas was checking his watch.

"It's just past six. Even though the gallery is nearby, I want to be ready to leave by seven. It'll take me about ten or fifteen minutes to rig up the wire."

She nodded, not trusting her voice yet. She felt so small and stupid. How could she have forgotten about his real reason for being here? And why had she thrown herself at him with such complete and utter abandon *again*? She drew in a deep breath, raked a hand through her hair. *Must be love...*

"Or a masochistic streak a mile long," she muttered.

"What?"

"Nothing." She stared at him, challenging him to contradict her. "I'll be ready."

He shrugged. "Fine. Wear jeans, a shirt, a baggy pullover sweater and sneakers. Don't wear a coat or jacket. I want you to be able to move fast." He crossed the bedroom, pausing in the doorway. "Come downstairs as soon as possible and I'll rig up the wire."

She hesitated only a moment after he disappeared down the hallway. Then switching on the lamp on the nightstand, she checked the time, shoved the blankets aside and got out of bed. If she hurried, she'd have time for a quick shower. If she was lucky, the pounding spray would not only wash away the last remnants of sleep, but still her steadily mounting fear as well.

She had started down the stairs a few minutes later, dressed except for the navy blue wool sweater in her hand, her hair scraped back from her face and clipped into submission at her neck, when the telephone began to ring. She cleared the last step and turned down the hallway toward the kitchen where Lucas waited. As she stepped through the doorway, he lifted the receiver, muttering a none-too-friendly greeting to the caller.

Dropping her sweater over a chair, she rested a hip against the kitchen table and crossed her arms over her chest. In the moment that Lucas's eyes met hers before he turned away, a prickle of unease whispered up her spine.

"What do you want, Kiley?"

Kiley? Kate glanced at her watch. What *did* he want? It was almost six-thirty, just over an hour before they were scheduled to meet at the gallery. Had he changed his mind? She drew in a breath, pressing her arms more tightly against her breasts, her heartbeat quickening.

"Yeah, sure, whatever you say." An angry scowl marring his features, Lucas dropped the receiver into the cradle. Hands on his hips, he stared at the wall for several seconds, then lifted the receiver again and punched in a series of numbers.

"Lucas, what—" Kate pushed away from the table, moving to stand beside him, but he didn't so much as glance at her.

"Tell Matt he's changed the meeting place. He wants us at the Galveston warehouse no later than seven-thirty or the deal's off. I'm leaving now." Cradling the receiver again, he turned on his heel, pushing past Kate without a word, his eyes glittering, his mouth set in a narrow line.

"Lucas, wait...." Kate whirled around, grabbing her sweater with one hand, reaching for his arm with the other, but he was already out of the kitchen and halfway down the hallway. "What about the wire? What about Matt and our backup?" she asked, trying to control the rising note of hysteria in her voice.

If she had been frightened before, it was nothing compared to the sick feeling clawing at the pit of her stomach now. Facing Jonathan Kiley at his gallery, knowing that every sound they uttered would be monitored and recorded, knowing that other agents were nearby waiting to rescue them was one thing. But facing him at the Galveston warehouse at the end of a dark, deserted street completely on their own was something else altogether.

"You're staying here." Lucas grabbed his sweater off the stair rail and pulled it over his head, mentally cursing Kiley. Whatever the bastard was up to, it wasn't anything good, and he didn't want Kate anywhere around when it went down.

"Oh, no, I'm going with you. He wants me as much as he wants the evidence. If you go alone, he'll know something is wrong. He could do anything. You said yourself that he's out of control. If we follow our plan, we've got a chance of getting him. If we don't, we might never have another opportunity."

Ignoring her, he crossed to the hall table, picked up the manila envelope and shoved it into the briefcase Matt had given him. He checked his watch, muttering a curse as he started toward the door. He'd have to break the speed limit by ten to fifteen miles per hour to make it to Galveston by seven-thirty. He reached for the door handle.

"If you don't take me with you, I'll follow you in my car."

She stood in the center of the hallway, clutching her dark sweater and her purse, her chin tipped up at a dangerous angle, her eyes challenging him. If he had time, he'd drag her upstairs and handcuff her to the bed. But time was running out....

Gritting his teeth, Lucas strode toward her, wrapped his hand around her upper arm, jerked her toward the door, opened it, and motioned her out ahead of him.

"Have you got your .38?" He slammed the door behind them and, without bothering to lock it, walked down the sidewalk to his car.

"Yes."

"Is it loaded?"

"Of course." She slid onto the passenger seat a bare second before he shoved the door closed.

"If you take it out of your purse, be prepared to use it," he advised as he climbed in beside her. He started the engine and pulled away from the curb. When she didn't respond, he glanced at her. "Did you hear me?"

"Yes." She knew what he was doing. He was scaring her...on purpose. But she wasn't go to back down. She wasn't going to let him face Jonathan Kiley alone.

"When we get there, I want you to stay behind me. And when we're with Kiley, I want you to keep your mouth closed. No matter what I say, no matter what I do. Got it?"

She twisted her fingers together in her lap and stared straight ahead. "Got it."

Chapter 12

He drove past the row of warehouses slowly, eyes scanning the area for anything out of the ordinary. Except for a black, late-model Mercedes, the street was empty. A scattering of streetlights did little to illuminate the area, and although there was a small globe burning near the side entrance of Kiley's warehouse, the rest of the building had the same dark, deserted look as those surrounding it.

"That's Jonathan's car," Kate advised as they cruised by. When Lucas continued down the street, she turned to face him. "Where are you going? It's almost 7:40. He said he wouldn't wait."

"He's waiting. He's sitting in the car."

Spinning the steering wheel, he made a U-turn, passed the Mercedes again, made another U-turn, then eased to the curb behind Kiley's car. As Lucas switched off the lights and engine, Jonathan opened his car door and stepped out. Lucas did the same, first cautioning Kate to stay put. Ignoring the gust of cold, damp wind that swept down the street

sending leaves and odd bits of paper scuttling, the two men
eyed each other silently for several seconds.

"I don't like being jerked around, Kiley."

In fact, he didn't like anything about the encounter—
from the sudden change in their meeting place, to Kate's
presence, to the smug half smile twisting the older man's
thin lips. But if he wanted Kiley, he'd have to let him call the
shots, at least for a while. The man was so sure of himself
of his power. Not only was he wealthy and respected, bu
he'd gotten rid of two obstacles already without any prob
lems. And Lucas had had enough experience with Kiley's
type to know that it was his intention to rid himself of two
more obstacles before the night was over.

But men like Kiley enjoyed showing off. First he'd flaun
his superior intellect, his foxlike cunning. Before he could
go any further, Lucas intended to bring him down. It was all
a matter of timing. Until then, they had no choice but to
play his game.

"Just a last-minute precaution on my part. There's been
too much activity around the gallery lately. A lot of coming
and going on a Sunday night would only arouse...suspicion
We'll have more privacy here." He gestured toward the
warehouse with one slim, fine-boned hand. "And you can't
be too put out. You didn't go to the police with your so
called evidence, did you?"

"I'd rather do business with you than the cops any day
For one thing, the pay's better. You brought the fifty thou
sand, didn't you?"

"Of course. And you brought Kate as I requested?"

"She's in the car."

"Well, then, Mr. Hunter, get her and come with me. A
I said earlier, I have something to show you." He reached
into the Mercedes, pulled out a thick, leather briefcase
closed the car door and started toward the side entrance o
the warehouse.

Lucas walked around to the passenger side, opened it and, taking Kate by the arm, helped her out of the car.

"Remember what I told you about keeping your mouth shut. One wrong word could tip our hand," he whispered as he took the briefcase from her. "And whatever you do, hang on to your purse. You're all the backup we've got, sweetheart." He held her gaze for one long moment, willing her to be brave enough, strong enough for what was coming. "Now give me a little resistance. I want Kiley to think I'm his man."

He crossed the sidewalk to join Kiley, pulling her along none too gently. "Just do what I tell you, and you won't get hurt," he ordered in a louder, harsher tone of voice.

She had sat in the car, heart pounding, hands twisting together in her lap, trying not to panic while the two men traded barbs and vied for dominance like a couple of snorting, stamping bulls. Her trust in Lucas had held her together. But now the sudden change in his tone and manner sent her spiraling toward the edge. In the blink of an eye he'd become someone she'd never known, someone she didn't want to know. All she wanted was to get away. It was a stupid, utterly irrational desire. It was also so overwhelming that pretending to rebel wasn't all that hard for her to do.

Digging in her heels, she forced him to stop in midstride, as she pried at his hand on her arm with trembling fingers. "What are we doing here? Let me go. Lucas, let... me...go...." She clawed at him with her nails, her high, thin voice echoing up and down the deserted street. "I'll wait in the car. Please, in the car."

"I thought you said she'd do what she's told," Kiley taunted, his eyes narrowed, his lips turned down in a grim line of disapproval.

"She will," Lucas snapped. Then, turning on Kate, he caught her other arm, dragged her forward until their bodies were almost touching, and bent his head so that his face was inches from hers. "Behave yourself." He shook her hard. "Do you understand me? Behave yourself."

He saw the hurt and fear in her eyes as she flinched away from him, her face pale, her lips quivering, but he couldn't offer her the slightest sign of comfort or reassurance. If he gave Kiley any indication at all that he cared for her, that her feelings mattered to him in the least, the game would be up. He had to convince him that he was willing to sacrifice her for fifty thousand dollars. That she was convinced certainly helped his cause. And if he was having trouble quelling the pain welling up inside of him, threatening to cripple him when he most needed to be strong and whole, it was his problem.

"What are you waiting for? Open the damn door."

He spun around, glaring at the slender, sardonic man, daring him to argue. But Kiley seemed satisfied with his handling of Kate. Nodding his head, he took a ring of keys from his pocket, unlocked the twin bolts at the top and bottom of the door, pushed it open and stepped across the threshold. Lucas followed him, dragging Kate as if she were nothing more than a bothersome piece of baggage, grateful that she went willingly and without another word. Standing aside, he waited while Kiley closed and relocked the door. A moment later, with the click of a switch, fluorescent lights flickered on throughout the building.

The interior of the warehouse was smaller than Lucas had expected, having studied it from the outside the previous day. It was neatly divided into a storage area toward the front near the large, overhead doors and a work area toward the back. Past the work area there was a paneled wall inset with a couple of plain wooden doors. Offices, Lucas thought, or perhaps an office and the storage-work area for Kiley's sideline. He tightened his grip on the briefcase.

"Nice setup you've got here. Nobody would ever suspect . . ." Lucas scanned the open area, then focused on the doors in the back wall. "I suppose you keep the stuff back here. Convenient, isn't it? You can hide the product in the pieces being refinished for your special customers fairly easily, can't you?"

"What are you talking about?" Kiley gazed at him, his pale gray eyes wide and innocent, refusing to give anything away.

"I'm talking about your little sideline. The little sideline David Evans discovered because he was curious, too curious for his own good. Right?" When Kiley didn't answer, Lucas waved the briefcase under his nose. "It's all in here. He took notes and he took pictures, and just in case something happened to him, he left copies of both with his big sister."

Lucas grinned at Kate, his face twisted in a mockery of good humor. "Trusting little soul that she is, she showed me everything. Didn't you, sweetheart?"

Kate nodded, quite unable to speak. Only Lucas's hand on her arm kept her upright and in place. This was it. This was showtime, but her courage as well as her common sense were failing fast. She knew that he wouldn't let Kiley hurt her. But the man she trusted had turned into a stranger with such incredible ease that her confidence had been shaken to the core. As a result, she'd come close to letting him down.

He had warned her that the confrontation with Jonathan would be a nasty piece of business. Why hadn't she listened to him? Why had she insisted on being a part of it? She glanced at the slim, silver-haired man standing beside Lucas. He was dressed in dark gray slacks, a black turtleneck sweater and a tweed jacket, and he was as cool, as calm, as elegant as ever. Who would believe him capable of murder?

She would. She did. And she was here to prove it. That was why she hadn't listened to Lucas. Drawing a deep breath, she stood a little straighter, tipped her chin a little higher. She could have all the hysterics she wanted tomorrow. *And I probably will,* she thought ruefully. But for now,

her determination to see Kiley behind bars renewed, she re
alized it would be wise to concentrate on the conversatio
going on around her.

"Intrepid businessman that I am, I contacted you," Lu
cas continued, relieved by the almost imperceptible chang
in Kate's demeanor. He had been worried about her, afraid
she'd come apart, but she was going to be all right. "Nov
that I've seen your setup, I don't think I want your money
I think you and I ought to talk about a partnership. As
mentioned, the heat's on in Miami, and we already have one
friend in common. I'm sure Diego Garcia would be mor
than happy to consolidate his business with us in one place
and this place suits me just fine."

"Unfortunately, you've been misled, Mr. Hunter. Ther
is no *setup*. There is nothing here but antique furniture i
various stages of preparation for my showroom or my cus
tomers." He waved a hand at the odd assortment of piece
around them as he moved along a narrow aisle that angle
toward the back of the building. "And of course I have
small office here, also." He stopped in front of one door
opened it, switched on a light.

Stopping several steps away from him, Lucas tipped hi
head toward the other door. "Another *small office*?"

"Actually, it's just an empty room," Jonathan drawle
as he moved to the second door, opened it and switched o
the light. "See for yourself."

The room that in all probability, had held the drugs Da
vid had photographed, was empty. Not so much as a scrap
of paper littered the concrete floor and the walls wer
equally bare. A windowless door opening out of the back o
the building was bolted shut. Not only was the man smart
he was fast. And no matter how hard he was goaded, h
wasn't giving anything away. Smothering a vile curse, Lu
cas turned to face him.

"I thought I told you I didn't like being jerked around."

"And I told *you* that you've been misled." Kiley's eyes glittered like shards of ice as his lips twisted into a rueful smile. "I'm afraid David Evans's imagination got away from him. He made assumptions about my business dealings that have no basis in fact, and he proceeded to put together what he considered to be evidence against me. I found a copy of a list and some photographs in his . . . desk after he was killed." Gesturing for them to follow him, he started toward his office.

"If only he'd come to me with his suspicions. . . . But he didn't. And now, here you are, claiming you have evidence against me that might interest the police. I ought to let you go to them and make a fool of yourself. But then it might end up smeared across the front pages of the local newspapers, and you know how bad publicity can affect a business. So, Mr. Hunter, give me whatever it is you have, and I'll pay your price." He moved behind his desk, setting his briefcase on its bare surface.

"You killed my brother," Kate cried, unable to control her anger any longer. He was taunting them, taunting *her* with his silky smooth tone of voice and his casual manner, as if he'd invited them to tea and was about to serve cake. Ignoring the tightening of Lucas's hand on her arm, she took a step toward Kiley and repeated her accusation, hurling her words at him with careless abandon. "You killed David."

"Dear, foolish girl, of course I didn't kill your brother. Why would I? He was my trusted friend and business associate."

"He found out what you were doing." She glared at him, forcing herself to meet his cold, hard eyes. "He found out about the drug deal—"

"Kate." Lucas interrupted, his voice full of warning. He understood her anger. He was angry, too. The manipulative bastard was playing with them. But going for his throat wasn't going to get them the answers they needed.

"Better to have her thoughts out in the open, don't you agree? Then I can set her mind to rest. That's why I wanted you to bring her here tonight." Jonathan glanced at Lucas, then turned his attention back to Kate. "My dear, as you can see for yourself, the only dealing I do is in antique furniture. And since I have my reputation as well as my business to protect, I've agreed to pay Mr. Hunter for your...silence."

"I'd rather have a piece of your action," Lucas insisted.

"Sorry, I don't have any action to offer." He extended his hand, palm up, and nodded toward the briefcase in Lucas's hand. "You don't mind if I take a look at what's in there, do you?"

Lucas released Kate's arm, set the briefcase on the edge of the desk, opened it and removed the envelope. He dumped the contents on the desktop. "I never realized Diego was an antique lover." He picked up the appropriate photograph and pretended to study it for a moment before tossing it aside.

Without a word, Kiley shifted through the pictures and the list of names and dates, then picked up the diary and thumbed through the pages. "What's this?"

"It's a coded diary, and it's very interesting, lots of...details. Kate figured it out. Her notes are in the back."

"And these are all of the negatives?"

"Yeah, sure. But don't take my word for it. Check them out."

As Kiley did just that, holding one strip after another up to the light, Kate edged away from Lucas until she was standing off to one side of the desk. Anger and frustration warring inside of her, she shifted her gaze from one man to the other as her fingers dug into the leather bag hanging from her shoulder. How much longer were they going to allow him to have the upper hand? Lucas had been so sure that he'd admit to everything when in fact he'd admitted to nothing. And what if he took their evidence? What if he handed over the money and left? They might be able to make a case against him but it would take months, perhaps years. And as long as he was free, she would live in fear, knowing that he knew that she knew too much.

"It looks as if all the negatives are here." He tossed them on the small pile atop his desk, then reached for his briefcase and spun the tumblers on the combination locks until they snapped open. "Fifty thousand seems like a lot to pay for peace of mind, but as I said, I have my reputation to maintain." He removed a neatly banded stack of bills and set it on the desk.

Lucas picked up the money and fanned one end of the bills. "Hundreds in stacks of fifties, right? You owe me ten stacks." He tossed the first one in his open case as Kiley produced another, then another.

Kate watched as Jonathan's hand dove in and out of the black leather briefcase, producing four, five stacks of dull green, one-hundred-dollar bills. She glanced at Lucas as she shifted from one foot to another, but he didn't meet her gaze. He was intent on stashing the money. In a few moments the deal would be done, and they would be no closer to putting Kiley behind bars than they'd been four days ago.

Do something, do something, do something. The words screamed inside her head as she shifted again, her eyes on Kiley's hand moving, moving...six, seven...green on green on...gray... Dark, gun-metal gray...gun metal...*gun*—

From where she was standing she saw the glint of the gun nestled among the remaining stacks of money, saw him wrap his fingers around the butt and lift it slowly. She couldn't move, couldn't speak, her mind and body frozen with fear. She had to warn Lucas because he couldn't see it, *wouldn't* see until it was too late.

"Lucas! Watch out," she screamed, launching herself at Kiley. Ignoring the sharp pain of the desk corner gouging her hip, she threw her weight at him as he fired the gun.

Too late...too late.... From the corner of her eye she saw Lucas stagger back against the wall and slide to the floor, a blood red color blossoming just below his left collarbone. "You bastard. You rotten, stinking, lousy bastard." She clawed at Kiley like a wild woman, rage coursing through her, but she wasn't strong enough to defeat him.

As if she were no more than a pesky fly to be flicked away, he rid himself of her with a powerful shove, sending her sprawling on the cold concrete floor. "You stupid, little fool. You didn't think I'd let you walk out of here, did you? You know too much," he snarled, his eyes glinting with maniacal glee as he stood over her.

"You killed my brother, didn't you?" She gazed up at him, her eyes wide and clear. "You were dealing drugs and he found out, so you killed him."

"Just like I killed that fool, Jackson. Just like I'm going to kill you," he promised, his lips twisting into a vicious little smile. "As soon as I finish with your boyfriend. Then I'm going to dump over a few cans of stripper, light a match and burn this place to the ground. Terrible accident, too bad about the people who didn't get out." His laughter echoed with insanity as he turned away from her and started toward Lucas.

She pushed herself up on one hand, gasping at the sharp pain radiating through her right hip and upper thigh. Still stunned by her brutal fall, she turned her head. Lucas was half sitting, half lying against the wall opposite Jonathan's desk, one arm bent behind his back. The dark blotch of red on his sweater had grown considerably, but his eyes were open, and he was looking at her. His eyes shifted down and then up as Jonathan moved toward him, taunting him as he'd taunted her. He was trying to tell her what?

She wanted to call his name, to ask him, but time was running out. She dug her fingers into her purse, followed his eyes down and remembered. *If you take it out of your purse, be prepared to use it.* Damn Kiley to hell, she would use it.

Her hand unbelievably steady, she slid the zipper back. Wrapping her fingers around the butt, she released the safety and drew it out. Kiley was less than a yard from Lucas, doing what Lucas had predicted he'd do, pumping himself up on his own power, crowing like the only cock in the chicken coop as he lifted his hand and aimed his gun. Pushing herself to her knees, she gripped the .38 in both hands.

"Shut up, Jonathan," she shouted. "Shut up and die."

His concentration broken, he swiveled to face her, then staggered back a step under the force of a bullet slamming into his upper right arm. He touched the bloody hole in his arm, his look of surprise almost comical as he met her gaze. Then his eyes hardened and his lips thinned as he started toward her.

She had to fire again, but her hands were shaking, her heart was pounding. Lucas was just behind him. If she missed Jonathan . . .

He was raising his arm, the barrel of his gun pointing at her as he drew closer and closer, moving as if in slow motion, his eyes glittering, his mouth flattened in a grim line of determination. "Wrong, Kate," he murmured. "You die—"

"I don't think so, Kiley," Lucas interrupted, his voice as cold and deadly as the bullet that slammed into Kiley's head.

With a cry that was part fear, part loathing, Kate scuttled out of the way as Jonathan spun and fell to the floor. "Oh, no.... Oh, God..." she whimpered, staring at the dead man's ruined face, her stomach churning, shivers coarsing through her body one after another. "Lucas," she whispered, her fingers locked around the .38. "Lucas...."

She wanted him, needed him. Why didn't he come to her now that it was over? She whimpered again, afraid to take her eyes off Jonathan, unable to believe that he was really dead. "Lucas, please..." Very slowly she turned her head, saw him slumped against the wall, his face deathly pale, his eyes closed, his automatic dangling from one limp hand as the circle of blood on his sweater spread. *"Lucas!"*

He was dying. God in heaven, he was dying. She tried to stand but her legs buckled under her. She gagged, her stomach heaving as the stench of blood and death filling the small office rolled over her. She was shaking so hard her teeth chattered. Tears blurred her vision and wet her cheeks. She had to go to him. But she couldn't get up; she couldn't walk. On her hands and knees, still clutching her revolver in one hand, she crawled across the concrete floor.

"You...can't die." She drew as close as possible to him, careful not to bump his wounded shoulder. She smoothed the thick, dark hair from his forehead. "Lucas, please, don't die."

His eyes fluttered open, his right hand moved to cover hers. He turned his face, pressing his lips to her palm. "Katie...." he murmured in a low voice. Still holding her hand, he met her gaze. "Are you...all right?"

She nodded, trying to blink away the hot tears from her eyes as she squeezed his hand. "I'm fine."

"Kiley?"

She glanced at the man sprawled on the floor just a few feet away. He bore no resemblance to the man who had been alive a few seconds ago. She had wanted him to pay for her brother's murder. But had she wanted this? Had she wanted to see him lying in a pool of blood? A shudder racked her body as she gripped Lucas's hand. "He's... I think he's...dead."

"Sorry, Kate. Sorry it had to end this way." He took a deep breath, his eyes drifted closed, then opened again. "My fault, my own damn fault. Read him wrong. But we got him, didn't we? Got him...job's done...safe now. You'll be safe now, sweetheart. Matt...Matt will take care...of...you...." His eyes closed once more as his hand slipped from hers. His head tipped to one side, then he lay still.

For one long, agonizing moment she thought he was dead. Then she saw the faint pulse throbbing at the base of his throat. He was alive, but how much longer could he hang on? Damn it, where was Matthew Owen? She couldn't wait for him. Clinging to the last shreds of her self-control, she stumbled to her feet and staggered toward the desk, trying unsuccessfully not to look at Jonathan Kiley.

No matter how much she wanted to block it out, he was dead, and she had been a part of his dying. She would have to live with the knowledge for the rest of her life. And she could. He had killed her brother. But if Lucas died... She turned her attention to the telephone on the desk. She dialed 911 and, in a voice she didn't recognize as her own, gave details and directions to the operator who answered.

Then, like a sleepwalker, she returned to Lucas. Bracing her back against the wall, she slid down beside him and gently eased her arms around him. His breathing was slow and shallow, his face frightfully pale except for the dark shadows beneath his eyes. But it looked as though the bleeding had stopped. If she could keep him warm until—

Someone was shouting, but she couldn't understand the words, and in the distance she could hear the sound of something crashing against a door. There should have been sirens, but there had been none. Heart thudding with renewed terror, she tightened her hold on Lucas as she groped for her revolver. Ignoring the trembling in her hand, she lifted it, leveling it as best she could at the open office doorway. Somewhere inside the warehouse, wood splintered. Then she heard the sound of someone running.

Matt Owen skidded to a halt just inside the small office, his sharp eyes taking in the bloody scene before he met Kate's steady gaze. She hovered over Lucas, shielding him with her body, and though her hand shook, she didn't lower her gun. Barring the doorway with one arm to keep the other agents out, he spoke to her in the soft, low voice he rarely used.

"It's all right, Kate. It's me, Matt. Everything's going to be all right. Just...put...the gun...down. No one's going to hurt you. We want to help you and Lucas."

She stared at him a moment longer, then did as he'd asked, setting her revolver on the floor beside her. Turning her face away, she rested her cheek on Lucas's head and closed her eyes. In the distance she could hear sirens. Maybe he was right. Maybe everything would be all right.

After ordering the other agents to secure the building and take care of Kiley, Matt moved toward the couple huddled on the floor. Crouching in front of them, he checked Lucas's pulse, then lifted one of his eyelids. "You called an ambulance?"

"I dialed 911," she muttered.

"Good girl. I think they're here now. Are you hurt?"

She shook her head. "I'm . . . okay. But Lucas—"

"He's going to be fine," he assured her. He glanced over his shoulder, hesitating a moment, then spoke again. "Want to tell me what happened?"

She turned her head slightly, opening her eyes so she could meet his gaze. "He called at the last minute. He wanted us to come here. He . . . he intended to kill us all along. He was going to set the warehouse on fire." She shuddered at the memory of Jonathan's madness as he spewed out his plans. "He killed David and the man . . . the man we saw in the paper." Had it only been that morning? It seemed as if it had been forever.

"Where's the ambulance?" She turned away from Matt, her eyes darting up and over his shoulder to meet those of a uniformed attendant.

"Right here, ma'am." He was tall and slender, with angel-of-mercy blond curls and a warm, reassuring smile. Pulling on a pair of protective rubber gloves, he knelt beside Matt and turned his attention to Lucas. "Gunshot wound?"

"Yeah."

"How long ago?" He signaled to another attendant to start an IV.

"Kate? How long ago?" Matt repeated the question, his voice rough, demanding her attention.

"I'm not sure." She had no concept of time anymore. Minutes had seemed like hours. But for Lucas's sake she had to try to remember. "Ten, maybe fifteen minutes."

"He's lost some blood, and I think the bullet's lodged under his collarbone. But it doesn't look like it did any major damage." The attendant smiled at Kate again. "He's going to be fine, ma'am." Then he turned to Matt. "Get her out of here, will you?"

"No." She clung to Lucas, not wanting to let him go, afraid that if she did, somehow she would lose him forever. And she couldn't lose him again.

"Yes, Kate," Matt ordered, reverting to his normally caustic manner as he took hold of her arm. "Let them do their job." Ignoring her slight resistance, he pulled her to her feet and slipped an arm around her waist when she swayed against him. "You've done everything you can," he added in a gentler tone of voice as he led her through the warehouse, past the probing eyes of the Galveston police officers talking to his men. "We'll take care of him for you, and we'll take care of you."

She wanted to argue with him, wanted to insist on staying with Lucas. But her knees wobbled and the maze of furniture dipped and twisted as a wave of dizziness swept over her. Too little sleep and nothing to eat, she thought, stumbling along beside Matt. This was so crazy. She pressed her face against his chest and started to cry as they stepped out into the cold night air.

"That's good. Let it go," he urged as he guided her toward one of the waiting ambulances. "It's over, it's all over now."

He spoke to the attendant, but she had no idea what they said. She was sobbing, her body shaking, hot tears blurring

her eyes and running down her cheeks. When he handed her
into an attendant's care, she didn't protest. She let the mar
help her into the ambulance and clung to the blanket he
wrapped around her. As if from a great distance she watched
him roll up the sleeve of her sweater, then her shirt, watched
him insert the needle into her arm, too numb to really no
tice the sharp sting as the sedative shot into her. At his
direction, she lay back on the stretcher. As he moved away
she curled onto her side, drawing up her knees, closing her
eyes, her tears soaking the starched sheet beneath her cheek.

"Don't die, Lucas," she murmured, the numbness in her
mind and body deepening as the drug claimed her
"Don't . . . die. . . ."

She awoke in a bed that was too hard and narrow to be
her own, in a small, pretty room filled with sunshine. Although she was lying on her back, the mattress was tilted up
just enough to give her a view of something more than the
ceiling. A pale, wooden door that was closed, a small dresser
that was bare, a narrow doorway opening into what ap
peared to be a tiny bathroom,

She blinked, wet her lips with the tip of her tongue and
shifted against the coarse cotton sheet, trying to relieve the
throbbing ache in her right hip and thigh. Something tugged
at her left hand, something uncomfortable. She blinked
again and turned her head, saw the IV bottle hanging from
a metal frame, the slender tube ending in a wad of tape or
the back of her hand. She closed her fingers into a fist, then
spread them wide against the soft, cotton blanket, watch
ing the tube quiver.

Somewhere in the back of her mind she knew she was in
a hospital, but her mind was too fuzzy to put together how
and why. She stirred again, her head rolling on the pillow
restlessly. Her leg hurt, and the feeling of being bound, if
only by a tube and tape, was almost unbearable. What had

happened? Had she been in an accident? She remembered riding in a car . . . on the freeway . . . with—

"Well, girlie, I was beginning to wonder if you'd sleep the clock around," Grace declared, a teasing note in her rough, gravelly voice.

Turning her head to the right, Kate met her friend's bright, blue gaze as Grace rose from a chair near the window and moved to stand beside the bed. Then, a sudden wave of dizziness washing over her, she closed her eyes.

"Hey, are you okay? Want me to call the nurse?" Grace asked, her voice full of concern as she smoothed a hand over Kate's hair.

"I'm . . . okay. Just a little dizzy." She opened her eyes, offering her friend what she hoped was a reassuring smile. "Where am I? What happened? I remember riding in a car."

"You're in the medical center in Galveston." Grace hesitated, reaching for Kate's hand.

Clinging to her friend, searching her face for some hint of what had happened, Kate forced herself to think, to remember.

"Oh, God," she murmured as the fuzziness suddenly slid away. As if it were happening all over again, she could hear the gunshots, see the blood. *"Lucas . . ."* She pushed up on her elbows, ignoring a second, less intense wave of dizziness. "Where is he? Grace, where is he?" she demanded.

"He's here, in the hospital. He's . . . he's all right." She put her hands on Kate's shoulders, trying to comfort her.

Kate shrugged away from her hold, struggling to sit up, clawing at the tape on the back of her hand with trembling fingers. Grace, normally so cocky and sure, had responded to her question about Lucas with too much reluctance, too much uncertainty. They would tell her anything to pacify her.

"I want to see him. I've got to see him."

"And you will." As if on cue, the wooden door opened with a whoosh as Matthew Owen entered the room. He stood next to Grace, studying Kate with his sharp eyes. "As soon as the doc releases you, you can get dressed, spend a few minutes with him, then we'll take you home."

At Matt's mention of dressing, Kate stopped tearing at the tape on her hand and glanced down at the pale blue hospital gown she was wearing. She shook her head. No way could she roam the hospital corridors in it. Shoving a hand through her hair, she glared at Matt. "Where are my clothes? I want my clothes now. And I want to be released *now*." She pounded her fist against the mattress for emphasis. Then, groaning as another mild wave of dizziness washed over her, she closed her eyes and tipped her head back against her pillow.

"I think she's feeling better." Matt turned to Grace, one bushy brow waggling.

"Hmm, a little. But she's still awfully pale, and I think she's having another dizzy spell."

"Don't talk about me as if I weren't here," Kate muttered through clenched teeth. "I'm much better. The dizziness is gone. Now get me out of here."

"She reminds me of you, Gracie," Matt muttered. Then ignoring Kate's scowl, he propped a hip on the edge of her bed and took her hand in one of his. "They operated on him last night. Got the bullet out. No major damage, but he lost a lot of blood. They're going to keep him in intensive care for a while longer. Later this afternoon, if there aren't any signs of infection, they'll move him into a private room. You'll be able to see him then. All right?"

Oddly calmed by Matt's brusque manner, Kate nodded her head as he squeezed her hand.

"And in the meantime, you stay here. You've had a bad shock. You need the rest and the fluids." He gestured toward the IV bottle. "Grace will stay with you. In a little while they'll bring you something to eat. You can take a shower, get dressed. Grace brought some fresh clothes for you.''

She glanced at her friend, offered a thankful smile. Then, her smile fading, she turned back to Matt, still holding her hand, still sitting on the side of her bed, with still more to say to her.

"Now...Kiley..." He gazed at her intently for several seconds, as if trying to gauge her response to what he was about to tell her. "Unfortunately, Jonathan Kiley was killed by an unknown assailant during a robbery attempt at his warehouse. Although the circumstances are similar to those surrounding the murder of his associate, David Evans, the police don't think the two incidents are related. Neither case will ever be officially closed."

"He killed my brother. He bragged about it," Kate cried, trying to pull away from Matt.

"And you want the whole world to know, don't you?" he asked, his voice suddenly cold and hard. "Do you also want the whole world to know Lucas Hunter is a DEA agent? Several extremely nasty types in Miami would find it quite interesting, especially Diego Garcia, the man who's been selling cocaine to Kiley."

"I didn't think—"

"Then think about this. With a little time and effort we should be able to make cases against the eight people listed in your brother's diary. They're dealing drugs. They aren't going to stop because one middle man is dead. With a little time and effort, we can also take down Diego Garcia, a major supplier. And you can get on with your life."

"As if nothing ever happened," she murmured, turning her face away.

"It's better, *safer*, that way, for you and for Lucas. And at least you know your brother's murderer will never harm anyone again." Releasing her hand, he stood up and glanced at his watch. "It's nearly noon. I'm going to check on Lucas, then I've got some business to do. I'll be back for you around five.''

Grace slipped her arm through his as he turned away, and they walked out the door together.

Kate leaned back against the pillow and closed her eyes, glad to be alone for a few moments. He was right, about everything. But even if she hadn't agreed with Matt, she wouldn't have said or done anything to endanger Lucas. Once he recuperated, he would go back to Miami, back to his life as an undercover agent. He'd done what he'd come to Houston to do. And this afternoon, before she left the hospital, she would stop by his room to say thank you and goodbye.

She wasn't going to cry. Despite the hot tears pricking at the backs of her eyelids, she was *not* going to cry. She was going to pick up the telephone, call the library and in twenty words or less, explain why she wasn't at work. If she was lucky, she'd still have a job. It would be better than nothing, and it would help to fill all the long, lonely days stretching ahead of her.

Chapter 13

His room looked more like a hospital room than hers, Kate thought, as she stepped through the door and allowed it to close behind her. The blinds at the window were drawn to block out most of the late-afternoon sunshine, but in the dim light she could see several machines blinking and beeping as they monitored the man sleeping in the high, narrow bed. He was just sleeping, she reminded herself as she crossed the room, but his face was so pale, the shadows beneath his eyes so dark.

She stopped by the bed, resting her hands on the cold, metal rail barring the side. An odd assortment of tubes and wires were attached to his body, and above the plain white sheet and blanket covering him, most of his bare chest was swaddled in heavy bandages. He was so still, his breathing shallow, but the nurse had warned her that the sedative he'd been given probably hadn't worn off yet.

So much for saying thank you and goodbye. She had planned to do it quickly, easily. Smiling ruefully, she reached out to touch his beard-roughened face and smooth a lock of thick, dark hair away from his forehead. Nothing about her relationship with Lucas had ever been quick or easy. For most of their growing-up years, they had been too shy and uncertain to do more than speak to each other. And then the war had taken him away. And when, at last, she had thought that he'd finally come home to her, she had been mistaken.

She had loved him for as long as she could remember. She would love him until the day she died. But she knew, as surely as she knew her own name, that she wasn't going to see him again. He hadn't sought her out because he still loved her. She had been nothing more to him than part of a job to be done, a job that *was* done. He had said as much in the warehouse. And not once had he said that he loved her. Even if he had, she wouldn't have believed him, not after the way he'd deceived her. She couldn't believe anything he'd said . . . or done.

Drawing her hand away, she blocked out the taunting memories of the night she'd spent in his arms. Later, much later, when he was gone, she would remember, but not now, not when she might be tempted to cling to the hope that it had been real. Not when going away and staying away was the wisest thing she could do.

He stirred in the bed, moving his good arm, rolling his head on the pillow. His eyes fluttered open, then closed, as he groaned deep in his throat. She clenched the metal railing, her knuckles turning white as he opened his eyes again and turned to meet her gaze.

"Katie?" His voice was little more than a dry croak, his eyes bleary with sleep. "Katie . . . you're okay."

"Yes, I'm fine." Unable to stop herself, she smiled tenderly and stroked his shaggy hair.

With surprising speed and strength, he caught her hand in his and held it against his face.

"Still . . . mad?" His eyes searched hers with a sudden probing intensity.

"No, I'm not mad. You saved my life, Lucas."

"And you...saved...mine...." His eyes closed, his grip on her hand slackened.

"Guess that makes us even," she whispered, tucking his arm under the blanket. "Except that I love you." Wiping a tear from her cheek, she touched his face one last time, then started toward the door.

"Still even," he muttered. "I love you, too, little...girl." He opened his eyes, turned to look at her. But the place beside his bed was empty, and the only sound he heard was the gentle closing of a door.

He was supposed to be released from the hospital on Saturday, but by Friday morning Lucas had had enough of cheery nurses shoving thermometers in his mouth and wrapping blood pressure cuffs around his arm, usually just about the time he'd finally managed to fall asleep. There had been no sign of infection and his wound was healing without complication. Yesterday he'd managed a stroll to the solarium not once, but three times. The third sojourn last night had left him weak and sweating, but he was stronger today.

And today he was out of here, doctor's release or not. He had places to go, people to see. As he eased his left arm into his shirtsleeve, he glanced at the telephone on the stand beside the bed. She had come to him on Monday, and she'd spoken of love. But she hadn't waited long enough to hear his reply. And she hadn't come back—not once—nor had she called.

Each time the door had swung open he had hoped to see her face. And each time he'd answered the telephone, he'd expected to hear her voice. But it had been Matt who'd brought his bag, the one he'd left at her house, and it was always Matt's voice on the other end of the line. As if by unspoken agreement, neither man had mentioned her name. And no matter how many times he'd lifted the receiver, Lucas hadn't dialed her number.

What if her visit on Monday had been her way of saying goodbye? Though he didn't want to admit it, as one day had flowed into another and another, he'd begun to believe it. Perhaps he'd misunderstood her. Perhaps when she'd spoken of love it had been in the past tense. The distance between Houston and Galveston wasn't that great, but as long as she stayed away, it was as if they were worlds apart. And when all was said and done, he couldn't blame her for not wanting him in her world any longer.

She had a life of her own, a job, a home, friends. Into that he'd brought nothing but chaos. Ah, but what wonderful chaos it had been, he thought, feeling his wicked grin edging at the corners of his mouth. The days he'd spent with Kate had been a tempting, teasing taste of what it would be like to share her life, to live in the warm glow of her love and laughter, the love and laughter that had drawn a young boy, that still drew the man he had become. The days with her had been a taste of heaven for a man who'd lived too long in the outer reaches of hell.

Those days were over now. His job was done, he reminded himself, as he tucked his shirt into his jeans and cinched a narrow leather belt around his waist. He had no reason to stay in Houston, no reason at all. Unless you counted the fact that the woman he loved more than anything in the world was there.

With a muttered curse, he turned to the black bag on the rumpled bed and poked through it to make sure he had everything. If he loved her, and he did, the best thing he could do was leave. Use the plane ticket to Columbus Matt had given him, spend a few weeks with his parents while he recuperated, then head back to Miami. Or he could take Matt's offer of a promotion out of Miami and into an office. If he gave up undercover work, he could think about settling down, he could think about a wife and family, he could think about . . . Kate.

No, not Kate, not anymore, not after what he'd done to her. He closed the suitcase with unusual force and slammed the locks shut. He'd deceived her, he'd endangered her life. If she'd wanted anything more to do with him, she would have come back to the hospital to see him. At the very least, she would have called. If he went to her now, she'd slam the door in his face.

Wouldn't she?

He punched the call button, letting the nurses know he was ready to go so they could get a taxi for him and organize the usual nonsense with a wheelchair. Then he picked up the airline ticket Matt had given him along with a lecture about taking it easy for at least a month. He was scheduled on a flight out tomorrow, but it shouldn't be too hard to change. He hadn't called his parents, so they weren't expecting him. They'd be surprised and, despite the circumstances, very pleased to see him.

He tucked the ticket in his shirt pocket. He ran a hand through his dark, shaggy hair as he paced from the bed to the window and back again.

Yeah, he'd go to Columbus, get some well-earned R and R, make some decisions. It was the best thing to do. Wasn't it?

She sat in her office, sifting through a stack of papers, reading not a word, much as she'd done for most of the past couple of days. Grace had insisted that she stay home from work on Tuesday, but she'd come back on Wednesday, unable to stay in the town house any longer.

Matt had taken Lucas's things on Monday night, but Lucas had remained a very real presence, lurking in the shadows of her mind and heart when she sat at the kitchen table or tried to sleep in her bed. She had hoped it would be easier at work, but it wasn't. She had caught herself searching for his face among the crowds, listening for his voice, and she had developed a bad habit of staring at her telephone.

Of course he wasn't going to show up at the library. He was still in the hospital. And he wasn't going to call her. She had been part of a job, a job that was done. Through Grace she knew that he would be discharged from the hospital tomorrow, and that he had a plane ticket to Columbus. He was getting on with his life, and she should do the same. Just as she'd done so many years ago.

"And you did such a good job of it, too," she muttered, tossing the papers aside so she could rub her forehead with her fingertips.

She had curled up in a ball of pain and anger and let him walk away from her once. And now she was going to do it again. She was going to ignore the fact that she'd never felt as alive as she had during the few days they'd been together. She was going to block out every kind and caring thing he'd said and done, she was going to forget the tenderness, the intimate possessiveness of his lovemaking. After all, he was an undercover agent, trained to deceive, used to living a lie. And she had no reason to believe—

"No!"

Pounding a fist on her desk, Kate stood up, grabbed her purse and headed for her office door. She wasn't going to do it again. She wasn't going to give up without a fight. She was going to face him, one-on-one. If he never wanted to see her again, he would have to tell her, face-to-face. At least then she wouldn't spend the rest of her life wondering "what if." She stopped at the front desk and left a message for her supervisor. Then she stepped into the elevator that led to the underground parking garage where she'd left her car. She'd be at the hospital in less than an hour, and then she would know.

He had gone, gone without a word. Gripping the steering wheel with both hands, she guided her car out of Galveston along the Gulf Freeway. As she neared Houston, the sun dipped into the horizon off to her left. On the opposite side of the highway vehicles heading out of downtown were bumper to bumper, signaling rush hour was in full swing. But heading toward town the drive was quick and easy, at least until she passed through the city and entered the freeway that led to her town house.

He had left the hospital early in the afternoon, probably while she was debating whether or not to see him. According to the nurse in charge, he'd been quite anxious to go, insisting on it even though his doctor warned that he was pushing it. And right now he was probably somewhere in Columbus, Ohio, surrounded by his family.

It had been one thing to go to the hospital to confront him. Had he been cool and distant, she would have slipped away with a wave and smile, pretending to have done nothing more than her Christian duty by visiting him. But flying to Columbus would reek of hot pursuit. She had too much pride for that. She wouldn't force herself on any man, especially Lucas Hunter. Surely if he'd wanted any kind of…relationship with her, he would have found a way to let her know, just as Matt had let Grace know in no uncertain terms that they were going to have a second chance at love.

At least Grace would live happily ever after, Kate thought, as she drove down the alley behind her town house, flicked the automatic garage door opener and pulled into her usual place. Moments later she crossed the small courtyard and patio, punched in the appropriate numbers to release the alarm system, slid her key into the door lock and opened the French door. She stepped inside without hesitation, closed and relocked the door. Now that she knew who had instigated the invasion of her home, now that she knew he was gone forever, her fear of the empty house had disappeared.

But as she switched on lamps in the living room, she paused, her head tipped to one side, listening. Something was wrong. No, not wrong. Something was…missing. A quick survey of the room assured her everything was in place, everything except . . . Caesar.

"Where are you, buddy?" she murmured as she headed for the kitchen. Although he'd stopped leaping at her out of the dark, he always greeted her at the door in some way. "Caesar?"

He responded to her call with a pitiful mewling, followed by an audible attack on the laundry room door with his claws.

"Well, what are you doing in here?" she asked as she opened the door.

Ignoring her completely, he darted across the kitchen, down the hallway and up the stairs, his ears flat, his tail high. Kate watched him go, a puzzled frown on her face. She couldn't remember putting him in the laundry room that morning before she left for work. There had been no reason to do it. Of course, he might have gone in there, gotten behind the door for some reason and accidently closed it himself. But Caesar wasn't fond of the laundry room. He only went in to eat and use his cat box, and neither his food dish nor the box were anywhere near the door.

Shrugging, she slipped off her suit jacket, tossed it over a chair, then stepped out of her pumps. She stared at the refrigerator for a moment, fidgeting with the high collar of her plain, white blouse, then smoothing her hands over her slim, black skirt as she thought about dinner.

She wasn't really hungry. Maybe a shower and fresh clothes would help. Maybe throwing herself on her bed and sobbing her heart out would help, too. Then again, maybe not, she admitted with a rueful sigh. He was gone and she'd found out fifteen years ago that tears wouldn't bring him back.

She padded up the stairs in her stockinged feet, switching on the hall light as she headed toward her bedroom. She was almost at the doorway when she heard a violent sneeze, followed by a muffled curse, followed by Caesar stalking past on his way downstairs. She stood still, her heart pounding. It wasn't possible, was it? He couldn't be . . . here. . . .

Forcing one foot in front of the other, she stepped through the doorway. Yes, there was someone sleeping in her bed, someone who looked more like Lucas Hunter than Goldilocks in the dimness. For one long moment she was sure she was hallucinating. Then he stirred and sat up, settling himself on the pillows piled up along the headboard as he switched on the bedside lamp. His name a whisper on her lips, Kate sagged against the door frame.

"Sorry, I didn't meant to scare you. I was kind of tired, but I thought I'd be awake by the time you got home from work. Wanted to be rested in case you decided to kick me out."

His face was pale, his dark, shaggy hair a rumpled mess, his silvery green eyes still shadowed with sleep, but he'd never looked better to her. Yet she couldn't quite believe he was really there. "Lucas?" She took a step toward him, then another and another, waiting for him to vanish into thin air. Finally she was standing next to the bed. "I thought you'd gone to Columbus. I . . . I went to the hospital this afternoon and you were gone."

His smile held just a hint of his wicked, wolfish grin as he reached for her hand and pulled her onto the bed. "I checked out early. And I was going to Columbus. But you know as well as I do that we've got unfinished business. So, I stopped by Grace's bookstore, borrowed her set of keys and here I am."

"What kind of unfinished business?" She tried to pull her hand free, but he wouldn't let her go. Instead he drew her down beside him, gently but firmly, slipping his good arm around her.

"I think you know. That's why you went to the hospital, isn't it? You had something to say to me. And I have something to say to you." He stroked her hair, pressed his lips to

her forehead. "Something I tried to say a few days ago, bu
you slipped away before I could. So..." He paused again
gathering his courage. This time he was going to trust he
with his heart and soul.

"I came to Houston to do a job, but from the very be
ginning I knew it would mean being with you. I tried to deny
it then, but now I know I took the job because I wanted t
see you again. I wanted to prove to myself that whatever w
had so many years ago was gone." When she stirred agains
him and started to speak, he hushed her with a quick kiss
"But it wasn't, was it? We were drawn to each other as i
we'd never been apart, as if we'd never stopped loving eacl
other. And we haven't, have we? I've always loved you
sweetheart, and I always will. We've been apart so long, and
it hasn't been good for me. I don't want to spend the rest o
my life without you. But I'll understand if...if yo
don't—"

She reached up to cover his lips with her fingertips. "Bu
I do," she murmured, rubbing her cheek against his chest
"I was hurt and angry that you didn't trust me, and for
while I thought that you'd used my love, that you'd use
me. But you didn't. I wanted to find my brother's mur
derer and you helped me do it the best way you could." Sh
tipped her face up, meeting his gaze. "I love you, too, Lu
cas. I love you so much. Don't leave. Don't ever leave m
again."

He bent his head and claimed her mouth with his, ravish
ing her with his lips, his teeth, his tongue with the hunger o
a starving man until they were both breathless. "Matt's bee
pushing to promote me, put me behind a desk. The agenc
has an office here in Houston, or we could go anywhere
anywhere at all." He kissed her again, shifting on the bed
groaning slightly at the jarring ache spreading through hi
sore shoulder.

"As long as we're together, I don't care." At her words
she eased her body closer to his, but in the lamplight Kat

saw the edge of pain in his eyes. When he bent his head to kiss her again, she pressed her palm against his chest ever so gently. "Are you sure this is a good idea? Your shoulder..."

He dropped a quick, light kiss on her lips, then drew back. "It shouldn't give me any trouble as long as we go slow and easy. And I want to be inside of you, sweetheart, so deep inside of you . . ."

"Well, then, this seems like a good time to explore those other, gentler ways, doesn't it?" She quirked a smile at him as she pushed him against the pillows and started on the buttons on his shirt.

He covered her hands with his for a moment. "Before we go any further, I want you to know we're getting married just as soon as we can. And something else." He hesitated for an instant, then continued. "What do you think about having kids?"

"I think if we're going to have kids, we better shut up and get busy." She nibbled at his neck as she eased his shirt off his shoulders, then started on his belt buckle. "What do you think?"

"I think you're right. And, Kate?" He'd managed to unbutton her blouse and release the front clasp of her bra.

"Yes, Lucas?" She moved down the bed, taking his jeans and briefs with her, then dealt with her own clothes just as quickly.

"I think we ought to get a dog, a big dog. Kids love...ah, Kate...kids love...dogs..."

"Caesar is not negotiable, Lucas." Straddling his hips, she braced her arms on either side of him, then leaned forward until her bare breasts grazed his chest. Her eyes holding his, she traced his lower lip with the tip of her tongue as she took him inside of her.

"Ah, Kate...I don't know—"

She tightened around him, drawing him deeper and deeper, her smile soft and very sure.

"Oh, sweetheart, that's good, so good." He arched up to take her mouth as his hands cupped her bottom, guiding her movements.

"So..." She raised her head, a new, teasing edge to her smile as she went very still. "We'll have a dog *and* a cat and kids. And a house with a white picket fence. And...ah, Lucas, each other...always..."

"Anything you say, little girl. Anything you say...." With his own special brand of wickedness, Lucas shifted to his good side, rolled her onto her back and filled her with his love.

*   *   *   *   *

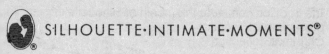

SILHOUETTE·INTIMATE·MOMENTS®

COMING NEXT MONTH

#361 LORD OF THE DESERT—Barbara Faith

Public relations consultant Genevieve Jordan's job was to ensure that oil-rich Kashkiri's international conference met with success. Nothing, not even the desire darkly handsome Prince Ali-Ben-Hari aroused in her, could distract her from that achievement. Yet it wasn't long before passion proved that this lord of the desert was the lord of her heart, as well!

#362 BLUE ICE—Marilyn Tracy

Caught up in a whirl of espionage and mysterious deaths, art expert Aleksandra Shashkevich accepted embassy official Jon Wyndham's offer to help in her search for the missing art she'd flown to Moscow to purchase. The dangers they encountered only enhanced their discovery of a love more valuable than the most priceless art.

#363 SAFE HAVEN—Marilyn Pappano

Protective custody in the hands of virile U.S. Marshal Deke Ramsey wouldn't have been so bad if Tess Marlowe hadn't found herself so attracted to a man whose only interest in her was professional. But when betrayal and corruption struck, Tess realized that the only true haven lay in Deke's arms....

#364 FORGOTTEN DREAM—Paula Detmer Riggs

Mateo Cruz intended to be the best Chief of Tribal Police Santa Ysabel had ever seen. He never expected to be confronted with angry Susanna Spencer, the woman his amnesia kept him from remembering. The blazing sensuality between them seemed impossible to forget, and he soon found himself wanting to right the wrongs of yesterday....

You'll flip . . . your pages won't!
Read paperbacks *hands-free* with

Book Mate · I

The perfect "mate" for all your romance paperbacks

Traveling • Vacationing • At Work • In Bed • Studying • Cooking • Eating

Perfect size for all standard paperbacks, this wonderful invention makes reading a pure pleasure! Ingenious design holds paperback books OPEN and FLAT so even wind can't ruffle pages — leaves your hands free to do other things. Reinforced, wipe-clean vinyl-covered holder flexes to let you turn pages without undoing the strap . . . supports paperbacks so well, they have the strength of hardcovers!

Pages turn WITHOUT opening the strap

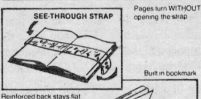

SEE-THROUGH STRAP

Reinforced back stays flat

Built in bookmark

BOOK MARK

BACK COVER HOLDING STRIP

10" x 7¼" opened
Snaps closed for easy carrying, too

PASSPORT TO ROMANCE VACATION SWEEPSTAKES

OFFICIAL RULES

SWEEPSTAKES RULES AND REGULATIONS. NO PURCHASE NECESSARY.

HOW TO ENTER:

1. To enter, complete this official entry form and return with your invoice in the envelope provided, or print your name, address, telephone number and age on a plain piece of paper and mail to: Passport to Romance, P.O. Box #1397, Buffalo, N.Y. 14269-1397. No mechanically reproduced entries accepted.

2. All entries must be received by the Contest Closing Date, midnight, December 31, 1990 to be eligible.

3. Prizes: There will be ten (10) Grand Prizes awarded, each consisting of a choice of a trip for two people to: i) London, England (approximate retail value $5,050 U.S.); ii) England, Wales and Scotland (approximate retail value $6,400 U.S.); iii) Caribbean Cruise (approximate retail value $7,300 U.S.); iv) Hawaii (approximate retail value $ 9,550 U.S.); v) Greek Island Cruise in the Mediterranean (approximate retail value $12,250 U.S.); vi) France (approximate retail value $7,300 U.S.).

4. Any winner may choose to receive any trip or a cash alternative prize of $5,000.00 U.S. in lieu of the trip.

5. Odds of winning depend on number of entries received.

6. A random draw will be made by Nielsen Promotion Services, an independent judging organization on January 29, 1991, in Buffalo, N.Y. at 11:30 a.m. from all eligible entries received on or before the Contest Closing Date. Any Canadian entrants who are selected must correctly answer a time-limited, mathematical skill-testing question in order to win. Quebec residents may submit any litigation respecting the conduct and awarding of a prize in this contest to the Régie des loteries et courses du Quebec.

7. Full contest rules may be obtained by sending a stamped, self-addressed envelope to: "Passport to Romance Rules Request", P.O. Box 9998, Saint John, New Brunswick, E2L 4N4.

8. Payment of taxes other than air and hotel taxes is the sole responsibility of the winner.

9. Void where prohibited by law.

PASSPORT TO ROMANCE VACATION SWEEPSTAKES

OFFICIAL RULES

SWEEPSTAKES RULES AND REGULATIONS. NO PURCHASE NECESSARY.

HOW TO ENTER:

To enter, complete this official entry form and return with your invoice in the envelope provided, print your name, address, telephone number and age on a plain piece of paper and mail to: Passport to Romance, P.O. Box #1397, Buffalo, N.Y. 14269-1397. No mechanically reproduced entries accepted.

All entries must be received by the Contest Closing Date, midnight, December 31, 1990 to be eligible.

Prizes: There will be ten (10) Grand Prizes awarded, each consisting of a choice of a trip for two people to: i) London, England (approximate retail value $5,050 U.S.); ii) England, Wales and Scotland (approximate retail value $6,400 U.S.); iii) Caribbean Cruise (approximate retail value $7,300 U.S.); iv) Hawaii (approximate retail value $ 9,550 U.S.); v) Greek Island Cruise in the Mediterranean (approximate retail value $12,250 U.S.); vi) France (approximate retail value $7,300 U.S.).

Any winner may choose to receive any trip or a cash alternative prize of $5,000.00 U.S. in lieu of the trip.

Odds of winning depend on number of entries received.

A random draw will be made by Nielsen Promotion Services, an independent judging organization on January 29, 1991, in Buffalo, N.Y. at 11:30 a.m. from all eligible entries received on or before the Contest Closing Date. Any Canadian entrants who are selected must correctly answer a time-limited, mathematical skill-testing question in order to win. Quebec residents may submit any litigation respecting the conduct and awarding of a prize in this contest to the Régie des loteries et courses du Quebec.

Full contest rules may be obtained by sending a stamped, self-addressed envelope to: "Passport to Romance Rules Request", P.O. Box 9998, Saint John, New Brunswick, E2L 4N4.

Payment of taxes other than air and hotel taxes is the sole responsibility of the winner.

Void where prohibited by law.

1990 HARLEQUIN ENTERPRISES LTD.   RLS-DIR